THE HOUSEWIFE ASSASSIN'S TIPS FOR WEDDINGS, WEAPONS, AND WARFARE

JOSIE BROWN

A BOOK BY

SIGNAL PRESS

Library of Congress Cataloging-in-Publication Data is available upon request

Cover Design by Andrew Brown, ClickTwiceDesign.com

Digital Formatting by Austin Brown, CheapEbookFormatting.com

Trade Paperback ISBN: 978-1-942052-21-0

Hardcover ISBN: 978-1-942052-23-4

V022319

can't wait to read the next in the series. Highly Recommended!"

—*CrimeThrillerGirl.com*

"This was an addictive read–gritty but funny at the same time. I ended up reading it in just one evening and couldn't go to sleep until I knew what the outcome would be! It was action-packed and humorous from the start, and that continued throughout, I was pleased to discover that this is the first of a series and look forward to getting my hands on Book Two so I can see where life takes Donna and her family next!"

—*Me, My Books, and I*

"The two halves of Donna's life make sense. As you follow her story, there's no point where you think of her as "Assassin Donna" vs. "Mummy Donna', her attitude to life is even throughout. I really like how well this is done. And as for Jack. I'll have one of those, please?"

—*The Northern Witch's Book Blog*

Novels in The Housewife Assassin Series

The Housewife Assassin's Handbook (Book 1)

The Housewife Assassin's Guide to Gracious Killing (Book 2)

The Housewife Assassin's Killer Christmas Tips (Book 3)

The Housewife Assassin's Relationship Survival Guide (Book 4)

The Housewife Assassin's Vacation to Die For (Book 5)

The Housewife Assassin's Recipes for Disaster (Book 6)

The Housewife Assassin's Hollywood Scream Play (Book 7)

The Housewife Assassin's Killer App (Book 8)

The Housewife Assassin's Hostage Hosting Tips (Book 9)

The Housewife Assassin's Garden of Deadly Delights (Book 10)

The Housewife Assassin's Tips for Weddings, Weapons, and Warfare (Book 11)

The Housewife Assassin's Husband Hunting Hints (Book 12)

The Housewife Assassin's Ghost Protocol (Book 13)

The Housewife Assassin's Terrorist TV Guide (Book 14)

The Housewife Assassin's Deadly Dossier (Book 15: The Series Prequel)

The Housewife Assassin's Greatest Hits (Book 16)

The Housewife Assassin's Fourth Estate Sale (Book 17)

The Housewife Assassin's Horrorscope (Book 18)

You Do—But Does He?

You answered, "Yes, I do!" when he proposed? Well, huzzah!

Now if you both can forget you had the barrel of your gun nudging up against his forehead when he asked, you may have a chance to live happily ever after!

By following these three must-do tips, neither of you will bolt (or be murdered) before the big day:

- *Tip #1: So that you're not disappointed, be prepared to take on the important things yourself: finding the venue, hiring the photographer, and choosing the cake, his tux, and the menu. All of these items call for an attention to detail that…well, let's face it, he lacks in regard to everything—other than the planning of his bachelor party.*
- *Tip #2: Don't sweat the small stuff. For example, don't let his mother get under your skin. And certainly don't get depressed if the ring is somewhat less than you hoped, just grin and wear it. You can always "lose" the*

*ring in a hole in the backyard—and perhaps his
mother too.*

- *Tip #3: Just the facts, ma'am, that's all he needs to
know. Give him the date, time, and a map, so that he
knows what to do and where to go on the big day.*

If he doesn't show, call out the posse.

And, yes, it's okay if they shoot to kill.

∾

"SOMEONE IS SHADOWING YOU." THIS DECLARATION COMES
from my limo driver, Abu Nagashahi.

That is to say, someone is shadowing the person I'm
pretending to be: Liang Xia, a freelance spy and hit woman
who successfully executed a contract killing of Catherine
Martin, a former United States congresswoman with valuable intel on the Quorum, an international terrorist organization.

Abu isn't really my hired ride. Like me, he works for
Acme Industries, a black-ops organization sanctioned by the
United States government for the kind of wet-work that gets
the CIA hauled in front of Congressional committees for
more than a mere slap on the wrist.

I hold up a makeup compact and look through it. Yes, I
see the car: a black Lexus sedan.

"How close are we to the rendezvous location?" I ask.

"Just a few blocks," Abu assures me. "Should I try to
shake him before we get there?"

"Don't bother," says Jack, our mission partner—who also

just so happens to be my fiancé. We hear him via our ear buds. He is already situated next door to our final destination: an elegant two-hundred year-old Federal-style mansion located in Washington D.C.'s most prestigious neighborhood, Georgetown. "Dominic is two car-lengths behind you. He can tail him and find out who he is. Besides, if the tail is working for the target, he knows where we'll end up anyway. The only thing the driver will be able to do is confirm 'Xia's' entry and drive off."

"Righto," Dominic Fleming, another one of my backup assets, is quick to confirm. "If I do say so myself, Acme's prosthetics department did a passable job with Donna's mask. Had I not known better, I'd have presumed Xia had come back from the dead."

Abu nods at me through the rearview mirror. "Even from a few feet, I'd say you're the spitting image of Xia."

I shrug. "Let's hope so."

Xia left China's Ministry of State Security for a lucrative retainer with the Quorum, the worst kind of terrorist group there is—in other words, well-funded.

There is a lot about Xia that is nothing like me. For starters, she's Asian. Ergo, the need to wear a mask of her face.

Also, she's dead.

I know this because I killed her.

Only a few others know it too, including Jack; our boss at Acme, Ryan Clancy; the rest of our Acme team; and Lee Chiffray, the President of the United States.

If Lee is also a member of the Quorum, God help us all.

In truth, this is a reconnaissance mission to determine whether he's one of the bad guys. Since he knew of Xia's death, he won't be her mystery date. But if no one shows up, we have even more reason to suspect him.

Right now, the odds are in his favor. Texts coming into Xia's cell phone from her client's Caller ID—362433—haven't stopped.

Whoever it is doesn't want her for another hit. He's looking for a booty call.

Before she died, Xia indicated that she was more than willing to oblige. The phone-sexting between them, monitored by Acme since her death, was much more than flirtatious. It was downright vulgar, detailing every role-playing sex act to be performed. Based on their mutual fantasies, it would be a full week before Xia and her mystery date came up for air.

Acme's ComInt director, Emma Honeycutt Locklear, now monitors Xia's texts. Between reading them and groaning, she plays along, lacing her responses with language so titillating that Emma's husband, Arnie, finally asked her, "Hey, um, did you ever work as a sex phone operator? I mean, it's okay with me if you have…" his voice trailed off hopefully.

"Wishful thinking," Emma retorted.

For Arnie, perhaps, but not for me. Unfortunately, I'm elected to take Xia's place since I'm the only crack shot in our mission team who can squeeze into the size four gold metallic twist-front backless jersey gown, sent by her mystery date as a gift to inaugurate what he calls their "virgin tryst."

Yeah, I know—lucky me. I'd much rather have been planning my upcoming nuptials than memorizing Mystery Date's sadistic bondage fantasies. If he has his way, I'll be tied up for quite some time. Is the "downstairs media room" really an S&M dungeon? If so, I'm sure I'll find out first-hand. I've never stepped foot in their well-appointed love nest. It is owned by Graffias International, a shell for the Quorum. Emma was able to pull up the architectural plans on record with the city from its most recent renovation. I've been studying it too.

To make this charade believable, I flew in from Xia's home base of Beijing via a private jet with untraceable ownership. The plane's flight plan was altered three times while winging its way over the Pacific towards the United States—a necessary precaution if Acme was to throw off anyone who may not already know Xia's final destination.

We landed at Manassas Regional, a smaller airport outside of D.C. that might not have been watched. By then my prosthesis was in place and accessorized with brown surveillance contacts.

I'm certainly dressed to kill, and I don't mean that figuratively. But if all Mystery Date is expecting is a few sex toys, he'll be sorely disappointed. Instead, Acme has sewn in a few hidden pockets for such little items as a knife, a capped syringe with liquid Rohypnol—the knockout drug also known as a "roofie," for the goal of taking the target alive—and the smallest Glock available: the 43.

"We're here," Abu says finally.

I lift my head and put a smile on my face in order to steel myself for the mission at hand: taking down one more link in the Quorum leadership chain—

Even if it turns out to be Lee.

THE DOORBELL OF OUR DESTINATION—THE MANSION THAT TAKES up the whole block of Thirty-ninth and P Streets—sounds like Christmas church bells.

I wait a few minutes, but no one answers.

Strange.

I try the doorknob. It opens to my touch, but still, no one is there to greet me.

Hmmm.

Slowly, I cross the entry threshold. Before I'm six feet into the foyer, the door closes gently behind me and I hear the click of the doorknob—

And then the slide of a lock, followed by the latching of another.

I turn around to find that the door has automatically bolted itself in two places: near the top frame of the door, and near the bottom, close to the floor.

I also notice that the hinges on the door are held into place with twelve bolts apiece, so they aren't going anywhere.

Not good.

As quickly as I can, I move into the living room. A stack of logs crackles in the five-foot-tall fireplace. It is fronted by a nine-foot empire sofa, and flanked by two Queen Anne wingback chairs. The windows are covered by thick floor-to-ceiling swag curtains, tied back on each side by braided tasseled ropes draped over ornate hooks to reveal sheers made of stark white silk.

I walk over to them and pull back the sheers to find that the windows aren't glass inside of pane, but steel panels.

Okay, yes, I'm scared.

"Do you see what I'm seeing?" I murmur.

"Try another room," Jack answers matter-of-factly. But the silence that follows tells me that he has muted my ear bud. I presume he's giving the rest of the mission team orders to find a way to get me out of this hellhole.

Under any other circumstances I'd enjoy roaming through the exquisitely decorated rooms of this mansion. Not today. I jog through the downstairs to find the windows in every room the same: in lockdown mode.

The kitchen is in the rear of the house. The back door is also bolted shut from the outside, as are the double doors leading from the dining room to the backyard. By the time I get to the library, I realize that I'm back around to the front of the house. Its doors, which lead out onto the sun porch, are also made of steel.

Frantically, I tug at them, as if that's going to do any good.

In regard to its height and depth, the library's fireplace is almost identical to the one in the living room. It also houses a roaring blaze—too hot in fact, as if someone has set the gas starter beneath the grate on high. The flames lick the wood mantel jutting out above the opening. As one log crumbles into red-hot coals, two more roll beyond the hearth onto the varnished floor.

Embers catch hold of a plush Persian rug. I try to stamp out the flames, but I'm too late. "The ground floor is on fire!" I scream.

"Donna, the fires are deliberate! Some sort of accelerant has been used, for instant combustion and a quick burn!"

By now, smoke is also pouring out of the living and dining rooms.

"I'm heading upstairs!" I shout.

I take the staircase two steps at a time, since the ground floor is now an inferno, and each previous step incinerates behind me.

I am running for my life.

~

THE UPSTAIRS HALLWAY HAS AT LEAST SIX DOORS—THREE ON each side. I try the one closest to me: a well-appointed bedroom. I run to the window, only to discover that the opening is solid concrete.

I run back into the hall, toward the staircase—

Only to find that the bottom half of the stairs has disintegrated in the flames.

I hear a crash and turn around, just in time to see a fireball jump out of a hole in the hall floor.

"I've got to go up to the third floor!" I yell, in the hope that they hear me over the snap, crackle, and pop of the flames.

"Donna, don't!" Jack shouts. "This place is stone on the outside, and all of its exits are airtight—in other words, it's a mausoleum! Whatever air is left will draw the fire straight up like a wick! If you go up there, we may not be able to reach you—"

"Jack, I have no other choice!"

I hustle up the stairs to the third story. From the look of the simple rooms, it was previously the servants' quarters. But it's certainly too much to expect that the windows have regular glass-and-pane sashes. They too are filled with solid cement.

I run into the room closest to me. It takes up most of the

attic. Beds line the wall. Unfortunately, like the ones on the other floors below, the small garret windows have been cemented over.

I circle the big room desperately, like a caged animal. There are no other exits.

Jack is right: the fire, contained within the mansion's impenetrable stone walls, is sucking up the oxygen. Exhausted, hot, and weak from lack of air, I freeze. So, this is how it all ends?

Like a warm shawl, the finality of my life settles over me. Its threads are my dearest memories: the smiles and voices of my three children—Mary, Jeff, and Trisha; Jack's gentle kisses; and the heady euphoria of our lovemaking.

Those sensations will be lost to me forever.

And I'll be lost forever to those I love most.

No. I won't let it end here, like this.

Exhausted, I slump against the wall.

Ouch. The small of my back hit something—

A handle of some sort, to a metal panel in the wall.

I pull it open, expecting to find a cabinet, or perhaps a safe. I reach inside. Just like the door, the sides are made of sheet metal—not as heavy, and there is no bottom panel.

"I found a laundry chute!" I don't know if Jack or anyone else can hear me, but it's worth a try. "I'll meet you in the basement!"

I look around the room. Mattresses and sheets are bundled on top of the twin beds throughout the room. I grab one of the mattresses and stuff it down the chute. It's too dark to see how far it has fallen. Still, I do the same with a second mattress. Afterward, I hoist myself into the chute, curl up into a cannonball, and leap off into oblivion.

I pray for a safe landing, but, for all I know, I've tossed myself into the heart of the inferno.

By the count of three, I'm riding the second mattress down the chute. Two more seconds go by before I catch up with the first mattress. But I'm still flying down into the abyss, so I guess my weight, coupled with the speed in which I'm falling, may still earn me some pain.

I brace for it—

Oomph.

Not so bad.

In fact, bounced on my heels, I rise a foot into the air.

This time, when I land, my feet slip out from under me. I find myself on my backside.

I roll onto my knees. One of the four walls within the chute contains a door from which a laundress would have removed soiled linens. I shove my right arm below the mattresses and move it around until I find the door, which is also metal.

But it is latched from the outside. I kick it—hard—again and again.

I'm exhausted.

Then I hear it: the roar of a fireball. It's coming down the chute.

Damn it, the metal door at the top of the chute was left open.

I brace myself against the wall opposite the laundry room door in order to give it one more big kick—

It gives.

I roll out, slamming the door behind me.

The flames gasp for air. Finding no more, their whispers die in the chute.

I'm safe—for now, anyway. The basement is cinderblock on all sides. Besides a laundry room, it holds a large wine cellar. In this case, that's a good thing, not because I feel like celebrating, but because the wine cellar's metal door and cooling system—metal ducts that line the ceiling—create a barrier to the heat. It is the only thing standing between Death and me.

So how do I get out of this hellhole?

The only door leads up into the house, to and from the kitchen. Like the others, the opening is solid concrete. In this case, I breathe a sigh of relief.

Still, the room is heating up. Ah, I see why now! A gap between two of the metal ducts directly above me is bulging from the heat above it.

Just at that moment, the fire burns a hole through the ceiling, dropping sizzling embers at my feet.

I spot a solitary glass-pane window on the far wall, above a room-length laundry table. The window is high on the wall, and certainly not the ideal size: three feet wide side-to-side, but only two feet high, top-to-bottom.

Too bad. It's the only way out, so it'll have to do.

I grab an iron. Holding on to its electrical cord, I hurl it at the window. It crashes through an old glass pane, but the wooden sash holds firm.

As if trying to lasso a wild horse, I swing it over my head again and again and again—

Then I let it rip. This time, the iron crashes through the sash's wooden grid. All of it lands on the sidewalk.

I hop up on the table. The heat from inside the house is so intense that the stones and cinderblock are now hot. Still, I heave myself through the window.

My landing is anything but gentle. I'm scorched, scraped, bruised, and charred.

But, hey, I'm *alive.*

Jack runs toward me. Whereas my stone prison made it virtually impossible to hear my mission team's chatter, the words he utters now come in loud and clear. "She's on the P Street side! Meet us there!"

He lifts me into his arms and holds me as if he never wants to let me go. "I thought I'd lost you forever," he whispers through his kisses.

I laugh. "What, are you kidding? I'm almost Mrs. Jack Craig! There's not a team of assassins alive who can keep me from my happily ever after." I give him a come-hither wink. "Wait until you see what I have planned for our wedding night."

"I'm counting down the days." Tenderly, he tears the mask off my face. It is covered with soot. He stuffs it in his pocket.

I shudder. "I guess I can use it again, come Halloween."

He laughs. "I'm glad to see your sense of humor is back."

I roll my eyes.

"Hey listen, 'Almost Mrs. Craig,' I vote we don't wait for the honeymoon for some curl-your-toes sex. Not that we need the practice, but now that this shindig is over, what do you say to us taking the rest of the night to explore the few Tao sexual positions that are not yet part of our repertoire? I've heard tell that the one known as 'Silkworm Spinning a Cocoon' has women screaming from the rooftops, begging for more."

I feel my right eyebrow arch. "'Heard tell,' or 'heard it for yourself?'"

In mock shock, he raises his hands. But it would be easier to buy his innocence if he weren't chuckling at some distant memory. "A gentleman never kisses and tells," he concedes. Leaning into me, he adds, "As consolation, I hope you'll join me tonight in the attempt of a never-before-initiated Ananga Ranga position known as 'the Dragon Turns.' I promise you—"

Just when he's about to say something that I'm sure will keep my heart fluttering in anticipation, we hear a loud crash:

The first floor has collapsed into the basement.

The force of the roiling blaze spews from the broken window, throwing Jack to the ground, with me still in his arms.

My landing is softer than his: on top of my mister.

Really, not so soft—where it counts most. "You're always so *happy* to see me," I purr.

"Donna! Jack! Are you okay?" Abu runs up to us. Dominic is right on his heels.

I nod as Abu helps me to my feet. "Thank God, yes!"

Dominic taps his cell phone. "Ryan is on the line." He frowns. "He says POTUS somehow found out we're here— and he wants to see us, *pronto.*"

Jack mutters, "Why am I not surprised that Lee knows our whereabouts?"

Still more proof –at least, in Jack's eyes—that Lee is Quorum.

For now, the honeymoon is over.

2

Breaking the News to Your Bestie

There is a right way to break the news of your impending nuptials to the world. When telling, specifically, your bestie, here's how to do it with sensitivity and care:

First of all, do it in person. This way, you can see for yourself the range of emotions created by your wonderful news. You're sure to see the surprise in her eyes (along with the tears. How many times did she claim you were wasting your time with him?); anxiety (she's under the assumption that things will change between you. Funny, you feel the same way, but for different reasons. Whereas, before you envied her belle-of-the-ball exploits, from now on she'll be jealous of your happily-ever-after ending); doubt (if she insists he'll get cold feet before the wedding, tweak her nose and tell her how cute she is when she's got your back), and finally resignation. (Don't be surprised if she chooses a funeral theme for your wedding shower. And please don't be miffed should you discover that she's asked the rest of your friends to chip in for a gift card to the best divorce attorney in town.)

He will also have to break the news to his best bud. Make sure you're there when it happens, so that you can hear for yourself what his friend thinks of you.

Gentle hint: words like skank, hag, whore, and bitch are not a good thing. However, proving him right won't get you the results you want: veto power on any and all jerks in his posse.

Of course, you know that the best posse for him is just one other: YOU.

With all that has happened tonight, Lee is the last person I want to see.

While I stood vigil over Jack when he was in a coma, Lee came to the hospital room. I confronted him with Catherine's accusations that he was Quorum.

Angrily, Lee grabbed me. He wanted me to believe him when he told me she was wrong.

Despite his rage, he longed for me. It was obvious in his eyes. In his touch.

At that moment, Jack woke up from his coma. I ran to Jack's side. I smothered my beloved with kisses. Then I proposed to him.

For the past weeks, Jack had been proposing marriage. Each time, I'd said no. Foolishly, I presumed that where and how he popped the question was more important than the fact he'd proven his love for me, time and time again.

It's funny how your beloved's near-death experience puts everything into perspective.

Jack accepted my proposal with a kiss that promised a lifetime of love.

When I looked up, Lee was gone.

Now, I'm face-to-face with him again.

Jack doesn't see me giving Dominic the cutthroat sign: a finger swiping my throat. I can't face Lee, not after the ordeal I've gone through. I need time to put something else in perspective: If Lee is a Quorum member, Ryan will want to use me as the bait to trap him.

Dominic nods, then proclaims into his cell phone, "No problem, Chief. Yes, okay, got it: We're expected at the West Wing, but we're to take only one car. Local operatives will retrieve the other vehicles. And I assume they'll take Donna to our hotel? After her ordeal, I'm sure she's too shook up to…" He frowns. "But—but, Chief, to put it politely, she looks beastly! If I had no personal knowledge of her usual shopworn frumpishness, I'd mistake her for some skanky Fourteenth Street slagger—"

My "usual shopworn frumpishness?" The nerve of that wanker!

The only reason I'm not smacking him silly is that Jack bared his teeth when Dominic compared me to a "skanky slagger." He may beat me to the punch, literally.

I guess I should calm down, considering the favor Dominic is supposedly doing for me.

"—Seriously, Boss, despite the fact that she is in *no condition* to meet with POTUS, no one can deny that her continual surliness will certainly—"

Dominic pauses. His omnipresent smile has faded. The way Ryan is yelling, he could be heard across the Virginia state line.

Finally, Dominic sighs. "The president insists, does he? Ah! Well then, our liege has spoken. His knights—and handmaiden—must obey." He gives me the slightest shrug, as if to say *I'm sorry.*

I won't argue that point.

Abu pops the trunk to retrieve my overnight valise. He hands it to Jack, who hops into the back of the limousine after me. Dominic is about to join us, but Jack blocks the door. "Donna has to change before we get to the White House. She looks—let's see, how did you put it? Oh yes: 'beastly. Like a skanky slagger.'" He twists a thumb toward the front of the cab. "Abu has plenty of room up there."

Abu shakes his head. "I dunno. I doubt he's ever sat in the front seat of one of these things. What if he gets seasick and tosses his cookies?"

Dominic shifts his eyes in my direction. I mouth the word, *Sorry.*

He starts to say something, but holds his tongue. Instead, he slams the door as he gets into the cab's front passenger seat. My guess is that he'd rather not wave down a cab or hop an Uber to the White House, since it's not exactly smart spycraft.

I'll have to make it up to him somehow.

Note to self: purchase a Swedish massage at the Hotel Bel-Air's La Prairie Spa, followed by afternoon tea and crumpets for two, as I'm sure he'll talk the masseuse into joining him.

The cottage suite is on him.

"IT'S A GOOD THING YOU BROUGHT A SUITCASE OF CIVILIAN

duds on this mission," Jack says encouragingly. He opens the case—

Where he finds a sheer nightie.

The fantasy that puts a naughty grin on his face is replaced by a frown that reflects the reality of our situation. "Um…no. Okay, let's see what else we've got here."

He holds up a bra and panties with peek-a-boo cutouts in strategic places: not exactly a proper change of clothes for a confab at the White House.

They are made of chocolate.

When Abu stops short, a can of whipped cream rolls out of my case and onto the floor.

Jack stares down at it, mesmerized. I know what he's thinking:

This is what we could—what we should *be doing right now.*

Hell, right here, for that matter.

As tempting as that is, calmer heads—mine, as opposed to the one beneath his waist—must prevail. To bait the truth out of Lee, we've both got to stay on task. I snatch the canister off the floor. Tossing it back into the case, I murmur, "It might be quicker if I look."

I rummage in my valise and pull out a bra, panties, a slip, and a demure navy Tadashi Shoji lace sheath dress. "Close your eyes," I command him, knowing full well that he'll do nothing of the sort.

Instead, he leans back into the seat, a grin of anticipation on his face.

I've just unzipped what's left of the gown from hell when Abu turns a corner so sharply that I'm thrown off the seat.

My squeal gives Dominic an excuse to crane his neck

backward—just in time to see my double nip slip before I right myself and cover up my naughty bits.

Dominic is so entranced that he totally misses Jack's glare —until my betrothed commands Abu to roll up the privacy glass. As it rises, Dominic finally turns around, but first he grins approvingly.

I forgive him, only because I know he can't help himself. It's primal, in the same way in which a male dog must lick its balls.

There will be no more peek-a-boo. A bigger game is afoot: Risk.

At stake: our futures.

"DON'T BLOW YOUR STACK," I WARN JACK. WE'RE OUTSIDE THE Oval Office, waiting for the president's secretary, Eileen Woodley, to beckon us in.

"Give me some credit," he hisses back. "I've been waiting for this day for a long time. I won't blow it now."

Egad, Eileen must have overheard him too, because she looks up from her computer and gives me a whisper of a smile. I like Eileen. She's one of those women who men describe as solid, which every woman knows is Man-Code for, *she wasn't hired for her looks.*

Considering she's been with Lee since his very first dotcom success, I would guess her skill set is much more important: say, helping him stay focused, initially in the tech world and now at the White House. Despite what Jack thinks of POTUS, Lee's loyalty to the person who has always had his back says a lot about him.

Acme has also shown him loyalty. If Jack accuses him of being in league with the country's worst enemy, I hope he remembers this.

"Let me take the lead," Jack murmurs.

I smile demurely. "But, of course." Like, duh. The smartest thing I can do is keep my mouth shut and let the men duke it out.

Dominic will also be in the meeting, and Ryan will be on speakerphone.

But Abu has opted out. "In case you want a quick pick-up, I'll leave on my tracker," he reassures us. Like Houdini, he's always planning his next escape.

I can't say I blame him. When Abu was an infant, he and his folks caught the last plane out of Baghdad before the Shah's regime fell to the Ayatollah.

Eileen may not be a looker, but the fact that she is ignoring Dominic makes her as tempting to him as a raw steak to a beagle with a tapeworm. Only when he sits at the edge of her desk does she turn to face him, and that's in an attempt to scare him with a withering stare. Had he been looking at her face instead of her bosom, he'd have been as frightened as Jack and me.

Instead, he murmurs, "That is a simply stunning brooch, milady." His finger hovers much too close to the black opal in the center of a gold setting. He waits for the usual response: A giggle, perhaps; or a shyly stammered thank-you. The best of all would be a flirtatious double-entendre—

But no, not a peep.

Just a frosty glare.

Oh shit.

Dominic stares back. It's oh-so-primal for him. I feel as if

I'm in the Serengeti, waiting for a lion to take down a gazelle with one mighty pounce and one sweep of its claw.

But this time, Dominic is the gazelle.

Jack and I exchange glances. From the look on his face, I can read his mind:

He's insulted the person closest to Lee. We are so fucked.

But just then, Eileen shrugs, lifts her hand and pats the brooch. "Old family heirloom. It's my lucky charm." She nods toward the Oval Office doors. "The president will see you now."

Dominic slides off the desk. Before she can protest, he bows slightly, lifts her hand, and brushes it with his lips.

"Fresh," she mutters under her breath.

But she's smiling.

Now that it seems all's well that ends well, Jack smacks Dominic in the back of the head.

Lee will be harder to charm and it won't be Dominic who can do it.

LEE STANDS TALL. HE FACES THE WINDOW, LOOKING OUT ONTO the Rose Garden. When he finally turns around, he isn't smiling, and he doesn't offer to shake hands. Instead, he nods curtly at the couches flanking the coffee table that sits dead center on the beige carpet bearing the presidential seal.

He's not alone. A Secret Service agent—broad-shouldered, over seven feet tall, his copper-toned hair buzzed in a military cut—closes the door behind us, then positions himself in front of it. I guess that's in case we try to make a run for it. I recognize him from my previous meetings with

Lee. His last name is Muldoon, but I think his first name, Lurch, is a joke on Lee's part.

An aide is also in the room. The man sits in the wingback chair farthest from the president's desk. The other wingback, closest to the desk, is where Lee will sit when he chooses to join us.

The aide is tall. He has dark hair and deep blue eyes. He can't be more than twenty-six, if that. It's easy to envision him wowing the girls with his WonkSpeak on First Thursday at Lounge 201; in other words, he's a real heart-breaker.

He swipes furiously at an iPad, but his eyes aren't on the screen. They are on us. He is following his boss's lead. In other words, the most we're granted is a grimace and a soft declaration, "Todd Courtland."

"Jack Craig," Jack responds with a nod. He points to me. "And this is—"

Todd raises his hand. "No need for introductions. The president has already given me the lay of the land."

Okay, gotcha. So that's how it's going to be.

Jack and I sit together on one of the couches. Dominic takes the other, but positions himself close to Lee's chair.

The silver tray on the coffee table holds a Waterford crystal pitcher and six cut crystal glasses. I pour some for myself. Dominic follows suit.

No one says anything until Eileen's husky voice announces via speakerphone, "Mr. Clancy is on the line."

"Put him through," Lee responds.

"Mr. President, I hope all is well with you and the family." Ryan isn't much of a talker to begin with, so I'm surprised that he opts for happy-pappy patter.

"Happy and healthy, one and all." Can Ryan detect the ice on the line?

If so, he pretends otherwise. "I hear that you'll all be spending a good six weeks at the Western White House for the summer."

I met Babette when she and her first and now deceased husband, Jonah Breck, built their palatial compound in Hilldale: Lion's Lair. Later, she married Lee there. It's where they make their home when they aren't at the White House.

"In this case, your reconnaissance is right," Lee concedes, as if it isn't always the case. "We leave D.C. in a day or two, now that Janie is out of school for the summer. As you well know, that doesn't mean the world stands still." He frowns as he considers the implication. "With that in mind, let's do this."

He takes his seat. He turns to me, not Jack. His tone is congenial, in fact, conspiratorial—but his eyes are ice cold. "Donna, tell me: what brings you to D.C.?"

I KNOW BETTER THAN TO LIE TO LEE. HE AND I ARE BEYOND IT.

But that doesn't mean I can't couch my words in such a way that he doesn't necessarily learn or guess the truth: that we don't trust him.

That is, Jack doesn't trust him. Not since Lee's name popped up on an eight-year-old stock prospectus for Graffias International, the Quorum's legitimate financial arm.

I'm on the fence until we find evidence that he knew of Graffias' connection with the Quorum.

As for Lee's trust of us, here goes everything:

"We're following the trail of Xia's White House contact."

I watch Todd out of the corner of my eye. He scowls, and the scrolling has stopped, so I guess I have his attention too.

Lee leans in, as if I've made the most intriguing statement. "If I remember correctly, you accused me of being her contact."

My face flames hotly. "Our intention was to rule you out."

A slight smile rises on Lee's lips. "You said, 'was.' Does this mean you've done so?"

His question hovers menacingly in the air like a vulture over fresh road kill.

Jack leans back into the couch. His eyes are lowered, as if he's drowsy.

As if he hasn't a care in the world.

Nothing could be further from the truth.

On the other hand, Dominic could be a corpse, now that all the blood has left his face. Gitmo isn't the tropical resort he has in mind for his upcoming vacation. Besides, his kind burn so easily.

Will Lee recognize Dominic's lack of rosy pallor as his gambling tell? I pray not, but he has seen it before: when they faced off in a high-stakes Baccarat game on Fantasy Island, a resort financed by one of Lee's companies. In truth, it's how Dominic looks when he goes into anaphylactic shock. But Lee may not have known it was happening at the time—

Unless he had something to do with it.

I look down at the water glass in front of Dominic. He hasn't touched it.

Come to think of it, I'll pass too.

Slowly, I lower my glass onto the table and take a deep breath. "Mr. President, I don't think we'd be sitting here if we hadn't. Do you?"

He thinks for a moment. Finally, he smiles. "What did you find out?"

"Our one lead went nowhere because our contact knows Xia is no longer among the living." *Gee, Lee—you knew it too.*

"I'm sorry to hear that. It's vital to national security that you find the culprit, at all costs—and no matter where the trail leads."

"We feel the same way, Mr. President," Ryan's God-like declaration booms over us.

"I thought so. That's why I've asked Todd to join us. He is my liaison to the National Security Council. Feel free to call on him for any access you'll need for your investigation. All of the country's resources will be at your disposal."

Jack nods. "Will do. And as for vetting White House staff, who can we count on?"

Before Lee can answer, Todd replies, "I'll be glad to handle that as well, Mr. President."

Ah, *such* an eager little beaver.

"And who at Acme will be our point person?" Todd asks.

"Jack is the team's mission leader," Ryan informs him.

"I'd prefer Donna." Lee's tone makes it very clear that there will be no more discussion on the matter.

Okay, enough of this. Lee needs to accept the lay of the land. "As flattered as I am at your confidence in me, I may be taking a personal furlough," I smile demurely. "Jack accepted my hand in marriage."

Jack's eyes, open wide with surprise, swivel in my direction. They seem to scream, *Where in hell are you going with this?*

My eyes answer, *Trust me on this.*

Lee's smile falters. "Yes, I remember. I had the honor of being in the room at his…awakening."

"I remember you were there, Lee. I appreciated your concern on my behalf," Jack says.

Gee, even I believe him—well, almost.

Lee turns to him. "Had you not recovered, it would have been a great loss, both to me and to the country. You've always been a good friend and a strong ally."

"We feel the same about you and the first lady—" Jack's voice is as warm as I've ever heard it.

Okay, what the hell is he *up to?*

"—Which is why we'd be honored if you were in our wedding party."

What?

I know it's Ryan's dream come true, especially if we're to determine if Lee is, in fact, Quorum. But, to use my wedding as a trap?

Ain't gonna happen.

So that Jack gets the message, I grind a fingernail into his side.

He grimaces, but it doesn't shut him up. "Would it be too much of an imposition to ask you to perform the ceremony?"

Lee opens his mouth, but says nothing. Instead, he looks at me.

He is waiting for my consent.

From the moment we entered the room, my mouth has been cantilevered into a convincing grin. But Lee's gaze is scrutinizing my eyes, as if they are hieroglyphics that hold some momentous secret.

Perhaps the truth of how I feel about him.

For that reason, I can't glance away. Otherwise, he'll realize that I don't trust him.

I *can't* trust him. How could I, after what I've just heard? After what I've just been through?

I deepen my gaze. The flecks of gold resemble faraway planets frozen in the ice blue galaxies of his eyes.

Whatever it is he's seeking in mine, I pray that he sees it.

Apparently, not. His answer is a regretful shake of his head.

I realize why when he adds, "The honor is all mine."

"Great!" Jack feigns relief with a wide open grin. "Wow! Well then, we've got a lot to do between now and then."

"As soon as possible, send all the details to Eileen." I've never heard such sadness in Lee's voice. He stands up. Holding out his hand to Jack, he adds, "I wouldn't miss it for the world. Babette will be thrilled too. You're her closest friend in Hilldale."

Following Jack's lead, I rise too.

As the men shake hands, Lee asks, "Mind if I kiss the bride?"

Jack pauses only a second. "Not at all."

Still stunned at all the bullshit flying around the room, I say nothing as Lee leans down.

Instinctively, I tilt my face toward his. I'm expecting a chaste, brotherly kiss on the cheek. It is anything but. His lips find mine, and linger there—

So long.

Too long.

At least, long enough that my embarrassment in having Jack witness this—even after he set me up as bait—has summoned up Babette Chiffray's syrupy sweet voice in my head: "Well, well! Isn't this a surprise!"

A chill runs up my spine as I realize it's not my guilty conscience I hear, but the real deal.

Oh, hell—she's here.

To make matters worse, Babette has been embarrassed in front of one of her aides. The slack-jawed woman, right on Babette's heels, is so taken aback that she drops her iPad.

So much for Lee's attempt at positioning me as Babette's BFF.

If looks could kill, right now I'd be six feet under.

3

Choosing Your Bridesmaids

Bridesmaids are women who are close to the bride, either by relation or by friendship, but not necessarily both. You may have as many bridesmaids as your budget allows and your popularity merits. As you narrow your choices, should it come down to choosing between a cousin you can't stand and a lifelong friend, choose the latter.

A harder choice is between the annoying cousin, and the girlfriend who once dated your betrothed and who you suspect still carries a torch for him. While it would be nice to rub the supposed gal pal's nose in your great fortune, doing so and making her pay for her own dress and shoes may be enough to have her coming on to the groom as payback. In this case, the annoying cousin is a safer choice.

However, if you must choose between the same distasteful cousin and some bag lady plucking garbage from a bus stop trashcan, again, go for the cousin. Odds are, she'll still be more annoying, but she'll smell much better.

Now, if your choice is between the torch-carrying hussy and the homeless woman, this time go for the bag lady. Even if she makes a move on the groom and he acts on her advances, he'll certainly reek of Eau du Bag Lady, and you'll know immediately what the future holds, no matter who comes on to your husband.

At that point, you can deal with the problem accordingly: castration.

(Helpful Hint: the Wüsthof Classic 7-inch Hollow Ground Santoku Knife you've received as a wedding gift will do the trick quite nicely.)

"BABETTE, DARLING—YOUR BRUNCH IS OVER ALREADY?" Unlike me, Lee isn't embarrassed at her presence. He's annoyed.

"Wives of foreign diplomats are such timid creatures, especially those from the Middle East." Babette rolls her eyes. "It's hard enough to entertain one wife of a foreign diplomat, let alone five of them! Frankly, I don't know where Salem Rahmin al-Sadah finds the stamina for his harem." She raises a brow playfully at Jack.

She was entertaining the wives of Graffias International's CEO? *Cha-ching!* Maybe it's time for a little chitchat with my BFF and neighbor. Better yet, if I can plant a bug on her—

Oops, wait a minute. She just caught me in a lip lock with her husband. My bad.

No, really, his bad, but she'll hate me just the same. And so will Ryan, when he realizes that Lee's move blew the best up-close surveillance op ever.

"So sorry you found it such a bore. Funny, since you get

along so swimmingly with Salem." Lee shrugs as he beckons Babette to his side. "No matter. You're just in time for the great news."

"Considering your response, it must be spectacular," Babette purrs. Despite her icy response, I can only imagine her eyes narrowing warily, and her forehead pursed with suspicion. But alas, with three eyelifts and a forehead reinforced with Botox, I'll never know for sure.

"Donna and I are getting married," Jack explains.

"Oh." Babette tears up. "I...I can't believe it!" Why, because she never thought that Jack, her fantasy fuck, could fall in love with someone as imperfect as me?

"Well then, congratulations are in order!" She throws herself into Jack's arms and puts him in a lip lock. Frankly, she's buried her tongue so deep in his throat that she could be licking his tonsils.

One would think her blatant flirtation would bother Lee. Oddly, he seems oblivious to it.

Todd, on the other hand, is seething. *Interesting.*

"In fact, I'll be marrying them," Lee informs her.

Babette's head whips around so quickly that you'd think she was due for an exorcism. "I beg your pardon?" It takes momentous effort on her part to raise a brow. I commend her for even trying. "Lee, really! You're the leader of the free world! When will you have time for"—She tries to smile, but it's more or less a grimace—"them?"

Lee's dark stare shuts her up, and fast. "Their nuptials are imminent, so they should coincide with our retreat to Lion's Lair. And considering all that Donna and Jack have done on our behalf—even before we met, when Jonah was still alive—I think we can both take time to celebrate their happiness."

Babette winces at the name of her deceased first husband. Of course, Lee is right. In fact, attempted to kill the son of a bitch, but one of his rivals—my terrorist ex-husband, Carl—beat me to the punch. Had I told the world the truth about Jonah Breck's treasonous acts as one of the original thirteen Quorum leaders, Babette's reputation would have been ruined.

"Yes, the timing is certainly convenient," she murmurs. Suddenly, a thought strikes her. She grabs both my hands in hers. "And, of course, Janie will be your flower girl! It'll be a family affair!"

I shake my head. "Yes, well, this *is* about family—*my* family. I'm sure you realize it's Trisha's role in our wedding."

"Why not double your pleasure, and double their fun? Won't they look adorable, going down the aisle together? We can dress them as twins. I'm sure Trisha would love that!"

Behind her back, Jack catches my eye and shrugs, as if to say, *She has a point.*

"Well…" I sigh. "If Trisha agrees, then I guess—"

"Wonderful!" Babette snaps her fingers at her aide. "Narcissa, make a note to text Janie to call Trisha and tell her the good news."

What nerve! Like hell she will—

"Excellent!" Ryan booms through the speakerphone. "Babette, your offer is tremendously generous. How could Donna turn it down?"

Watch me. "Really, Babette, I can't let you do it. I mean—we've already asked so much of your family—"

She swats away my protest as if being annoyed by a moth. "Nonsense! I'll hear no more about it!" Her smile widens to the point that she bares her teeth at me. I'd never noticed how pointy her canine cuspids were until now.

Jack moves between Babette and my clenched fist. He's afraid I'll miss my own wedding if I end up in a maximum-security prison for the first lady's murder. *As if.* "What Donna is trying to say is that this is awfully kind of you, Babette."

What the hell?

"I'll bet! And, on such short notice! For shame, Donna!" She cocks her head to one side. "What is the date, exactly?"

"We were discussing the last weekend in June," I mutter.

"Oh, my God! You haven't yet locked in *the date?*" She shakes her head in wonder. "Then I guess it means you haven't got a location, either."

"Yes, well, what with Jack's near-fatal coma and all—"

"Excuses, excuses." She wags her finger at me. "Of which there are none for a lazy bride." She sighs. "How perturbing. Why, this little endeavor may not come off after all." The hope in her voice matches the longing in her eyes for Jack.

He and I answer, adamantly and in unison, "Oh, yes, it will!"

"Ah! Well then, it's settled. I insist on planning it for you."

Just as I say, "No, you won't—" Jack proclaims, "That would be great!"

"Narcissa, call Chantal Desmarais. She does me for weddings."

The aide nods frantically. Another flurry of iPad swiping ensues.

"Why do you feel the need to hold on to your wedding planner's number? You're already married—to the leader of the free world," I point out.

Babette strokes Lee's arm like a favored pet. "Sadly, I'm attracted to men for whom assassination attempts are an occupational hazard." She cocks her head to one side. "Oh, my God, Donna! I think I've stumbled across the one thing we have in common."

She's got me there.

Todd takes it upon himself to hustle Jack, Dominic, and me out of the Oval Office. "The president was kind enough to pass along your personal email, Donna. I've sent you a secure missive, so that now your emails and texts to me will get through the White House server."

"I'll open it, pronto," I assure him.

It's not lost on Jack when Todd places his hand on the small of my back and murmurs, "The two of us will make quite a team."

Jack grits his teeth, but keeps his arms at his sides.

He thinks he's pissed? He's not the one who has to deal with Babette.

At least, not if I have any say in the matter.

I better not find her measuring his inseam for a tux.

"We've been airborne for a full hour, and you haven't said a word." Jack holds out a peace offering: a gift box of sea-salt caramels from Lula's in Santa Cruz.

"Here's one: fuck off."

"That's two words," he points out.

"Consider the second word a bonus. It's a hell of a long ride."

Still, I snatch the chocolates from his hand and cram one in my mouth. I'm starving, but I refuse to grab grub from the plane's galley with the rest of the mission team.

Abu and Dominic have taken the hint. They stay clear of my compartment in the Gulfstream 650ER. Instead, they've grabbed the couches in the front of the plane. A rugby match is on the television. They watch it out of one eye, while keeping the other on their laptops, where they write their case notes on our operation.

My own case note was sent when we hit cruising altitude. It was short and not so sweet:

TO: R. Clancy, CEO

> *FR: D. Stone, Senior Operative*
>
> *CC: J. Craig, Operation China Doll Mission Leader*
>
> *You sold me out.*
>
> *Don't expect an invitation to the wedding, because the way it* looks now, there probably won't be one. —Donna Stone

"I admire the brevity of your case notes," Jack says, trying hard not to smile, but he's failing miserably.

"I wish I could say I appreciated how you handled Babette today, but I can't," I mumble through a jaw full of chewy caramel.

He kneels beside me so that we are eye to eye. "It's the chance we're looking for to get close enough to her, to prove that you're right: that she's Quorum." He reaches for one of the chocolates.

I slap his hand away. "Or to prove me wrong, and that it's Lee," I counter.

"Whom, by the way, you played very well." Jack shrugs. "Appealing to his ego worked like a charm."

"As it does with most men, you included." I bat my eyes at him. Then, in my best imitation of Babette's baby-doll patois, I coo, *"Oooh Jack! Pucker up for a kiss that will knock your socks off, and prove that you're marrying the wrong woman—"*

He knows one way to shut me up: he kisses me.

His lips taste of the coarse pink Himalayan salt that laces these yummy candies, and the longing that makes me want to set my anger aside. I fight the urge to lick them—not because I still crave the sweetness of dark chocolate, but because I can't suppress my desire for him.

As if reading my mind, he takes my hand and pulls me into his arms.

Our lips never part. Instead, our bodies mesh as one.

He carries me into the last cabin, kicking the door shut behind him before falling with me onto the only piece of furniture in it: a bed.

"Ouch!" I roll over onto my stomach in order to get away from whatever is poking me in the back.

Turns out that it's Dominic's hairbrush.

If he thinks he can lay claim to the room by strewing the contents of his valise all over the place, he's got another think coming. With one arm, Jack sweeps all of Dominic's crap back into his case. With the other, he opens the door.

The suitcase lands in the hall with a thud.

"Blimey wankers!" Dominic shouts. Then: "Bollocks! My Hermês Body Wash went all over the place!"

The pungent scent of *Eau d'Orange Verte* wafts our way.

I'm sure we'd be queasy from the overwhelmingly sweet stench if our empirical senses weren't already stimulated with the touch and smell and taste and sight and sounds of each other in an orgasmic climax.

~

I SIT STRAIGHT UP IN THE BED. "TRISHA IS GOING TO HATE ME!"

Jack opens an eye. "It's a rite of passage. It was bound to happen sooner or later."

I shove him—hard. "I was praying for later. And, no, I don't mean she'll hate me in general. She's going to hate me *specifically,* because I have to renege on my promise to have her as my one and only flower girl—thanks to your open invitation to all the Chiffrays."

My declaration has roused him into an upright position. "Oh, hell. If you tell her how it went down, she'll hate me too!"

I choke on my laughter. "Get used to it, Daddy Dearest."

"No need to have her hate us both, right? One of us has to be the good cop. What say you take the fall for my misdeed"—To entice me, his lips roam over my shoulders —"just this once?"

"I say dream on. We're in this together." I stroke Jack's chest. "Okay, listen, we'll get home in time to pick up the kids from school. Ryan doesn't expect us back in the office until after dinner tonight. I'll text Aunt Phyllis to grab Trisha from ballet class. Why don't you pick up Mary and Evan, while I do middle school carpool? We'll grill burgers and catch up on all we missed while we were out of town. Then tonight, when we tuck her into bed—together—we'll break the news to her."

He lifts my hand and uses it to scratch his five-o'clock shadow. "Despite her—and our—feelings about Babette, maybe she'll think it's exciting, and historically significant that she stood beside the President of the United States at her parents' wedding. And if it turns out that Lee is fronting the Quorum, we'll give her something else to remember the Chiffrays: our Medals of Honor."

"And if he's not, she can visit her parents in jail," I remind him. "Either way, it'll be a memorable event."

4

Four Reasons Why You Need a Wedding Planner

The best way in which to enjoy your wedding ceremony is to stay oblivious to all the hard work and effort that, in the end, make it a rousing success. That's just the first reason why you want to hire a wedding planner! Here are three more:

- *Reason #2: You'll be too busy thinking about more important things—like how to lose another ten pounds, so that you fit into the wedding dress you bought almost a year ago.*
- *Reason #3: You'll need someone to blame if (a) the canapés are soggy, (b) your mother hates the seating arrangement, or (c) the florist brings the wrong flowers; and*
- *Reason #4: Someone needs to play "bad cop." Case in point: your mother would never forgive you for bitch-slapping your bridesmaid-slash-sister out of her giggles before she promenades down the aisle in front of you, but she'll accept seeing li'l sis pummeled by your*

wedding planner. After all, the woman is simply doing her job!

W‌HEN J‌EFF'S PAL, C‌HEEVER B‌ING, HOPS IN MY SUV, HE DOES the unthinkable: he shoves my son aside so that he can plop down in the front passenger seat.

This is *verboten* for two reasons. First, this specific seat is reserved either for my youngest, Trisha, or my son, Jeff. Cheever knows quite well that the rabble—that is, he and my other carpool charge, Morton Smith—sit in the back.

Secondly, I don't need his baseball practice stench wafting in my direction.

I'm just about to remind him of this (my guess is that a twist of the ear will do it) when I realize that he's fixated on me.

Well, on my stomach, anyway.

Surprising, since I usually catch him looking at my boobs. (For that, he's learned to expect a kick in the pants.)

To break his trance, I snap my fingers in front of his eyes.

He shakes his head, confused. "You don't look ready to pop. I mean, you're carrying a small tire, but that could be your advanced years."

I grab his collar, jerking him so close that we're eye to eye. "What the heck do you mean by that?"

"You know: knocked up, bun in the oven, baby on board. All I'm trying to say is that you look almost normal." His curiosity gets the better of him. His hand moves toward my stomach—

But I grab it just before he commits another unthinkable act: *touching me.*

My goal was the count of ten, but I only make it to six before I have to ask: "Why, in the name of sanity, would you think I'm pregnant?"

"My mom says it's the only reason Mr. Craig would marry you—so that the kid won't be a bastard."

Why, that *bitch!*

I'm no stranger to the fact that Cheever's mother, Penelope, despises me. Her snide asides to others about me are made just loud enough for me to catch them. Her meanmommy posse—Tiffy Swift, and the unfortunately named Hayley Coxhead—are her Greek chorus in recounting my mommy misdemeanors and my public indiscretions to everyone in Hilldale.

My children are no exception to their snide asides.

On the other hand, I've been the soul of discretion when it's come to the discovery of Penelope's peccadillos, many of which expose her as a third-rate mother and a first-class slut.

I've cut her some slack because I'm a lady.

Okay, yeah, and because I've accidentally set her on fire at least twice.

Well, the honeymoon is over. If pyrotechnics is her fate, who am I to stand in the way?

Usually, it takes fourteen minutes to get from Hilldale Middle School to Penelope's rambling cottage. I make it in eight. Even Cheever would have applauded the way in which I outran the two cop cars on my tail. However, he's now shaking in his boots as he contemplates all the ways in which I could make his mother suffer, including any attempt on my part to disembowel the apple of her eye:

Him.

He shouldn't worry. I've never been one to shoot the messenger. However, on several occasions, the perpetrator of the message has been blown to smithereens.

By the time I turn onto Cheever's street, he's wet his pants.

I was already resigned to the need for a full fumigation and detailing of the passenger seat. Now, I guess I'll have to replace it altogether.

Still, it's a small price to pay for putting Penelope Bing in her place, once and for all.

DESPITE THEIR OWN DISGUST AT CHEEVER'S LACK OF BLADDER control, Jeff and Morton haven't had the nerve to chide him about it. Neither wants to deflect my anger in their direction. Smart boys.

I swerve into the Bings' driveway, barely skidding to a stop in order to avoid hitting Penelope, who stands dead center in it as she plucks through a stack of envelopes she just pulled from a mailbox entwined with pale pink climbing roses.

"What the heck?" she squeals, as she stumbles backward, breaking a heel off of her Louboutins. "Damn it!" She swats the air in frustration.

Two bees, obviously upset that she's invading their nectar reconnaissance, swoop in different directions before regrouping to hover menacingly over her head.

The two neighbors who stand across the street admiring the rhododendron bushes of a third are now enthralled enough to freeze their chitchat mid-sentence. This is quite frustrating, since the last thing I need are a couple of witnesses to a murder. Note to self: *Play. It. Cool—*

Cheever jumps out. Running to his mother, he howls, "Mom, save me from the fat pregnant psycho lady!"

Penelope clasps him to her bosom. The imperious smile on her surgically-enhanced mug is proof that she's accomplished her goal:

Once again, I am Hilldale's social pariah.

I can think of one way in which to wipe off her sneer. But, no, I fight the urge to lift my foot off the brake and mash it onto the gas.

Instead, I put the car in park and leap out. It's finally time for our long-awaited heart-to-heart. "Did you tell your son that I'm getting married because I'm pregnant?"

Penelope smiles. "But…aren't you? Do you mean to say that those extra pounds you're packing are just plain old fat?"

"I am not fat," I growl. "I'm *healthy.*"

"'Healthy?'" Her emphasis on the word is accompanied by air quotes. "Is that what we're calling obesity these days?"

"Give it a break, Penelope! For God's sake, I'm a size four! Just because I don't heave after every meal, like you and the rest of your coven…Wait! Don't try to change the subject!" I'm so angry that I'm stuttering.

I take a step forward, so that she's within throttling distance, should my otherwise gentle powers of persuasion fail to achieve the desired result. "I'm tired of you implying that I've somehow roped Jack into some sort of—*shotgun wedding!*"

She pats my arm sympathetically. "But *of course* you haven't, dear! The fact that he's stuck by your side this long has nothing at all to do with the fact that you'd murder him in his sleep otherwise."

It would be easier to assassinate her in her sleep—or shower, or while she's shopping, or driving…you name it. But why tip her off to this fact?

Or the rest of my Hilldale neighbors, for that matter, three whose eyes gleam in anticipation of an impending mom-on-mom smack down. They hate Penelope as much as I do. Still, it ain't gonna happen. At least not in public.

I shake off all my (and their) bada-bing-to-Penelope-Bing fantasies—for now, anyway. "Let me make this crystal clear to you," I hiss, just loud enough for her to hear. "If I you say one more cruel word about me to anyone—Tiffy, Hayley, a teacher, a neighbor"—I yank Cheever up by his collar —"even your evil little spawn here, I'll make your life so miserable that you'll—"

One of the bees lands on Penelope's forehead. Of course, with the amount of Botox injected there, she doesn't feel it. But to anyone who may be nose-to-nose with her, it's quite distracting, to say the least. I reach up in order to flick it away—

But the bee is quicker than me, and flies off safely.

I flick Penelope instead.

Furious, her eyes widen. The next thing I know, she's slapped me.

Thrilled, Cheever yells, "Cat fight!"

Nah. I mean, let's face it, it's not much of a cat fight when your opponent's swipe at your face lands as lightly on your cheek as a dandy dueler's glove. It's not because I want to encourage her to put some effort into it that I slap her with the back of my hand, but an inbred defense mechanism.

My smack catches her by surprise.

Fear dilates her eyes. Her natural instinct is good—to back off.

But how can she do so, when the little apple of her eye shoves her forward while cowering for safety behind her? Penelope feels obligated to take the hint:

If there was ever a time to be a tiger mom, it's now.

Proof that she's more adept in verbal sparring than outright mortal combat comes with her next move: a fist aimed at my gut.

Before it reaches its destination, I grab it and twist it so high behind her back that she doubles over from the pain. Penelope may be able to squeeze into a minus-two dress size, but her bony ass is still a large enough target for my foot. One kick puts her face down on the ground.

That shows her who's boss.

I take a triumphant breath and look around, only to find that there are no spoils in my victory, just spoiled relationships:

With my neighbors, whose mouths are slack-jawed with horror.

With my son, whose eyes glisten with tears.

"You all saw it!" Penelope shouts. "She attacked me—for protecting my poor baby! I'll never let him near her, ever again!"

Miffed, Cheever whines, "Mom, I'm not a baby,"

My walk of shame to the SUV is only a few feet, but every inch of it burns with my new reality:

I've set the worst example for my child.

By the time I reach the door, Morton has already jumped out. Thrilled, he pumps his fist ecstatically. "You kick ass, Mrs. Stone! But I'll walk home from here. I'd hate for my mom to be snubbed because I'm still riding with Jeff."

Ah, well. I should look on the bright side. No need to send out obligatory wedding invitations to my neighbors, now that I know I'm *persona non-grata*.

JEFF DOESN'T SAY A WORD THE WHOLE WAY HOME.

My attempts at small talk are ignored. During my apology, which begins with a blathering attempt to explain about the bee, and how my survival skills work instinctively, he holds up a hand. "Mom, please! Don't make it any worse."

"Worse?" As if that were possible. "Jeff, please listen… You're right. I have no justification for my actions back there. I'm sorry I embarrassed you in front of your friends."

"They aren't my friends." He shrugs. "Maybe Morton—depending on how the wind blows." He doesn't have to tell me that, right now a gale force tornado is on the horizon, and both of us are in its path.

Should Penelope have her way, it will be a direct hit.

We've just pulled onto our street when Jeff puts his hand on my shoulder. Our eyes meet in the rearview mirror. "Mom, I know how hard it is to be normal, after…after all that you've been through since…well, since our birth father left us."

It takes one to know one. Jeff's ordeal as a terrorist hostage pushed him front-and-center onto a stage no child should ever trod upon: senseless violence, and its horrible *entr'acte*: the death of innocence.

I pull over to the curb. After letting the car idle in park, I put my hand over his and force my mouth into a semblance of a smile. "I can always count on you. Still, I wish I'd kept my cool. Penelope lives to make my life miserable."

Curiosity furrows his brow. "But she can't, really, can she? Not if you don't care what she thinks."

"You're right. Her opinion means nothing to me. But yours—and Mary's and Trisha's and Jack's and Evan's—means everything. When I let Mrs. Bing goad me with her cruelty, I let down those whom I love the most."

He shakes his head. "You have it all wrong. We love you —we will *always* love you—no matter what you do or say, even if it's just embarrassing or stupid or…deadly."

"It's what I have to do—"

Before I can say anything else, he stops me by raising a finger to my lips. "We know, Mom. We accept it because you do it to protect us"—he points out the window—"and them too, even if they don't know it." He sighs. "Frankly, I'm glad we aren't inviting the Bings. They live to hate us." Finally, he smiles. "And besides, Cheever would eat all the cake."

I laugh. "Speaking of which, so that this event goes off without a hitch, I'm assigning everyone a wedding task. Do you want to be in on the cake decision?"

Jeff shakes his head. "We'd better leave that to Trisha. It's all she talks about—well, that, and dress shopping for her role as official flower girl."

Oh heck. I just remembered. Trisha will soon get wise to the fact that I had Aunt Phyllis block Janie's calls to her. In any event, tonight I break the news to Trisha in person that Janie wants to horn in on her role in my wedding.

"Besides," Jeff continues, "I'm doing a spreadsheet of the guest list."

"I guess we can forget the rest of Hilldale too," I opine.

"Great, even more cake for us."

I kiss his cheek. "That's one way to make lemonade from lemons."

The sooner Jack and I get married, the better. Is it wishful thinking to think I can annihilate the Quorum before I walk down the aisle?

Yeah, okay, maybe I'll save that for after the honeymoon.

THE CONVERTIBLE AUDI R8 SPYDER SITTING IN OUR DRIVEWAY IS the color of bubbly champagne. Because Jack left the garage door open, I can see that its owner chose to park behind his BMW i8 on the left, as opposed to Aunt Phyllis's vintage Volkswagen Beetle, which is parked on the right.

The driver, a statuesque brunette in an elegant Aquilano Rimondi sheath, stands on our front stoop. The colors in her two-tone Phillip Lim satchel match the blues of her dress.

She must have just arrived, because her long manicured finger is poised to ring the doorbell. She pauses, though, when she hears my wheels crunch on the driveway as I slide my SUV behind the Beetle.

I've never seen her before, and she's not any of the usual suspects—a local realtor, Hilldale's Avon representative, or the Welcome Wagon lady.

When I open my car door, her poker face rearranges itself

into a wide smile, but she waits until we are close enough to shake hands to hold out hers. "You must be Donna Stone— or I should say, the future Mrs. Jack Craig."

I nod slowly. "And you are?"

"Your wedding planner!"

My shocked stare prompts her to add, "Oh…yes. Chantal Desmarais. Babette's, er, friend."

Chantal winces. To be expected. After dealing with Babette on two weddings, I'm surprised she doesn't have a permanent tick. "Yes, she is—*was*—a client. By that, I mean in my line of work, there is little repeat business, mostly referrals."

I open the door and motion for her to enter. "Here's hoping that in the first lady's case, two times is the charm."

"Yours as well," she murmurs, as she walks through.

Strike one.

Then again, I've only got less than a month to plan a wedding and get married. At the same time, I have to take down an international organization that funds terrorist groups.

Maybe it's time I learn to delegate.

"YOU WANT TO GET MARRIED *WHEN*?" CHANTAL'S BROWS ARCH over her eyes like frightened gulls.

"Four weeks from now?" I shrug. "But…we're flexible. Earlier works well too."

"Ah, well, that's a relief." The sarcasm is unbecoming.

Having wrangled Aunt Phyllis, Evan, and the soon-to-be-Family-Craig in the great room, shushed us into silence, and linked her laptop to our large-screen television, Chantal now reveals a calendar for all to see.

"Okay, people, we're on a very tight deadline, so listen up!" She stops mid-sentence until Jeff looks up from his computer and Trisha has stopped humming the tune from *Frozen*. Her trick for taking Aunt Phyllis's attention away from her *Crazy Taxi* digital game is to grab her phone and toss it on an empty chair.

"What the hell, lady!" Aunt Phyllis stands up, furious. "My fare was up to six-hundred bucks!"

"It can wait. Isn't the happiness of your niece more important to you?"

"How much effort does it take to find a dress, order a cake, and throw a party?" Aunt Phyllis grumbles. However, when she sits down, she mouths, *I'm sorry* to me.

To show forgiveness, I mouth *I love you.*

By the time I look back at the TV screen, three June weekends have been exed out. "Ouch! How did that happen?"

Chantal heaves an exasperated sigh. "Your timetable has put us in a box. Most of the acceptable venues have already been booked, or are at odds with POTUS's or FLOTUS's schedules."

The calendar morphs into a photo of a fancy hotel ballroom. "Our first choice is the Beverly Hills Hotel. It will easily accommodate the three hundred guests—"

"Wait!" Jack's brow furrows. "Why would we need something so large?"

Chantal's blank stare is followed by a sigh. "Besides the attending dignitaries, celebrities, and statespersons, I'm sure you'll also want a table or two for your family and friends— if they pass the security clearance, of course. And then there's the Secret Service detail. While they won't be noshing with guests, they'll be mingling—unobtrusively. But they count as attendees, since they're made of ectoplasm and take up space too."

Smart ass. "Why would famous people show up at our wedding?" I wonder out loud.

"You've got a point there," Chantal conceded. "But, keep in mind—they're not really there for *you*. They are there to bask in the glory of the first couple. You're just...well, simply put: 'icing on the cake.'" She's trying much too hard to hide her smirk.

I'm trying much too hard not to goosestep her out of my house. What she really means is that we're the excuse for others to rub shoulders with Lee and Babette. For that matter, it might as well be some foreign dignitary's funeral.

With that in mind, I rise from the couch—

But Jack holds tightly to my wrist and yanks me down.

"Celebrities?" For the first time since Chantal entered the room, Mary's frown disappears. "Who, exactly?"

"Well, certainly George and Amal—"

Aunt Phyllis and Mary squeak in unison. Okay, yes, I must have too, because Jack pinches me.

Chantal rolls her eyes. No stardust there. "And Tom and Rita. Sean and Charlize, of course." She frowns. "Matthew McConaughey has requested an invitation, but the president is sure to veto it. We don't want to have a 'Magic Mike' moment at such a decorous occasion, now do we?"

Aunt Phyllis nods adamantly. "Hell yeah, we do!" Noting Chantal's stony silence, she asks, "But if he wants to co-host the bachelorette party with me, I'd agree to that."

"I've no doubt," Chantal murmurs.

"What about Prince Harry?" Mary begs. "Can you get him here, too?"

Evan's smile fades. "While she's at it, why doesn't she see if she can round up Jennifer Lawrence?"

"Hey, don't ball players like to come to these things too?" Jeff pipes up. "Mom, can we invite Steph Curry?"

"This isn't a 'thing,'" I grumble. "It's my wedding."

"Now, now, children, no promises, but I'll do my best." Chantal smiles conspiratorially. "So, it's settled. The Beverly Hills Hotel it is—on the only day it still has open."

"But...but..." I'm stammering—not because I want to put my dibs in for the Duke and Duchess of Cambridge (okay, yes, maybe I wouldn't mind having Wills and Kate tear up as Jack and I swap vows and spit)—but because this is turning into the wedding of the millennium—

On Jack's and my dime, since our Acme *per diem* ain't gonna cover this shindig.

Jack is on my wavelength. "Excuse me, but how much exactly is this event going to cost?"

She rolls her eyes. "Money is no object."

"Says who?" he counters.

"Why, the first lady, of course."

"Oh...well then." Jack shrugs.

Hmmm. Okay, but even if one of the Chiffrays is kind enough to offer the event as a wedding gift, if it turns out we can, in fact, pin a Quorum membership on one of them, the other is sure to renege on the promise.

Hell, I know I would.

I'd point this out to Jack, but it's too late. Jeff, Mary, and Evan are exchanging high-fives.

Perhaps this is a conversation Chantal and I should have

in private. I can break the news about the smaller wedding to them later.

"If I'm to understand correctly, Jeff will be giving away his mother, the bride, and Evan will be one of the groomsmen," Chantal continues. "I've got this in mind for them."

Suddenly, the TV screen is broadcasting front-facing, full-body photos of Jack, Evan, and Jeff. All of them are wearing jeans and tee shirts, but it's obvious that the photos were taken at different times, and in different locations.

Jack's eyes narrow darkly. "Where did you get these?"

"At the first lady's behest, the CIA secured them for us." A second later, the clothes in the photos are replaced with tuxes. "Givenchy with satin-trimmed lapels for Jeff and Evan, and perhaps Dolce & Gabbana for Jack." She tilts her head to one side, but then shakes it. "Nope, sorry. There's that McConaughey connection again. Let's go with Hugo Boss instead." A new tuxedo flies onto the picture of Jack's torso. "And John Lobbs on everyone's feet." Out go the sneakers, replaced by the brand's *Soirée Castilo* model.

"Do me next!" Trisha shouts.

"Not so quick, little lady," Chantal purrs, as she pats my Trisha's head. "Age before beauty! Let's take care of Aunt Phyllis first."

The next photo of my aunt shows her in a thong bikini, standing beside the Hilldale Country Club pool.

Evan, Jeff, and Mary smother their giggles in my sofa pillows. Trisha covers her eyes.

Aunt Phyllis holds her head proudly. "Since when are a few wrinkles so scary?"

Chantal nods vigorously. "I agree with you emphatically! That's why I think this gown is perfect!"

Instantly, Aunt Phyllis's body is clad in a cherry-red floor-length gown. It has long sleeves and a bateau neckline. It sparkles with strategically placed sprays of diamonds.

Phyllis's eyes gleam proudly. "Why, I look…*wonderful!*"

She should—considering her head has been superimposed on Cher's body in a Bob Mackie gown.

Apparently, I'm not the only one who has noticed this. The children nudge each other. Trisha gapes, then blurts, "Aunt Phyllis, I don't think that's—"

Before she can finish her sentence, Chantal declares, "And now, for our little princesses' gowns!"

Trisha doesn't pick up on Chantal's plural nouns. She's too enthralled with the picture of herself, wearing a silk frock splashed with hand-painted lavender, turquoise, and fuchsia blooms. "I love it," she whispers.

"Well, of course you do!" Chantal bows to her audience of one. "Janie picked it out with both of you in mind. She'd like to wear it with a turquoise bow—to match her eyes. You'll wear a lavender one—"

Trisha's tiny brow furrows. "Janie? Why would she be wearing my dress?"

"Not *your* dress, silly girl! A dress of her own. Exactly the same, but you'll have different bows in your hair—and matching shoes, of course. So that you walk down the aisle together—"

Trisha's stare shifts to me. "But…but Janie was already a flower girl—for *her* mommy's wedding! I thought I was going to be yours."

Now, everyone is staring at me.

"Of course you are! But then Janie's mother asked if it

were okay if Janie did it too, I told her I felt you wouldn't mind—"

Trisha runs out of the room, her cheeks damp from her tears.

I can't do this to my daughter.

"Trisha—wait!" Mary reaches for my hand. "Mom, don't worry, I'll take care of this." She runs out after her sister.

I'm right on her heels. Only I can answer to Trisha.

Chantal has the audacity to block my way. "We're not done! I've yet to show you what I've got for the bridesmaids! Oh, by the way, Kim Kardashian says she's available if you need another to fill out the wedding party—"

"I'll say," Evan murmurs.

I pull Chantal out of the room, into the foyer.

"I don't have time for this now! My little girl is upset!"

Chantal scolds me with a wagging finger. "I can't say I blame her. Donna, how could you do that to your daughter? You must have known I'd be bringing it up."

"For your information, Ms. Desmarais, I've been on a business trip for the past seventy-two hours, and you reached my home before me. So, why don't you cut me some slack?"

From the way she rolls her eyes, "slack" is not a word in this woman's vocabulary. "Yeah, yeah, okay, whatever. Look, this is a once-in-a-lifetime opportunity for the both of us: I get to plan a presidential wedding, and for whatever reason, you, Cinderella, have the most fashionable first lady in U.S. history as your fairy godmother. It's a win-win, right? So why don't we both just play nice-nice for a short while, at least until this shindig is over and deemed a rousing success?"

Sure, by everyone except Trisha.

I've got one foot on the staircase when Jack appears in the foyer. "Something's popped up. Donna, they need us in the office just as soon as we can get there."

I tear up. "But I should be with Trisha."

"Mary texted me. She's got things under control," Jack assures me. "And Aunt Phyllis is ordering pizza for dinner."

Chantal slides her iPad into her bag. "My, my, what busy lives you lead! Are you sure you have time for something as insignificant as a wedding?"

I've had just about enough of this bitch's sarcasm. Jack grabs my arm before I can give in to the urge to wipe the smirk off her face with my fist.

Well, Chantal has one thing right. This wedding will be memorable, but it may not be something she'll want on her résumé.

5

Three Reasons to Get Cold Feet

Any time before the wedding, it's natural to question whether your betrothed is right for you. But, wouldn't it be a darned shame if you allowed irrational fears of the future to ruin your Happily Ever After?

Use these tips as your litmus test as to whether you stay put, or hightail it out of there:

- *Tip 1: He refuses to share—anything. Whether it's a meal, a dresser drawer, an apartment, a bank account, or a bed, the fact that he can't give freely means he's hiding something—more than likely, a wife, so move on.*
- *Tip 2: He borrows everything of yours. You pouted when he used up your favorite shampoo. You winced when he roared off in your car. You were apoplectic when he borrowed your credit card. If you find him slipping into your Spanx and kitten heels, take off—*

perhaps to your old roommate. (She did the same, but at least she never stretched out your clothes.)

- *Tip 3: You catch him in lies. He's never where he claims to be. He fibbed to you about his past. You learned to take everything he says with a grain of salt. The best relationships are built on trust, demonstrated every day, in every way. If he can't be true, he won't be true blue, either. End it now, before one of you ends up regretting it. (That would be YOU.)*

"THIS WEDDING THING IS BAD IDEA." THERE, I'VE SAID IT.

Everyone on the mission team—Jack, Abu, Dominic, Arnie, and Emma—look up from their computers, where they've been busy assessing dossiers on White House staffers sent over by my liaison, Todd.

Even Ryan stops scribbling names of those most likely to have the ear of either Lee or Babette to hear what I have to say.

Jack swallows a grin. "Don't tell me you're reneging on your proposal."

"You're not getting off the hook that easily," I assure him. "I just don't think it's necessary to have Babette plan my wedding in order to get to the root of the Chiffrays' connection with the Quorum."

"Does that mean you're going to tell the first lady to stuff it?" Ryan's hand is grasping a dry ink pen so tightly that I'm afraid he might break it.

"I think 'stuff it' is a bit harsh. I was thinking more along the line of, 'Thanks, but no thanks.' Or perhaps telling her that we've decided to elope. Or…" From the look on his face, nothing I say is going to get me out of this debacle in the making.

Jack puts his hand over mine. "Why don't you put little Miss Wedding Hitler on ice until Babette gets here? That way, the three of you can have a meeting of the minds. You know, give them the lay of the land, and tell them our do's and don'ts—"

I'm trying not to laugh. "'Our' do's and don'ts? You weren't exactly vocal in Chantal's skull session. But if you care to join us, I'll be glad to give you a chance to redeem yourself."

Jack grimaces. "That might be too distracting for Babette."

"You're not joking," I mutter.

"Then, definitely, he should be there," Ryan insists.

"No!" Jack and I declare at the same time.

"Do I have to make it an order?" He points to the whiteboard. "From the most junior janitor to the chief of staff, the White House has over four thousand employees." Ryan rubs fatigue from his eyes. "What would it take to hack POTUS's cell, let alone plant a bug in his office?"

"The Russians hacked the last president's email. Cell phones are a step up, but still doable," Arnie admits. "All it takes is for him to download a Trojan from an app or a hyperlink, even if it comes from a known source."

Emma raises her hand. "Agreed. It's just a matter of access."

"In that case, Babette would be a piece…of cake." Dominic grins at the thought of what he really means by this.

Ryan faces me. "My point exactly. Anyone with access to Lee, Babette, or the Oval Office could figure it out. Even with the twice-daily security sweeps, a live bug might hide in plain sight." He shakes his head at the obvious.

"It sounds like we're trying to clear the Chiffrays," Jack mutters.

"Innocent until proven guilty," Ryan counters. "You'll have a better chance of finding out if you use what access you have to them. And considering how quickly this wedding is going down, you won't have it for long."

He's got a point there. Jack and I both know it.

I entwine my fingers with Jack's. "Okay, Ryan, convince me why the happiest and most personal day of my life is worth ruining. Why don't you start with how this mission breaks down?"

Ryan nods, pleased that I'm now toeing the line, but he and I both know that I'm waiting for the punchline.

He uses his dry ink pen to write the number one on the whiteboard along with the words *Archival Data.* "Arnie and his Tech-Ops team need access to West Wing security camera archives, so that he and his team can pull a list of everyone— both on staff and visitors."

Arnie nods as he types away.

Next, Ryan adds the number two on the whiteboard with the words *Background Checks/Persons of Interest.* "Those names will be given to Emma and her ComInt team, so that they can run background checks and look for behavior or financial anomalies within the past year. They'll start with the staff members who work specifically in the Oval Office and POTUS's private quarters. Remember, FLOTUS has her own staff. It includes a social secretary, a press secretary, a floral designer, and an executive chef. The woman you met, Narcissa Belmont, is her chief of staff. She's high on our list, as is POTUS's NSC liaison, Todd Courtland."

"On it, Chief," Emma murmurs, as her fingers tap her keyboard.

"Other POIs are any Oval Office guests whose visits took place within a certain time period: at least, since Salem's first visit," Ryan continues. "In other words, we've got a lot of ground to cover."

Ryan writes 3 on the board followed by *Surveillance*. Turning to Abu, he says, "In the meantime, we'll also initiate some real-time surveillance. Abu, you're getting a new job. I've pulled some strings with the Secret Service director. You're now part of the president's security detail."

"Secret Service? Cool! Does it come with a raise?" Abu asks.

"You are much better paid here, trust me," Ryan assures him. "But at least until this mission is over, you'll be double-dipping."

Abu's happy dance has a few gangsta moves. I'm impressed.

"Dominic, I've done the same to put you on FLOTUS's detail." Even as he says it, Ryan winces at the thought.

On the other hand, Dominic's smile runs ear to ear. "Simple, as my forte is undercover work."

Ryan sighs. "We're all well aware of that. Should you succeed, try not to get shot." He thinks for a moment, then adds, "And, for that matter, should you fail, try not to get shot."

The number 4 goes on the board, along with the word *Infiltration*. It's now my turn for a lecture. "Donna, no one here wants to take down the Quorum any more than you. And the timing couldn't be better."

Okay, I'll bite. "Really? Enlighten me."

"Emma, fill her in on the reason President Chiffray is heading to Los Angeles—other than out of his admiration for Donna…and, er, Jack."

Jack's lip curls into a smirk at our boss's faux pas.

Thanks for nothing, Ryan.

"POTUS is hosting a summit of Arab leaders at Lion's Lair. The White House is trying to keep it under wraps, but Arnie used Todd's initial correspondence with Donna to hack his email. Since Todd has access to POTUS's itinerary, well, now we do too."

Arnie stands up and takes a bow before Emma jerks him back down onto his chair.

Ryan ignores him. "The summit's timing isn't great for the president's retreat, but he can't postpone it. The Middle East is at a boiling point. There are so many sectarian conflicts and proxy wars that it's hard to keep count. Too much of Afghanistan is now in Taliban control. As we all know, Pakistan has convinced China to play middleman with the two, seeing how it also shares a border with Afghanistan."

"Just what we need—China making waves in the Middle East," Dominic mutters.

"Add to this al-Qaeda's attacks in Yemen. And let's not forget that Iraq and Syria have been overrun by Islamic State militants. In fact, rumor has it that ISIS is making an end-run for the nuclear bomb Iran adamantly denies it has. Ha! As if it's the lesser of two evils." The implication draws a heavy sigh from Ryan. "As we all know, ISIS is heavily funded by its kidnappings of international citizens within its reach. And it is heavily armed, mostly with U.S. munitions confiscated from Iraqi government caches."

"At the same time, the U.S. arms industry's most active clients are our country's Arab allies—Saudi Arabia, of course, along with Jordan, Egypt, Qatar, Bahrain, and the Emirates. All of them are on buying sprees," Jack says.

Ryan nods. "Exactly. If President Chiffray is a Quorum leader, this puts him in a quandary. If he doesn't accommodate our Arab allies with boots on the ground along with drones in the air, they'll look for their military toys elsewhere. Needless to say, this will put him at odds with the Congressional hawks *and* their largest financial benefactors: the defense industry."

"Putin will be happy to do so," Abu adds. "Anything to get back at al-Qaeda for aiding the Chechen rebels."

"And just as unthinkable, so will the Quorum," Jack replies. "They won't mind arming both sides with black market munitions."

"At the same time, playing the dove endears President Chiffray to his left-of-center constituency, who are tired of our participation in all these Middle East wars, in which our only stake is oil contracts," Arnie points out.

"All of this bullshit killing, and for what?" Emma declares. "For a fuel source that is so harmful to the environment. The really smart countries are shifting to solar and wind. OPEC's clout is the lowest it has been in years. Even the Arabs see the writing on the wall, and have begun shifting their investments to green development."

"It isn't just about oil. You forget that most of the Islamic States' jihadists consider this a holy war against all Christians, Jews, and Muslim Shiites," Abu counters. "Many of the citizens in those countries—moderate Muslims, non-Muslims, and non-sectarians—are being slaughtered for standing up to them, or for just living their lives."

"At the same time, by securing the oil pipelines in captured territories, ISIS can easily pay for its so-called holy war," Dominic reminds us.

Ryan frowns. "People, let's stay on task—finding the Quorum operative in the White House." He turns to me. "Donna, to do so, your mission and Jack's won't be easy. First, you'll have to gain access to the Chiffrays' cell phones. Unfortunately, the kind used by White House administration and staff does not store its data on a SIM card, but in a secure cloud."

"For that, you'll need this." Arnie hands us a tiny device. "This scanner can be connected to the cell phone's audio port," he explains. "From there, it reads the phone's passcode and opens the phone immediately. When the phone is open, a Trojan is automatically placed into its operating system. Emma's ComInt team will then access the cell's secure cloud remotely in order to search its archival data for text correspondence with Xia. If the texts were made from either of the first family's cells, we'll have proof of it."

"Getting ahold of the president and the first lady's cell phone—or that of any other person of interest—won't exactly be a piece of cake," I warn him.

Ryan nods. "If that's the case, your fallback position is to plant this on the Chiffrays and other POIs." He holds up a transparent disk. It's tiny—not even an eighth of an inch in diameter.

Everyone leans in. "Ah, a microdot audio transmitter," Dominic murmurs.

I look meaningfully at Jack. Before I knew that Carl was a Quorum operative, Jack placed one on me without my knowledge. He guessed, rightly, that Carl would try to turn me.

Carl didn't. But he had convinced me that Jack was Quorum instead, and couldn't be trusted.

I learned the hard way that Carl was wrong. I have the scar from his bullet to prove it.

Ryan nods. "Yes, but this specific unit is equipped with both audio and video capabilities. As you see, it's not only smaller, but its signal is clearer and it can transmit from twice the distance. We have several of these at your disposal." He shrugs. "In all honesty, the microdot is our fallback position. We'll only be able to deduce culpability by what is said or seen. Then again, considering Babette's involvement with the wedding, if you can't get ahold of her phone, you'll have ample opportunities to plant a microdot on both POTUS and FLOTUS, as well as any other POI who may be floating around Lion's Lair."

"Adhering the microdot may be tricky," Jack reminds him. "If I remember correctly, ideal placement is an area of skin that is hard to get at by the POI and can't be washed off."

I know why he's grinning. He placed mine high—*very* high—on my inner thigh.

"I'm sure you'll be creative in your methodology—that is, the mission is a go." Ryan looks me in the eye. "Donna, fortunately for Acme—albeit unfortunately for you—your nuptials put Jack and you in a unique position to carry out this mission and find the White House's mole." He puts his hand on my shoulder. "I'll understand if you want to pass in order to focus on the wedding. Still, for all our sakes, I hope you don't."

I shrug. "Okay, sure, I'll play along."

What choice do I have?

IT'S TEN O'CLOCK. I OPEN TRISHA'S BEDROOM DOOR, BUT SHE'S not there.

I find her in Mary's bed, cuddled in her older sister's arms.

Their chests rise and fall calmly and in tandem. There are smiles on their lips. Are they dreaming in unison too? I'll pretend that they are, though I know better.

Their lives are too rarely in sync. I make this my excuse to let Trisha sleep.

Tomorrow is soon enough for me to break her heart.

6

Couples Counseling

Prior to making your union legal, taking the time for relationship counseling is always a great idea. Besides helping you deal with the stress of a wedding, it will also reveal traits that can blow up your marriage before it even begins.

'Blow up' being the operative words here. Preferably him, as opposed to you.

That being said, if your counselor's assessment mentions any of these behavior patterns, call off the wedding, return the dress, and re-up your membership on Tinder:

Pattern #1: He refuses to give up his Little Black Book. (In other words, all former girlfriends' digits are still in his cell phone's contact list.)

- *Your Fear: He's not ready to settle down.*
- *A More Likely Reason: He views its readiness (and maybe theirs too) as his security blanket, reinforcing his need to know that he's still desirable.*

- *Solution: Reassure him with random acts of romance.*
- *Tip: If that doesn't convince him, try not-so-random acts of violence instead.*

Pattern #2: He takes too many business trips.

- *Your Fear: He's working much too hard.*
- *A More Likely Reason: When you ask to tag along, he claims you'll distract him from his work.*
- *Solution: Follow him. That way, should he need stress release, you'll be there to give him a massage.*
- *Tip: Should your rap on his hotel room door reveal him in the midst of a massage from a buxom young woman, don't apologize for knocking—because it's an inopportune time, or for the bruise he'll have when their heads collide.*

Pattern #3: He kisses every woman he meets hello.

- *Your Fear: He misses being single.*
- *A More Likely Reason: He's a straight-out lech.*
- *Solution: Blind him.*
- *Tip: Get him a sturdy cane and a good seeing-eye dog.*
- *Better Tip: Get yourself a new boyfriend.*

WE'RE HAVING CHOCOLATE CHIP MICKEY MOUSE PANCAKES FOR breakfast.

It's Trisha's favorite.

As for me, I'll eat my words.

On the side of her plate, I place a long pink plastic skewer with slices of bananas and strawberries, and fry an egg in a star cookie cutter. I put the pure maple syrup in the pitcher, which is adorned with a painting of Betty Boop.

This morning, Mary has helped Trisha get dressed, and holds her hand as she walks down the stairs toward the kitchen table. Trisha hugs Jack before taking her place at the table. She blushes when I bid her a good morning, but she keeps her eyes on her plate.

Only when I sit down beside her does she finally look over at me. "I hope you can forgive me for agreeing with Mrs. Chiffray that it would be alright for Janie to be a flower girl too. I—"

Trisha holds a finger to my lips in order to silence me. "Mommy, it's okay. I do forgive you and I'm fine with it."

"Oh! Well…thank you."

My relief is so obvious to her that she deigns to kiss me on the cheek. "You're quite welcome. Mary told me that our biggest job during the wedding is to make you happy. So, if it makes you happy to make Mrs. Chiffray happy, I guess I can share my part with Janie." She forces a smile onto her face. "Sometimes Janie wants to be the boss of me, but as long as she knows up front that we are to be even-steven, everything will be okay."

"Agreed. Even-steven." I hold out my hand. "Shake on it?"

She does, and even better than that, she rewards me with a big hug.

As she digs into her pancakes, I pull Mary aside. "Thank you, from the bottom of my heart."

"Mom, not to worry. You've got enough on your plate.

Besides, that's what the maid of honor does—puts out the emotional fires before and during the wedding."

I kiss her cheek. "You're much more than that to me. You're quickly growing into my closest girlfriend."

Despite her ear-to-ear smile, tears well up in her eyes. "That means the world to me…because you've always been mine."

She hugs me as if she never wants to let me go.

This is what I live for. This is what I fight for.

Jack's arms go around both of us. He's just as relieved as me. "Donna, why don't you take Evan and Mary to school? I'd like to take Jeff and Trisha."

Jeff pumps his arm. "Alright! The BMW! Oh, and don't worry, Dad—we no longer pick up Cheever, now that Mom punched out Mrs. Bing."

Everyone turns to gawk at me.

"It was an accident…sort of," I stammer.

"What do you mean by sort of?" Trisha asks. "Can I sometimes use 'sort of' too?"

Jack smothers his smile. "This happened yesterday and you're just telling us about it now?" he murmurs.

I'm saved by the bell, literally.

"You had to be there!" Jeff shouts, as he runs off toward the front door. "But the great news is that we never have to carpool with Cheever or Morton again—and that's fine by me."

I'd rather clear away the breakfast dishes than suffer my family's stares. I've just stacked the plates in the sink when Jeff runs back. "Mom! You better come quick! We're being raided!"

Jack's eyes meet mine. If Lee somehow discovered

Acme's game plan, we'll be hauled away in handcuffs in front of the children.

Jack leaps up and heads to the foyer. I'm right behind him.

The front door is open, and already they are swarming in and casing the place: men wearing suits, dark glasses, and ear buds, and talking into wrist mics.

One is heading our way.

Like me, Jack's stance shifts as his muscles tense up, despite the welcoming smile on the man's face.

We are also assessing the situation: flight or fight? The kids' presence means one of us should do the former while the other attempts the latter in order to get them out of harm's way.

And perhaps be taken down in the process, considering the number of the man's associates who are casing every room in the house.

Since women are considered to be less threatening, I take the first step forward. "May I help you?"

"Are you Donna Stone?"

But, of course, he already knows I am. Still I resist the urge to be a smartass and curtsey, and instead I nod benignly.

"And you're Jack Craig." It's a statement, not a question.

The man's eyes scan over me as if I'm a walking barcode. It's a safe bet that he's checking for weapons. Does a soapy sponge count? Frankly, it could if used right—say, crammed into his mouth to stop him from shouting out after I give him a sidekick to the solar plexus.

But Jack relaxes his hands and shakes his head to me. There are too many men in black to even try for a takedown.

Ever curious, the children hover in the doorway.

I'm a mother. Maybe I can shame our guests into keeping the cuffs off me until after the kids leave for school.

Evan is old enough to drive the others to school. I'll just ask him to take my mommy mobile. In case we need to make a quick getaway, Jack's BMW i8 can do zero to sixty in four-point-two seconds.

First Man in Black's eyes roam from one of the kids to the other. Finally, he asks, "Anyone else in the house?"

"My sixty-eight year-old aunt is asleep in the guest room." I don't think it's wise to confess that Aunt Phyllis stayed up until four in the morning on a Tongan online gambling website, playing Seven-Card Stud. We'll need her to bail us out of jail, not share a cell with us.

Man in Black nods as he murmurs into wrist mic, "Phyllis Lindholm too. Cleared?" He frowns and adds, "Barely, eh?" He glares at me for the longest time.

I shrug. "You can't choose your family."

He processes that. Finally, he growls, "Okay send in Peacock, Parakeet, Puffin, Wren and Love Bird."

What the hell…

Ah, so that's who they are.

The men closest to the door stand even taller. It's a ten-count before we see whom they are protecting:

Babette. Of course, she is Peacock.

Janie is with her, which would make her Secret Service name Parakeet. A woman—in her mid-twenties, and wearing round owlish glasses—holds her hand. Her face, dimpled and freckled, is sweetly pretty. My guess is that she's Janie's au pair. Puffin, perhaps?

If so, Wren has to be Babette's aide-de-camp, Narcissa.

That would mean that the last of their entourage, Chantal, has the code name Love Bird.

Another woman carries in a portfolio stamped WEDDING INVITATIONS, as well as mini-speakers and an iPod, which holds samples of the music Babette has deemed fit to play at the wedding.

I wish I could give in to the part of me that is relieved to have help in planning, but it's much harder to do than I thought.

Yet another woman—large, and wearing a chef's jacket and cap—rolls a large silver cart laden with ten different wedding cakes.

"Dessert, for breakfast?" Jeff asks. "Double score!"

"You can put that down in the dining room," Babette points in the wrong direction.

I stop the baker before she heads off to the kitchen, where she's sure to be jumped by Lassie and Rin Tin Tin, who are probably on top of the kitchen table by now, scavenging everyone's leftover pancakes. "In there," I tell her, nodding to the room on the left.

Janie runs past her mother and all the Men in Black between her and Trisha in order to give her dear friend a neck-clinging hug.

Trisha's face shifts from surprise at seeing her friend, to wariness from the thought of any further concessions she may have to make for our wedding, and finally to joy at being adored. All is forgiven.

I wish I could do the same with Babette, but we were

never friends to begin with. I may soon discover that we are mortal enemies.

All the more reason for me to slap a smile on my mug, bat my eyes, and proclaim, "So glad you could make it back to Hilldale so quickly, Mrs. Chiffray."

I hold out my hand, but she pulls me in close for a hug and murmurs, "I wouldn't miss it for the world. It'll be…*killer.*"

Jack tosses Evan his set of our car keys. "Why don't you drive yourself and the kids to school in Donna's car?"

Evan acknowledges the request with a wave and then nods to the others as he heads off to grab his school bag.

After politely shaking Babette's hand, Mary and Jeff take off after him. Neither likes Babette. I guess they've inherited my Shit-o-Meter.

Trisha pulls away from Janie. "Got to go. Last week of school! We have our final math and spelling tests today." Trisha blushes. She's not a natural born liar. Her glance begs me not to rat her out. In truth, all tests have been taken. Today is the last day of school. All of the elementary classes are celebrating with a picnic at Hilldale Park, where the staff has set up a mini carnival.

Janie pouts, but Trisha stands firm. As consolation, she pats her friend's shoulder. "We can play when I get home from school." She runs after the others.

"Please, Mummy, may I?" Janie looks pleadingly at her mother.

Babette sighs heavily. "Frannie, why don't you remind Janie what's on her agenda today."

The au pair clicks open an iPad and scrolls to a calendar page. "This was simply to be a meet-and-greet," she reminds Janie. "Immediately from here, you're to go to East South Central for a ribbon-cutting ceremony of a new playground, then the Santa Monica Library to read to the preschoolers."

Janie wrinkles her nose. "Not *The Cat in the Hat* again!"

"*Green Eggs and Ham* is also approved," Frannie informs her, "and you read it almost as well."

Janie's lower lip quivers. "By now, shouldn't I be reading books like *Harry Potter*?"

A flick of Babette's slim wrist is supposed to whisk away her daughter's concern. "Maybe next year, darling. Without your two front teeth, your lisp is still far too pronounced. Such a display would just add more grist to the *SNL* mill."

By that, she's referring to some recent *Saturday Night Live* skits, which have poked fun at the first family's public faux pas. Granted, most of these have been Babette's doing, such as her curtsey to the Duchess of Cornwall on the Royals' first visit to the Chiffray White House.

Then there was the leak by a former aide of her clothing bill, which topped three million dollars in her first full year as first lady.

So far the most sensational scandal of all concerned is a paparazzo's photo of Babette caught in a clinch with a strange man. Apparently, it was taken while she was staying in a posh Manhattan penthouse apartment.

I recognized their supposed love nest the moment I saw the photo. It's on Riverside Boulevard, It belongs to Global World Industries, an international conglomerate that is part of the first family's supposedly frozen assets. Lee and I would rendezvous there when the need to swap intel on his treasonous Director of Intelligence—Carl—was mutually beneficial. Thank goodness our innocent liaisons were a thing of the past by the time some enterprising paparazzo figured out that the office building next door was a great place for a gotcha moment.

Because her paramour's head was buried somewhere below her waist, his face was never identified.

Although Babette's back was toward the camera, having a Samsung NX1 with an ISO setting of 3200 made it easy for the pap to capture an unmistakable identifier: an odd-shaped birthmark on Babette's right butt cheek.

"Yes, the first lady was in New York on the weekend in question," the White House spokesperson sniffed. "But having no *personal* knowledge of the identifying feature, I can neither confirm nor deny if the photo is, in fact, her."

Other than her alleged lover, Lee may be the only one who has personal knowledge of the mark. But, he refuses to talk about the incident in public.

In private, they lead their lives like two ships passing in a frigid sea: acknowledging the other, but giving as wide a berth as possible.

When Dominic saw the photo, he held it sideways, like a centerfold, then declared, "Poppycock! Of course, it's her!"

"As if you'd know," I murmured.

"In fact, I do," he stated grandly. "Since the moment she became a prime suspect, I've made it my business to memorize every 'detail' in her dossier—including this photo, which I procured directly from the pap himself, along with others he snapped at the time."

What he said didn't surprise me in the least. Dominic is obsessive-compulsive. I can just imagine the walls of some room in his Hilldale abode (the Tudor monstrosity he's nicknamed "Chateau Fleming") filled with such photos.

That is to say, nudes—albeit not all of Babette.

"None, I take it, with her lover's face in view," I chided him.

"Not surprisingly, the lucky sod wasn't keen on coming up for air. Not that I blame him." He pointed to the man, who was on his knees in front of Babette. "She got chill bumps before he acquiesced to moving her inside." He pointed to the grainy dots on her skin. "Certainly a sadistic sod."

I was more interested in the man's right hand, which held firm to Babette's left buttock. There was a crook in the index finger, and he was wearing a distinctive pinky ring. It was gold, and the center sported a black onyx stone adorned with the number "13" in gold filigree.

When I pointed it out to Jack, his whistle was long and low. "Bingo."

"I meant the ring," I said pointedly.

"Me too. I've seen one just like it before—on the pinky of a dead Quorum operative." Jack smacked Dominic's shoulder. "Mr. Fleming, it seems for once, your voyeurism has come in handy." But Jack had to pry the photo from Dominic's hand.

When I get Jack alone, I'll be sure to remind him that her Quorum mystery man is yet another strike against her.

In the meantime, I change the subject. "Janie has official duties too?" This surprises me since previous first families did what they could to protect their children from the harsh and endless scrutiny of the public.

"We're all in this together." Despite her syrupy sweet tone, Babette sounds as if she's mouthing some New Age mantra. "Every one of the Chiffrays must pull his or her weight. Besides, these ceremonial events are child's play, and my time is better spent on more meaningful tasks—like international diplomacy." She snaps her fingers at Frannie. "Speaking of which, the al-Sadah contingency arrives in a few days. It will include two children—girls, ages eight and ten, respectively. Janie's downtime can be spent entertaining them."

Jack's eyes meet mine. I'm sure we're thinking along the same lines: So another of our chief Quorum suspects, Salem, will be here for the summit as well.

This opens up new surveillance opportunities for Acme, perhaps giving us the evidence we need for the exposure and conviction of whichever Chiffray turns out to be his partner.

Babette pecks her daughter on the cheek. "Now, run along with Frannie to your little events. I'll come up and kiss you goodnight before your bedtime."

Janie's sigh is filled with doubt. Something tells me Babette's promises are as meaningless as her air kisses.

"Jack, why don't you show our guests into the living room, while I set up coffee and tea for everyone." At the same time, I'll grab a couple of microdots from my pocketbook. The sooner Jack and I can plant one on Babette—or better yet, snatch her cell phone, hack the passcode, and embed the Trojan so that Emma can access her secure cloud —the sooner I can prove him wrong.

Or, to my dismay, right.

Babette's eyes light up at the chance to preen in front of my guy without my hovering. She takes Jack's proffered arm and follows him in. As they head off, she turns around to tell me, "Make mine a latte, with a half-teaspoon of raw coconut sugar."

"Let me see what I can dig up." I wonder if rat poison can pass as coconut sugar.

Man in Black follows me into the kitchen. Drat, I guess he's making sure I don't spike her mug with anything she didn't request.

Why would I? If I'm right and she's Quorum, I'd rather see her hang for treason.

Rin Tin Tin growls when he sees my visitor. On the other hand, Lassie comes up to him to trade licks for pats. They divert Man in Black just long enough for me to pull the scanner and a couple of microdots from my purse and slip them into my pocket. I'll hand one off to Jack with his coffee. Odds are, he'll have no problem touching Babette, whereas she recoils when I attempt a mere air kiss.

The first latte from my Nespresso VertuoLine goes to my shadow, as a peace offering. "For you. Enjoy."

He looks surprised. "Why, thank you, Mrs. Stone."

"Please, call me Donna."

He shakes my hand. "Zeb Dunne."

"So, FLOTUS, eh?" I murmur. "Must be one hell of an assignment."

He shakes his head then looks skyward. "Ten months, twenty-two days, three hours, and"—he looks down at his watch—"forty-four minutes."

That's one way of deflecting the inevitable questions that

must come his way. Okay, I'll play along. "Really? You've only been on the job that long?"

He laughs as if I've said something witty, but he isn't smiling. "That's how long I have left before I can *retire*. There's a cabin on Chickahominy Lake with my name on it."

If I had to follow Babette around all day, I guess I'd be counting down the minutes too.

I knock his mug with mine. "Here's to retirement."

"You can say that again!" After a sip, he smacks his lips.

I grab my tray of lattes and head for the living room. If Babette is Quorum and he missed it, he'll get his wish even earlier. A win-win for everyone.

7

Sampling Wedding Cakes!

There is truly an art to choosing the cake for your wedding. So that it makes your guests oooh and aaah, do the following:

First, pick your baker carefully. For example, if he also makes porn cakes, the wrong delivery on the day of your blessed event may leave you with a rather embarrassing dildo as a cake topper.

Next, taste several cakes before you choose the one to serve on your wedding day. Hint: stay away from exotic flavors. How sad would it be to find out the hard way that your groom has a fatally allergic reaction to the peanut butter filling between that yummy double Dutch chocolate?

And finally, don't get carried away with the cake's shape or size. Yes, it would be unique for it to have tiers as tall as you, or perhaps even sculpted in the form of you and your betrothed. But, like most things in life, cakes are always subject to the old adage, "Anything that can go wrong, will go wrong—"

Especially around guests who are soused. If some drunken cousin doesn't trip headfirst into your sky-high tower of fondant and flour, a tipsy ex-boyfriend is sure to cop a feel of your pound cake lookalike's buttercream breast.

"Some subtle ingredient pops the flavor in this sample." Jack pauses between bites of a three-tiered naked wedding cake, adorned with strawberries and real roses. "Anise perhaps?"

"What a discerning palate you have," Babette coos, then licks her lips.

Frankly, I'm surprised she's not licking his, considering the dab of icing on the corner of his mouth.

By the way Jack's been going at the cake, you'd think he had a tapeworm. Thus far, his favorite is a three-tiered cake with a different icing slathered between each layer: a lemon one with blackberry jam on the bottom, and green tea layer with white chocolate icing in the middle. The top layer is strawberry cake smeared with strawberry preserves, and the whole thing is covered in a purple hombre buttercream frosting.

Initially, I was determined to pace myself, so I started off by taking tiny bites. But by my fifth sampling of cake, I was queasy—not from the cake, but from the sugarcoated bullshit these two were shoveling at each other. All this gooey cooing and Jack's yet to steal the cell, let alone plant the bug on her. It's not for lack of trying. He's cozied up to her in so many ways that if you didn't know better you'd think they were playing Twister.

He's admired her earrings (touched behind her ear) and her hairstyle (on the back of her neck). When his gushing compliment over her toned figure (hands on her waist) was met with a sigh bemoaning no time to get out to take a jog, he's offered to take her out onto Lion's Lair's private nine-hole golf course to show her a few moves guaranteed to lower her handicap (small of back; shoulders; elbows).

"*Oooh*, Walton wouldn't like that at all." She fakes a pout.

Jack raises a brow. "Oh? And who would that be?"

"My personal trainer. I take him everywhere. It's not easy staying a size minus two, but, I can at least make the attempt." Her tongue darts naughtily between her lips. "Someone has to be America's Royals. I guess Lee and I are elected."

I bite my tongue before shouting, *No, it was Lee who was elected—and only because Catherine stepped down for her murder rap. You're just along for the ride.*

"I'm sure this Walton guy is doing a great job." Jack shrugs—a broad hint that he thinks otherwise. "Tell you what—pick a day and we'll hit the links together. I'll improve your swing in no time."

"I'll bet you will," she simpers. "Okay, you're on. Come over later this afternoon." Suddenly, she remembers I'm here too. "Oh...you too, Donna. It'll give Walton something to do, other than curl his biceps." She titters at the thought. "Don't worry, he'll whip you into shape in no time." Her voice lingers a second too long on the word *whip*. At the same time, her eyes linger too long on Jack before slipping her fork into her mouth and sucking on it.

Jack takes the hint and smiles.

I remind myself that he's only doing his job, but that doesn't stop me from binging on cake.

I look at it this way: each slice I put in my mouth makes it less likely that I'll give in to the temptation to shove one into Babette's face.

~

An hour later, I have a tummy ache. Ugh! There are still three more cakes to sample.

Why bother? The choice isn't mine anyway. The way Babette has inserted herself into every decision, you'd think it was she who's marrying Jack, not I.

All the while, Chantal has been taking copious notes, but she's never once considered my protests, pleas, or sullen stares at her all too obvious slights. I am not at all pleased with my wedding colors (ice blue and gold), or my wedding invitations (monogrammed, and beveled in 24-karat gold leaf, on an ecru cotton stock). Add to this list the music to be played as I walk down the aisle (*Canon in D* by Pachelbel, plucked by a string quartet); or the guests' party favors (blue leather passport cases with our names engraved in gold on one side and the presidential seal on the other).

And I'm certainly not pleased with the wedding's theme. ("Vintage," Babette insists. "We'll decorate with iconography from the year you were born ...Which was...Egad! *Really?* You're *that* much older than me? Well then, you must be older than Jack as well. *No?* Sure, if you say so...")

I know for a fact that Babette and I are the exact same age, despite what she has on her official White House fact sheet.

"We should talk about Donna's dress," Chantal reminds Babette, as if I'm not sitting right beside her. "She *claims* to be a size four."

In unison, their heads swivel in order to scrutinize me—

Just as, in a pique of frustration, I've crammed a piece of the groom's cake into my mouth.

"Whot's wong?" I ask, through chocolate ganache.

Chantal bites her lower lip. Ignoring my question, she turns to Babette instead. "Maybe the dress is a discussion we should table until tomorrow, after Walton can do a full assessment of her."

I gulp down the last of the fondant icing. "I've got my own workout partner, thank you very much. It's Jack, remember?"

"And we've got just a few days to stuff you into some wedding gown in the size you claim to be."

Fuck off.

Just as I reach for another slice, Babette grabs my hands in hers. "Face it, Donna. You have a sugar obsession! But I'll be damned if I'll let you ruin the most important day in my —I mean, your life. No matter how many pounds you pack on between now and the wedding, Walton will be sure to get it off of you, one way or another."

Miffed, I straighten up. "For God's sake, how much weight do you think I can gain in just a few days?"

"If you keep eating like that, who's to say?" Babette's sympathetic look is aimed at Jack, not me.

"Honey, I think what Babette is trying to say is that the days leading up to the wedding are sure to be stressful, so perhaps we should try to, er, stay healthy." He shoves my cake plate just beyond my reach.

I yank it back. "I wasn't finished."

Jack inches away. He can take a hint.

"Call Mario Testino," Babette murmurs to Chantal. "I

want him to shoot the wedding photos. Be sure to warn him that some photoshopping will be needed. Oh! And before the stylist sends over the gowns I chose for Donna's consideration, make sure she knows what she's dealing with. Just tell her *zaftig*."

"Pray tell, what exactly does that mean?" I wipe the icing off my mouth with the back of my hand.

Jack's eyes open wide. He doesn't like the way I'm holding the cake knife.

"Just a little shorthand, darling," Babette reassures me. "It's a compliment! Think 'Kardashian,' only, well…flabbier."

Before I can retort, Chantal taps one of her bronze-coated talons on her laptop in order to rally everyone's attention. "Tomorrow—after your workout sessions, of course"—she grins knowingly at Babette—"we'll go over the deets on the engagement party."

Jack frowns. "An engagement party, on this short notice?"

"It's a way of extending an olive branch to those who didn't make the cut for the wedding ceremony," Babette explains. "In fact, let's set it for this weekend."

"But…that's only two days away," I point out.

"Even better. Guarantees that half the guests won't be able to make it." She chuckles at the thought. "At your earliest convenience, please text Chantal with a list of your closest friends and relatives."

Chantal chimes in, "Oh! And before we take off, I have some great news. Beyoncé has confirmed her attendance at the wedding, and she's consented to sing during your first dance as a couple."

"Wow!" I can't believe my ears.

"I approved, 'Put a Ring on It,' since, a, it's her signature song, and b, you're lucky to have her," Chantal declares.

I shake my head. "I agree that, a, we're lucky to have her. But, b, Jack and I have a song we consider 'ours.' It's—"

I'm dismissed with a wave of her wrist. As I simmer and stew, she adds, "And also great news! We've locked in the Beverly Hills Hotel as our venue—"

Jack's wince mirrors mine. Time to level with Babette: we don't have the money to rent the coatroom there, let alone a whole ballroom. I stammer, "Oh…um, yes, well about that. You see—"

"In all honesty, the venue doesn't make the Secret Service too happy," Babette sighs heavily. "Something about 'ingress' and 'egress' and vetting of the staff—" Suddenly, Babette leans in, ready to bust. "Oh. My. *Gawd*! I know how to make my little toy soldiers happy—"

"That's her little nickname for her Secret Service detail," Chantal giggles. "Isn't that adorable?"

"Yeah, adorable," Jack smirks.

The three men watching over us hang their heads in shame.

"As I was saying"—Babette's glare pierces Chantal into a momentary silence—"I have a solution that should make everyone ecstatically happy. Why not have the wedding at Lion's Lair?"

Where she can control the whole damn thing—

The damn thing that is supposed to be the happiest day of my life.

Like hell she will.

"No," I growl. "Really, Babette, I can't let you do that—"

"Sure you can! And I know Lee won't mind at all. However, it must take place within a few days after the engagement party. After that, our calendars are packed to the hilt—you know, with really important things—Oh! That's not to say that your little wedding isn't important." She nudges Chantal, who stifles a guffaw.

Ouch! Jack just kicked me under the table. He's tickled pink that we'll be so close to our targets.

But of course he is. Having the wedding there will give us much-needed access to every room in the Chiffray household, which is Ryan's wet dream come true.

One way or another, we'll get ahold of those cell phones.

Doesn't Ryan realize how hard it is to contemplate wedded bliss when you're planting a bug on the first lady, let alone doing so within the two-foot thick, ten-foot high walls of her compound, and with her private army of quote-unquote little toy soldiers watching your every move?

So much for a cozy, romantic ceremony.

I dimple up, ostensibly for Babette and company, but really because I've got to hide my anger that my wedding is turning into a train wreck. "You're much too generous…but we can never repay you!"

"I know," she declares smugly.

I'll sure as heck try, though. And it will hurt—

Her.

Babette pulls me in close for a squeeze that would have broken a rib if I'd had her infinitesimal Body Mass Index. "And, in answer to what is obviously your very next question: yes, I accept!"

Hmmm. "I beg your pardon?"

Babette's laugh rivals a glass chime tickled by a gentle

breeze. "Yes, Donna Stone, I *will* be your matron of honor." Babette rolls her eyes at Jack, as if he's caught her being kind to an imbecile—that imbecile, of course, being me.

No! No way in hell. I've already asked Mary to be my maid of honor!

Jack isn't smiling either. His ploy has backfired like a '47 Chevy running on sixty-three proof moonshine during an ice storm. "Yeah, er, Babette, now about that...I really don't think we can let you—"

"*Shhh!*" she insists. "I know where you're heading with this, but say no more. Donna and I go back too far, and we're much too close, to let something as trivial as the expense of what will soon be hailed as 'the most celebrated *wedding of the decade*' stand in the way of our friendship." Babette sheds a crocodile tear.

"Oh. Good, then the costs are being covered." He can't hide the relief in his voice.

Babette shrugs. "I'm sure that some political action committee will realize the goodwill aspect of doing so. Happy marriages, happy homes, and all that nonsense. Plus, they so love making me happy...and making *you* happy"— she pets him as if he's a calico kitten—"is what makes *me* happy too. Besides, my true gift to you is my presence, am I right?" She turns to me. "I mean, be honest, Donna: if I'm not standing beside you, the guests will be so disappointed."

Why...that *bitch!*

Before I can tell her that I'd call the wedding off before I let her highjack my special day (no, even better, that I'll take her out and chop her up into itty-bitty bits and drop the parts off a cliff into the Pacific Ocean and *then* have my wedding, after a respectful period of mourning...perhaps a

day) Jack stuffs what's left of the rum-soaked orange blossom cake into my mouth.

Yum.

It shuts me up—for now.

By the time Babette's cavalcade of black town cars with smoked glass windows is halfway down the street, my Hilldale neighbors have caught on to the fact that we're somehow Very Important People.

The very first person to ring my doorbell is Penelope Bing.

She comes bearing crow—I mean, a Bundt cake. After what I've just eaten, the last thing I need is a mouthful of her Betty Crocker crapfest. "Donna, dear, perhaps we should let bygones be bygones."

"And, why is that?"

Suddenly, she realizes this *mea culpa* is not going to be the cakewalk she had hoped for. She frowns. "Because we live in the same neighborhood."

"Feel free to move. Trust me, I won't stop you, and I look forward to anything that raises my home's property value."

Penelope's face turns red, but she knows better than to blow her stack. "Well then—because it would make our mutual friends more comfortable."

"We have none. You've made sure that everyone in Hilldale hates me."

A slight smile alights on her lips. She can't help but preen when someone recognizes her accomplishments. But it fades soon enough when she realizes the consequence: she's now banned from rubbing elbows with the first family.

"Donna," Jack shouts from the living room, "Babette's on the phone! She wants to remind you that she still needs to go over the guest list for the engagement party she's hosting for us this weekend!"

Naughty boy. He sure knows how to make a woman grovel—in this case Penelope, whose lip quivers at the thought that she may have insulted FLOTUS's bestie.

I'm closing the door on her face when she throws her Hail Mary: "Well then…for the sake of our sons!"

"I can do without Cheever in my car."

She winces as the door wedges the toe of her Michael Kors espadrille into the doorframe, but she holds firm. "I'll —make him wear a diaper for his, er, incontinence!"

"Really? You know he'll hate you for it, don't you?"

"He'll…get over it. Eventually." She purses her lips. Yet one more thing he can bring up to his therapist.

"You'd be okay humiliating your son if it allows you to rub elbows with Lee and Babette? Shame on you, Penelope!" Truly disappointed, I shake my head.

She opens her mouth to say something, but no words come out, because she knows I'm right.

"Let me think about it," I say, but we both know it's a hollow promise.

This time when I shut the door, she doesn't stop me. Her hateful glare proves I've made the right choice: keep your loved ones close, and your enemies far enough away to be target practice.

～

"I'LL TELL MARY, IF YOU'D PREFER." JACK WAITS ONLY A second after I shut the door firmly behind Penelope before manning up.

My laugh is anything but jovial. "You're a brave soul. I appreciate the offer, but this is something I have to do, especially if it puts the Quorum out of commission once and for all."

"On the other hand, if the bad news comes from me, it may soften the blow."

I shake my head. "Jack, Mary is going to shoot the messenger, no matter who it is. I need to take the bullet. She's my daughter."

He frowns. "She's *our* daughter. At least, I've felt that way about her since the moment she accepted me as her father, even before Carl tried to muscle his way back into her life."

"She feels the same about you," I insist. "All the more reason for me to take the heat. This way, when she seeks you out to cry on your shoulder, at least one of us can be the voice of reason."

"'The voice of reason?'" He shrugs. "That particular voice is whispering, 'Elope!'"

I put my hand to my ear. "Funny! I hear it too."

His lips find mine. I melt into his kiss.

But even this joy can't push aside the anxiety of my next task: foregoing my promise to my daughter.

Once again, on tonight's agenda: heartache for one of my children.

Maybe eloping isn't such a bad idea after all.

Texts ping on our cell phones.

Jack clicks onto his first. "It's from Ryan. 'Feel free to take off from work between now and the wedding. By the way, Emma is coordinating the wedding party details. You can pick up a list of what she needs from you at her place. Enjoy!'"

"I don't get it," I mutter. "Does he have a screw loose or something?"

"Frankly, it's a very smart move. It's his way of safeguarding the mission, and Acme itself, from prying eyes. Granted, it would have been easier to get the POI list via email or to head over to the office and pluck it off of Emma's desk. However, rendezvousing with our other mission operatives at Arnie and Emma's Venice Beach cottage passes muster with anyone who may be watching us."

I look at my message. "It's from Emma. It says, 'Pick up ice cream before you get here. Prefer Fudgsicle.'"

Jack chuckles. "We must be due for a brush pass with Abu. Are you up for ice cream?"

"After all that cake?" I stick my finger down my throat. "Oh hell, sure, why not?"

Babette is right. They'll need a crowbar to get me into any designer wedding dress.

That's okay. I'm sure it'll be worth it.

8

Putting a Ring on It

How exciting! You and your betrothed are going ring shopping! Here are a few tips for getting a bauble worthy of your love:

- *Tip #1: Ask politely for what you really want. After all, the ring is supposed to be yours for a lifetime. (You may not be able to say the same about the man who gave it to you if you catch him in bed with another woman.)*
- *Tip #2: Don't succumb to his pleas to settle for his heirloom ring—especially if it's the same ring he gave his last fiancée before she left him at the altar.*
- *Tip #3: If he uses the excuse that "no diamond is grand enough to grace the finger of my betrothed," take this as a very broad hint that his feet have turned to blocks of ice at the thought of seeing you walk down the aisle toward him.*

At this point, the only way to warm them up is to roast them with the smoking gun food torch you've already received as a wedding gift. As he dances a hot-footed jig, he's sure to change his tune.

"SO, SPILL IT. DID YOU DO THE DIRTY DEED?"

Jack winces at my question. Shame on him. Since starting our surveillance detection route, we've spotted two tails: most likely FBI, since we're on the Chiffrays' guest list while they're in town. It's a precautionary measure, considering that Jack and I were once on the FBI's Most Wanted List (another little gift from my not-so-dearly departed ex, Carl), I can't say I blame them.

We're taking a little stroll on Hilldale's Main Street in order to kill time before we're to pick up Trisha from her elementary school's end-of-year picnic. We'll stay in the park long enough to rendezvous with Abu, who's got his ice cream truck back on the streets for a brush pass: the fruits of Acme's ComInt division—a full list of our mission's Persons of Interest—can be found on a Fudgsicle stick.

Many of the POIs will be attending President Chiffray's Middle East summit, and are even now buzzing around Lion's Lair in preparation for it. If our target is among them, we'll now be in position to find him.

Or her.

Jack stops to gaze into Hilldale's Tiffany store window. "Hey, what's your guess—is that ring's diamond two carats? Three?" He points to a white-gold ring, crowned with a halo diamond.

"It's big enough," I assure him. "Now quit trying to change the subject."

"If what you're asking is if I planted the microdot on Babette while you stuffed your face with cake, unfortunately, the answer is no. Although, I have earmarked a couple of possible, er, locations. I'm supposed to work out with her later today, remember? If I'm showing her a few new strokes—"

"Ha, ha. I'm sure she'll figure out how to turn the tables so that she does the stroking." I keep a placid grin on my face as I point to another ring in the case: a Princess cut diamond in a scroll vintage cluster setting. "That one is prettier. So, tell me: where?"

"Are you sure you really want to know?" Jack bends down in the pretense of scrutinizing my choice. In reality, he's avoiding eye contact.

Now I feel guilty. I mean, heck, he's only doing his job.

Our job.

Which is rarely in sync with the rest of our lives. The wedding is an apt case in point. "I'm facing the same problem, so we may as well share trade secrets," I concede.

"You've got a point." He shakes his head, frustrated. "There's a fold between her ear lobe and the back of her neck. How about there?"

"Don't. We won't get video that we could use."

He nods. "Good point. How about on the neck, below the jaw?"

"She's sure to wash it off."

"Gotcha. She always wears low-cut tops. Maybe, you know, between her breasts?"

"Since when will you have a chance to touch her breasts? …Oh, yeah, I forget. We're talking about Babette." My smile belies the anger in my murmur.

He rolls his eyes. "Donna, please don't be jealous."

My eyes narrow into a glare. "Tell me, Jack Craig, how would you feel if I asked your opinion about planting a microdot on Lee's itchy and scratchy?"

"We're talking an audio and video feed here! Since he doesn't walk around with his boys exposed, I don't think we'll find what we need," he snickers.

I cover my angst with a shrug. "Sure then, go for it."

If the opportunity presents itself, he'll take it. We both know it.

I stare at the rings so that he and our government-sanctioned shadows can't see my tears.

An idea strikes me. When our eyes meet through the reflection of the store's plate glass window, I murmur, "Since our true goal is their cell phones, why work so hard to place the microdot?"

"Who says I am?" Through gritted teeth, Jack's voice cracks with exasperation. "I can't stand the woman. Whereas, let's face it—you care about Lee."

"I don't 'care' about Lee." I turn to face him.

Without the reflection of shadow and light, those brilliant green of his eyes take my breath away—

Until I notice the wariness in them. "Then why do you keep making excuses for him?" he asks.

"Because...because I don't want the wrong person to go down for this."

"I see: Lee, being the 'wrong person.' And you're convinced that Babette is such a brilliant evil mastermind that she could pull off control of the Quorum?"

"Why not?" I retort defensively. "Just because she plays the part of a lecherous airhead bitch doesn't mean she isn't all that *plus* a brilliant evil mastermind! In fact, what evil mastermind isn't also lecherous, or bitchy for that matter? Granted, airheadedness isn't usually part of the equation, but you catch my drift."

"You're rambling, but I've been around you long enough to decode DonnaSpeak. What you mean to say is you'll do everything in your power to prove me wrong." His smirk says, *Bring. It. On.* "And no doubt Lee will enjoy every minute of it."

"If—please take note I've used the conjunction 'if' as opposed to 'when'—I have to place the microdot on Lee, it's only because I failed to get his cell phone first."

"If any circumstance affords you the opportunity to place the microdot, do it."

My laugh sounds hollow, even to me. "You don't mean that."

"I'm not being flippant," Jack growls. "This is not a request, Donna. It is an order from your mission leader."

"I don't need your permission to do my job, Jack Craig. And you certainly don't need mine."

He reaches for my hand. "You're right. But I'd still like to know I've earned your understanding."

"To earn it, you first have to give it."

Despite his attempt to keep his face smooth as marble, Jack grimaces. "Fair enough."

I lean into him. Just shifting my body those few inches gives shade to one particular ring. Its two-and-a-half carat diamond, raised on six prongs above a band inlaid with channel-set diamonds on each side, and is backlit in such a way that its natural brilliance is even more dazzling. "So beautiful," I murmur—

Suddenly, I'm hit with an idea. "Oh, my God! We never—"

"I know, Donna." Guilt lays heavy in Jack's eyes. "Look—I'm sorry I've never taken you shopping for a wedding ring. But in all honesty, we've been so busy—"

"I wasn't going for a broad hint, silly!" I step up to kiss the tip of his nose. "Jack, I think I know where we can hide the microdots without…well, without having to put it where the sun don't shine, if you catch my drift."

"I'm all ears." His relieved tone makes me feel silly for even doubting him.

I point to the rings. "What I started to say is that we forgot the one thing the Chiffrays always wear: their wedding rings. If Plan B is inevitable, instead of attaching it on skin, why don't we slip the microdots on the settings of their wedding bands?"

Jack stares at the rings for a long time. Finally, he whispers, "Oh, my God, that's perfect! You are a genius, Almost Mrs. Craig! The dot will have enough glue to cling between the prongs and stone. And it's clear, so no one will see it!" He sweeps me up in his arms and smothers me in a deep, languid kiss.

When our lips part, he adds, "Of course, we may have to be creative in how we get ahold of their rings."

"By 'creative,' do you mean we'll have to hold hands with the targets? I'd expect that."

"And, you won't mind?" He's still staring at the ring in the window.

"What, if you hold Babette's hand? No—not if that's all you're holding." I shrug. "I presume you feel the same way about me and Lee."

He laughs. "And every other guy on Emma's list."

"Well, hopefully, the damn list isn't too long!"

"More to the point, they all better have rings." Jack frowns, but he still won't face me. "Otherwise, we'll have to come up with a Plan C, which we both know won't be as chaste as holding hands."

My mind shifts to everything a wedding band is meant to stand for: fidelity, trust, and eternity.

Happily ever after.

Can spies like us ever truly be happy, *ad infinitum*, knowing that we must trust each other, despite any infidelity our jobs entail?

A large part of why Jack hopes Lee is Quorum because of my feelings for him.

At every turn, I've given Lee the benefit of the doubt. I've trusted Lee.

But Jack has had no reason to be jealous, since I've never loved Lee.

I take that back: Jack doesn't trust Lee because it's so obvious that Lee has feelings for *me.*

And now, to prove Jack right, I may have to do the one thing he dreads: give in to Lee's feelings for me.

I pat Jack's arm. "Here's our Plan B: Trust. Fidelity. Eternity."

Jack nods. He gets it. "Always," he murmurs, as he kisses my hand. "Let's grab Trisha, then pick up our Fudgsicle." I sigh. "Then I'll work off this cake while you can play golf with Babette."

He rolls his eyes. He's not happy about it, but he knows it's what Ryan would want.

As for me, I just want this mission to be over.

THERE IS A LINE A BLOCK LONG AROUND ABU'S ICE CREAM truck. The line moves quickly, despite the mommies who meander forward as they gossip, and the indecision inherent in children with too many tasty frozen desserts to choose from on this hot summer day.

Abu has gotten his groove back.

Even as he makes chitchat and change, like all good bridge agents, his eyes scan the length of the park in search of anyone who will notice the hand-off of intel. When I catch his eye, he grins. At the same time, he smacks the hand of a fifth-grader who makes a grab for a kindergartener's special edition Disney Popsicle: the Blue Raspberry Elsa.

"Cut it out," Abu growls at the kid. "If you can't wait your turn, go to the back of the line."

Soon, there is only one family in front of us: a dad with an eight-year-old boy. After buying a Dreamsicle, the man hands Abu a twenty-dollar bill. Abu dolefully counts out his change in singles, just like the man asked. As thanks, the man takes the loose change—a dime and three pennies—and drops it in Abu's tip jar.

The coins tinkle as they hit the jar's glass bottom.

"Piker," Abu mutters under his breath.

Trisha asks for a White Cherry Olaf Popsicle. Armed with the frozen treat, she ecstatically runs off to catch some shade so that it won't melt so quickly.

"That, and a Fudgsicle," I bat my eyes at Abu.

He nods nonchalantly, as he reaches deep into the freezer for our very special pop.

Jack hands him a ten-dollar bill. "Will this cover it?"

Abu gleefully snatches it out of his hand. "You're a generous man, my friend." He holds it up for the other parents to see before stuffing it into the tip jar.

"I take it this hasn't been a lucrative day?" I ask.

Abu shrugs. "Beats driving an Uber car share."

He's got a point.

We aren't worried that the pop will melt before we get home. Most of it is dry ice anyway.

THE CODE IS PUNCHED OUT, LIKE BRAILLE, ON THE FUDGSICLE'S stick. After tracing over the stick and deciphering the message, we light a match to both, and let them burn down to ashes in the fireplace.

"There are only seven POIs?" I ask, as we watch them go up in smoke.

"You got your wish. It makes our job a lot easier," Jack points out. "Let's see…Todd Courtland. That's a no-brainer. And Eileen."

I shrug. "She's unlikely."

"I agree, but she's an obvious POI, based on her long affiliation with Lee, and her access to his personal effects, which include his cell." His gaze shifts back to the list. "The head agent in Lee's Secret Service detail is also on the list: Gerald Muldoon."

"You mean Lurch—the tall, solid guy who stayed in the Oval Office during our meeting with Lee."

Jack chuckles. "A colorful nickname, but yes. And on the flip side, there is Babette's chief of staff, and the head of her Secret Service detail as well."

"Narcissa Belmont, and Zeb Dunne. I'm more likely to believe it could be Narcissa. But, from what I could see, Zeb isn't all that fond of her."

"Whether he likes her or not isn't important. All that counts is whether or not he sent the texts to Xia."

He has a point—but I've got a great idea. "Hey, listen—Babette is expecting our friends and family list for the engagement party. I'd already decided to include the names of Ryan and our Acme team. While the whole mission team has access to Lion's Lair, why don't we put them to work? Arnie can get in early with the catering crew, so that he can fake out the security cameras and hack the computer system in order to monitor anything that reeks of Quorum. Later, he'll enter the party as a guest, along with Emma. During the party, you and I will snatch the cell phones while Abu, Dominic, and Ryan stand guard as Emma and Arnie pull off brush passes in order to scan them quickly, then pass them back to us to replace."

Jack kisses the top of my head. "That's a brilliant idea. Between the seven of us, we'll have a better chance of scrubbing Lion's Lair for intel. If we have to abort during the engagement party, we'll get a second chance during the wedding. But, how do we get the message to Ryan?"

"Easy," I declare.

I log on to Hilldale Library's website, through a member account I've established under the name *P. Lindstrom*. From there, I click onto the email account of the circulation librarian, Marion, who happens to be an Acme operative.

My note to her reads:

Which book has this quote? I'd like to reserve it, if you please, but

I won't be able to pick it up until Saturday. Thank you! –P Lindstrom

"When you look at me, when you think of me, I am in paradise." —William Makepeace Thackeray

Seeing this, Jack honors me with a thumbs-up. He's just remembered that Emma also accesses this account, and is alerted whenever correspondence goes between P Lindstrom and Marion.

Emma will decode the quote as follows:

- When: *known event, indicated in correspondence above, and via code word in this quote.*
- You: *Acme*
- Look: *Be on the lookout for*
- Think: *assistance needed*
- At me/of me: *involving me, your field agent*
- In Paradise: *at the Party*

Jack's grin melts into a frown as he looks down at his watch. "Let's grab Trisha and our workout clothes, then head to Lion's Lair."

Ah, back to reality. Hopefully, our sweat equity will pay off in successful spycraft.

"TWELVE MORE LUNGES, AND WE'LL CALL IT A DAY," WALTON says.

"Let's go for twenty-four," I counter, despite my huffing and puffing.

"A glutton for punishment, eh?" He grins wickedly. "I see we have that in common."

My sudden burst of energy has nothing to do with the fact that I'm bound and determined to prove Babette wrong about bulging out of my wedding dress, and everything to do with getting him to open up about his first client.

So far, nothing I've done has worked.

Yes, he was seething when he discovered that she has a new workout partner. To make up for the fact that his replacement is my betrothed, I'm being put through my paces. He hopes my pain will gain him something as well: Babette's jealousy.

I'm not complaining. I'll do everything in my power to prove Babette wrong. Not only will the dress fit beautifully on the day of my wedding, every eye will be on me, as opposed to her.

As a last resort to loosen his tongue, I turn around and fold at the waist into a wide-legged forward bend.

This at least earns me his appreciative gaze. Although my head is upside down, I can still watch him as he tilts his head, better to admire me from behind.

"Nice…" he murmurs. "But you'll get more out of it if you widen your legs a couple more inches"—he bends so that one hand can nudge my foot even further out. Why he feels he's got to cup my ass with the other is beyond me.

"Feel what I mean?" he whispers in my ear.

He is not expecting to feel my hand on his nutsack. I twist it so hard that he drops to his knees onto the gym mat.

I could kick myself for losing my cool until he whispers, "I…love you."

I put my hand around his throat. "What's that you say?"

"I needed to be…"—he blushes—"disciplined."

I let go, then ease down beside him. "You're right. Someone should take you in hand. *Especially for gossiping about my bestie.*"

His eyes light up when he realizes what he must pay for me to play. "I can be more indiscreet."

I circle his right nipple with my index finger and thumb before twisting it hard. "Prove it."

He groans ecstatically. When, finally, he opens his eyes, he has a new reason to whine: Jack and Babette have just come into view. They are walking arm-in-arm to the sixth hole.

If Jack hasn't placed that damn microdot by now, I'm going to be pissed.

Or maybe not, since it may have meant getting even more up close and personal with her than he is already.

"Since when has Babette taken up golf?"

Walton shrugs. "It gives her an excuse to hang with some dude from the Middle East." He sneers at the thought. "He gets a woody whenever she's around."

"Oh, really?" Salem is already on my radar, so no news there. My hand moves to the other nipple. As my fingers do their magic, I hiss, "You're gossiping again, you very bad boy."

"That's just…the tip…of the iceberg." He gazes down, where his own iceberg is growing. "Until the Sheik of Araby hits town, she amuses herself with Lucky Lee's chief of staff —that creepy Todd dude."

Hmmm. Jealous much? Again, he hasn't told me anything I don't already know. I slap his face, hard. "Of course, she'd be flattered. He's a man-ho. Still, it's no reason for you to be telling tales out of school," I purr. "If there was a desk in this room, I'd make you bend over it for twelve lashes."

"Just twelve?" He moans at the thought. "Wait…listen! There's more—like the head honcho with her Secret Service detail." He frowns at the thought.

I pause too, only because I know this dude is so off base. "But it's the man's job to spend time with her, isn't it?"

"Honey, he ain't hoppin' in the front of her Lincoln town car." Walton arches a brow. "And if the limo is a'rockin,' no one should come a'knockin.'"

"You don't say?" Has the ol' Donna-o-Meter missed something? Walton may be wrong about Zeb, but it would be interesting to have an extra pair of eyes on Babette, and he certainly has no qualms playing the Peeping Tom.

Which gives me a great idea…

I notice he's wearing a chain around his neck, holding a fob of some sort. "What's this?" I wrap it around my hand so that it chokes him.

"My…Saint Christopher's medal," he gasps.

Walton may not be on our POI list, but he's close enough to Babette to be our eyes and ears on her. I finger the medal lovingly. He assumes I'm mesmerized by it. What he doesn't know is that I've attached a microdot. As far as Walton is concerned, it covers the bases.

I let the chain fall to his chest. "A good Catholic boy, eh? I used to want to be a nun. I bet the abbess would have called me Sister Donatella."

Walton grins. "The nuns at school called me naughty as they rapped my knuckles."

"Do you always wear your medal?"

"No."

"The right answer is yes." So that he remembers, I twist his fingers straight back, almost to the breaking point. "If you forget, I'll take it as a sign that you don't really want me to be your friend."

"I'll always wear it! I promise!" He flinches through the pain, but he's certainly got a smile on his face.

I pat his cheek gently before slapping it again. "And leave it exposed, so that everyone can admire it."

"Yes, of course"—he hesitates, then whispers, "Sister Donatella."

"That's a good boy. And so that my best friend in the world looks her best for my wedding, do everything in your power to stay by her side. She needs you to remind her that she's got a few sags, that she's carrying a few extra pounds."

He nods vigorously.

As an incentive, I step hard on his toes.

He shows his pleasure with a howl.

"Yes, I know you'll look after her. And because of that, I'll look after you," I promise. "Isn't that what friends are for?"

I pick up my gym bag and head out the door.

9

Picking Out Your Wedding Dress

One mistake a bride must never make is in the choice of her wedding dress. So many choices, but only one body:

Yours, with all its assets and flaws.

So that your dress is all you've dreamed about for that very important day, avoid the following:

- *No-No Number One: Don't be afraid to go over your budget. If there's one dress you'll remember for the rest of your life, this is it. If there's one dress in which you'll be photographed more than any other, this is it. If there is one dress that will make you look like a million dollars, this is it. If there's one dress choice that you don't want to screw up, this is it, so please don't give a damn if you go over your budget by a buck or two (or ten...or a hundred).*
- *No-No Number Two: Don't follow any trends. Yes, the micro-mini, or granny gown, or puffy pirate shirtdress may have seemed like a good idea at the time, but let's*

face it: it's not a keeper for anything other than a Halloween costume.

- *No-No Number Three: Don't take the advice of others. Here's the bottom line: as much as you'd hope that your (a) mother, (b) sister, (c) best friend, (d) fiancé will know immediately which dress looks best on you, they have their own reasons for choosing one that may not be your ideal princess dress. Trust your own judgment!*

Think of it this way: twenty years hence, when you look at your wedding pictures, you don't need this to be yet another issue to blame on your mother. It'll be no one's fault but your own.

"IT SOUNDED AS IF YOU HAD QUITE A WORKOUT," CHANTAL IS leaning against the wall opposite the workout room.

The hall is broad, but Walton's howl was loud enough to shake the birds from the trees. I'm not surprised someone walked over to check it out.

I just wish it weren't her. The smirk on her face comes with a presumption that what went on in there is exactly what Babette had counted on.

"That shriek?" I shrug. "Walton dropped a barbell on his foot."

"Then I guess the first lady will have to get her exercise elsewhere." I follow Chantal's gaze out the window toward the golf course, where Babette is set to tee off.

Jack positions himself behind her. When he puts his hands on her hips to position them, she deliberately takes a step back in order to rub up against him.

Grrrrr…

I bend down to tie my sneaker, so that Chantal can't see my grimace. Unfortunately, she's still standing there when I look up. So that she takes the hint, I say, "Don't let me take you away from your coffee break."

"In fact, I came to find you."

I sigh. "What now?"

"Now we're getting into the fun stuff! I've got a room full of wedding dresses for you to try on."

"Oh! Well, in that case—"

"I've set them up in Babette's dressing suite, since it has wall-to-wall mirrors—as well as a bathroom with a shower stall." She leans in close in order to take a whiff, and wrinkles her nose. "Smells like it was quite a workout."

Bitch. "It takes sweat equity to have a body like this," I remind her coolly.

"You don't say." To get a full assessment, she circles me, then shrugs. "Sad isn't it? Look, seriously, so that you're not disappointed on your wedding day, I'll book you for double sessions with Walton every day between now and then." She writes something in her iPad. "There, done…Well, well, well, he must have enjoyed himself too. See? He sent a string of emojis."

She holds out the iPad so that I can see the smiley faces.

No wonder they're smiling. Each is demonstrating an X-rated sex act.

Now I *really* need that shower.

"THAT ONE IS PERFECT, DON'T YOU THINK?" I WON'T BE FOOLED

by Chantal's cheery chirp. This dress is just as fug-ugly as the last four.

I shake my head. "Nope, sorry. Not exactly what I had in mind."

"Seriously? What's wrong with this one?" By this point, she no longer attempts to smile. She just bares her teeth.

I stare at my body in the mirror. "You mean, besides the fact that it has a turtleneck? Isn't that enough?" Not to mention an endless train, and is wrapped so tightly around me that I could pass for a mummy.

"No, not really. Look, I'm just trying to protect you from the cruel whispers that bring most older brides to tears." She touches her throat and hisses, *"Turkey neck."*

I close my eyes and count to ten. Yes, I'm disappointed to see that she's still here when they open.

"Donna, admit it: you've become a bridezilla." She shakes her head in mock terror.

"I beg your pardon? How can you say that?"

"Easily! I mean, look at all the dresses you've vetoed!" She picks up one of the discards off the bed. "This one was perfectly fine, but you have a problem with the waistline."

"You mean, I had a problem with the fact that there *was no* waistline. I looked like an Oompa Loompa!" I hold up the dress, which could pass for a silk pillowcase stuffed and puffed with tulle, allowing strategically cut holes for the release of the bride's head and appendages.

Chantal shrugs. "You should reconsider. It covers a lot of sins."

Ah, sins. Would, say, strangling your bossy wedding planner with the ugly wedding gown she insists you accept count as one? I'm sure most brides would vote no.

"And what was wrong with this one?" She holds up another abomination. "The lacework is one of a kind, and the raw silk comes all the way from Italy."

"It looks as if it was designed by a Trappist monk!" I shake my head in wonder. "My God, I can wrap it twice around my body! I guess that's why it comes with a sash. By the way, did you notice that the sleeves were three inches longer than my arms?"

She rolls her eyes. "And all this time I thought you'd appreciate an opportunity to cover up your batwings."

I hold up my left arm. "I don't have any flab! ...Okay, maybe just a little." If I wasn't trussed up in three pairs of Boostie-Yay Spanx bodysuits, I might be able to sidekick that smirk off her face. As it is, I can barely move a muscle.

"Frankly, I thought the first one suited you the best." She holds up the dress I hated most: so low cut that a nip slip would have been inevitable. Then again, considering it's also got a micro-miniskirt, I wouldn't have been able to bend down anyway.

"Really? I'll be saying my wedding vows—not dancing in a go-go dancers cage in some Vegas strip club!"

"Another reason to choose the gown designed by Brother Francis."

I waddle over to her until we're nose to nose. "I knew it! You bought it in some monastery gift shop!" Trappist monks use sign language in order to honor their vow of silence. I do the same, to honor my vow of sanity: a one-finger salute.

She pretends she doesn't see it. "Granted, the dress is a bit boho. But even someone your age can be a fashion trend-setter." Before I can point out that I'm younger than she, despite the numerous operations to cover up this fact, she cuts me off with her palm to my face. "We're down to one last dress, and that's it. Make your choice of the lesser of all evils." She motions at the only gown hanging from one of the elegant wrought iron hooks.

"That's my point: they're *all* evil!" I motion toward the dresses tossed on the bed.

She crosses her hands below her non-existent bosom. She's not budging.

Frustrated, I hold up the last dress—

Yuck. It's a knock-off of Princess Diana's Eighties-era wedding gown: puffed sleeves, doily collar, and overlong train.

I hold it up, laughing. "This isn't a wedding dress! It's a Halloween costume!"

Chantal yanks it out of my hand. "This will always be viewed as an iconic classic! Dressing up as a princess on her wedding day is something every little girl dreams of. And, besides"—she sniffs—"*every* fashion maven on earth agrees with one thing: Babette Chiffray has wonderful taste. You'll just have to suck it up."

"Oh, yeah? Pray tell, just what will Babette be wearing to my wedding?"

Chantal stalks off toward the stadium-sized closet at the other end of the dressing room. "It's a Michael Kors. Stunning, isn't it?"

"I'll say," I mutter. Slim straps hold up the simple column that scoops low in the front, and is cut even lower in its vented back. Above the Empire waist, the dress is covered in silver sequins.

The body of the dress is white.

"But…why would she wear white at my wedding?" I stammer.

Confused, she mutters, "Why should the color of her dress matter?"

"Because only the bride is supposed to wear white! It's *my wedding, not hers, or has she forgotten that?*"

Chantal shrugs. "Considering that she's the first lady, frankly, dearie, all that should matter to you is that she's deemed the event worthy enough to attend in the first place." She jerks the dress away from me—

But I'm not letting go.

Hearing it rip, we freeze.

"Why, you jealous lunatic! It was one of a kind! Michael designed it especially for Babette!"

"Really?" I look at the designer's signature tag on the inside lining. "Then why is it in my size?"

"Oh! …Well…," she stutters, "because designers always send something a few sizes larger. It makes it easier in the off chance that alterations are needed."

"She'll be swimming in it. Admit it, she took it for herself, but it was meant for me."

I yank it out of her hand.

She snatches it back.

I grab it again—

But she holds tight—

Another loud rip freezes us both in our tracks.

"Oh, my God," Chantal murmurs. "Do you know how much this dress costs?"

"Well, you can certainly have it now." Babette's voice rings through the room.

We turn to the doorway to see her standing there with Jack, who is trying hard not to laugh—not at my predicament, but from the monstrosity that swaddles me from head to toe.

I toss the dress on the floor. "I'll pass on the honor." With my head held high in the turtleneck mummy wrapper, I turn on my heel, and take four steps—

Only to fall flat on my face. Somehow, I've tripped on the train of my dress.

It rips too.

Just great. Now I own two wedding dresses, neither of which are wearable.

My pride gives me the strength to hold in my tears. So, who's wailing?

Babette.

We can barely make out what she's saying through her gulps and sobs. "I...I didn't think you'd care if I kept one of the dresses for myself."

Jack is stroking her bowed head and murmuring, "There, there, Babette. Donna didn't mean it."

Wait...*What?*

I sure as hell did mean it.

How could he!

Jack's head turns so that he can scowl at me—

And give me a wink unobserved by the others.

I am not mollified, but let it be noted that I am a team player.

At least until I get him alone and can read him the riot act.

And cry on his shoulder for throwing me to that she-wolf.

"I'm...sorry. But of course you can wear whatever you

want." My apology is delivered with a shrug.

Her sniffling stops the second the words are out of my mouth. She gazes up at me, her eyes gleaming—not from tears, but from this latest victory. "So, you don't mind if I wear a similar shade?"

"By that, do you mean white? No. Knock yourself out." *Before I do it for you.*

I smirk as I hold up the torn gown. "Since this is ruined, I guess you'll have to go for something else."

If Babette had truly shed tears, they were now nowhere in sight—only the sly smile of a woman who knows how to get what she wants. "Oh, don't be silly," she admonishes me. "Michael will gladly send another one over, in the right size —that is, *my* size."

"But, won't he mind that the first one is now ripped?"

"Not at all. What designer wouldn't want his creation worn by the president's wife? Besides, I'll just explain that the dress ripped when we zipped you up. Heaven knows, it would have happened anyway."

Without a second glance, she heads for the door with her handmaiden, Chantal, beside her—a good thing, I guess, because neither sees me throw a hook punch at Babette—

Which is stopped by Jack's open palm.

It's great to see him share my pain.

He waits until they are out of the room before hissing a chorus of curses as he shakes his aching hand.

When he's through, I growl, "Considering all the up-close-and-personal time you've had with Babette, I presume your mission was accomplished."

Jack grimaces. "Well…almost."

"No? Do tell."

"It wasn't as if I could slip her cell phone out of her golf bag and scan it right there in front of her."

"From what I could see, you've had ample time for hand holding."

"We did, but she wasn't wearing her ring."

"I'm shocked, considering the splash it made in the society pages when international playboy and tech entrepreneur, Lee Chiffray, presented it to the wealthy widow Breck after a whirlwind courtship." I roll my eyes. "So, I take it you didn't get touchy-feely either?"

"Not anywhere that may stick permanently." He glances away. "But I'll have another opportunity. She's bound and determined to lower her handicap."

"Along with her thong, no doubt."

He winces at the thought as he grabs my hand. "I've had enough of Lion's Lair for one day. Let's get out of here."

Gladly.

So that I can avoid the inevitable phone call from Chantal asking which of the designer gowns I've chosen, I grab the dress least likely to make me upchuck during the ceremony: the monk's robe.

They say accessories make any outfit. Maybe finding the right belt will make all the difference.

If not, I can use it to hang Chantal from the nearest lamppost.

10

Engagement Party!

Now that your betrothal is official, it's time to tell the world—by throwing an engagement party!

Of course, not everyone will be pleased with the news that you're both off the mating market—all the more reason to keep a tight rein on your guest list. The following should certainly make the cut:

1. *Meet the parents (and the rest of the family). There is no better time to impress them than in an elegant setting where bubbly flows like Niagara Falls. That way, should you discover that his reason for keeping them at bay until now has more to do with their rap sheets, and less to do with their scintillating personalities, you can still run like hell.*

2. *Invite his closest friends? But of course! Here's your chance to meet his posse. Should one mutter a few lascivious comments in your direction, no problem! Feel free to respond with a few choice words of your own. As*

for a wandering hand or two (or three), all it takes is a quick slice of his tongue with the knife used for carving the roast beef to shut him up. Any bloodletting can be dismissed as, "Rare. But yes, if you're not careful, you can bleed to death."

3. *Should he insist on inviting his old girlfriends, acquiesce to the request. You're not doing it because it makes you secure in the relationship, or because you don't have a jealous bone in your body. You're doing it because getting the competition out of the way is easier when they're all in the same room: preferably one with no escape route.*

"As of this very moment, everyone on the engagement party list has RSVP'd," Chantal gushes. "Obviously, we saved the A-List for the wedding—you know, George and Amal, Beyoncé, Kate and Cate, Anne Hathaway, Madonna, Lady Gaga, Leo DiCaprio, and Melissa McCarthy. But lucky you, the B-List ain't so shabby, either. Granted, it includes a few of the Housewives of Beverly Hills, but, never fear, we also got all the Kardashians! Isn't this wonderful news?"

"Yep, truly super-duper! I have to pinch myself to believe it!" Really, I'd like to pinch her pinhead between my thumb and forefinger, just as I'd do to any annoying blood sucking tick.

But I can't. At least, not until the mission is over. At that point the wedding planner from hell *had better run for her life.*

"Now, add *my family* to the list, and everything stays

peachy-keen." The frost in my tone should have her reaching for a thermal push-up bra and thong.

"Oh…*hmmm*," she stutters. Her lousy attempt at damage control is to proclaim, "Well, you know how it is. We had to cut the guest list somewhere."

"You can't cut it *there*! Aunt Phyllis is family, as are Mary, Jeff, and Evan— not to mention that they're in the wedding party."

Only Trisha will join us, since she's been invited to sleep over with Janie.

Chantal stumbles through an explanation—something about a full house as is, what with the number of RSVPs received from all the glitterati on the guest list, including, "the whole cast of *Game of Thrones* and *The Hobbit* movies too! Not to mention all of the Secret Service detail wandering around—"

"Get real," I growl. "The ball room in Lion's Lair holds four hundred! Surely there's space for four more!"

"Sorry, but no," Chantal growls. "Babette is already concerned that this is turning into an OC housewife hoedown. Trust me, those rarely make the *Vanity Fair* party page." She sighs heavily, as if carrying the weight of the world on her bony shoulders.

"If that's what has you worried, feel free to cut any and all of Hilldale."

"Believe me, I wish I could, but Babette won't allow it. Or, as she puts it, 'We don't want the natives to get restless.'"

Or the voters, for that matter.

This wedding stuff is wearing me down.

Before I can give her my ultimatum—my family in attendance, or her head hanging from one of the spikes that top the ten-foot wall around Lion's Lair—she squeals through the phone, "Gotta go! We just scored a four-star general! Babette will be beside herself. The Armed Services have never forgiven her for telling Anna Wintour of *Vogue* that the U.S. Military's uniforms need a total overhaul by Ralph Lauren, so now it's time to make nice-nice!"

Click.

I turn to Jack. "Can we elope?"

"Sure. Let's leave now." He's serious.

We can't. It would mean giving up the opportunity we've been waiting for to take down the Quorum.

"No." I shake my head halfheartedly. "But you get major brownie points for saying yes."

He kisses the nape of my neck. "I'll collect them tonight, after the party."

Because I don't want him to stop, I bite my tongue to keep from saying, *not if I'm in jail for stealing POTUS's cell phone.*

If I do get caught, when will I get the opportunity feel Jack's lips on me again?

How often do they allow conjugal visits in federal prison? I hope I don't have a chance to find out.

"DONNA! ...DONNA!" TIFFY SWIFT WAVES FRANTICALLY AT ME from across the room, "Congratulations, girlfriend!"

As if I'm some long-lost gal pal? *Give me a break.*

She's waving, not to pass along her good wishes, but because Jack and I stand next to Babette and Lee.

Tiffy is obviously more star struck than Hayley Coxhead

or Penelope because she literally drags them over. To reach us, they have to duck and dodge through the crowd of Chantal's B-listers, as well as the legion of cater waiters, and an army of Secret Service agents, including Abu and Dominic.

Then there's the rest of our Acme team.

Ryan came in earlier than Emma and Arnie. He greeted the Chiffrays with formal handshakes, and was somewhat surprised when Lee pulled him in close for a bear hug. It would have been great if he could have picked POTUS's upper inside jacket pocket for his cell phone right then and there, but my guess is that he was too stunned to think about it, let alone try it, so that little bit of spycraft is still up to me.

Emma and Arnie spaced their entrances so that they were dead center in the receiving line, which included Lee, Babette, Jack, and me. Arnie walked through first. He was oblivious that his formal bow to the Chiffrays drew a smirk from Babette, as did the manner in which he pumped Jack's hand, like a long-lost brother.

He practically lifted me off the ground with his hug, whispering, "Good luck, Don! ...By the way, if you get caught, head for the panic room. It's through the shower in Lee's office. The tunnel drops you outside the gate next to Hilldale Park."

Now he tells me. I guess he's just as concerned about my odds of pulling this off as I am.

Emma's smile wavered as we shook hands, when she handed off the iPhone so similar to Lee's that he'll never know the difference. I slip it into a pocket buried deep in the voluminous folds of my pleated tulle tea-length skirt.

Seeing the concern in her eyes, I whispered, "Don't worry, it'll all be fine."

I wish I meant what I said.

"I guess I'll have to take your word for it," Emma muttered. "This place has more security than Fort Knox!" She shuddered slightly.

Surely she's dreading the fate of her infant son, Nicky, should our mission fail and she and Arnie are implicated in it. "A heads-up: the cams are on a loop, and the security sensors have been turned off."

In other words, the mission is a go.

The Acme operatives are equipped with contacts and ear buds that allow for constant visual and audio, respectively, on each of us. Dominic is shadowing Jack, and Abu is shadowing me.

Should I get ahold of Lee's cell, I'll use a code phrase, "It's warmer in here than it is outside…"

This signals Emma and Arnie to move past me to retrieve Lee's iPhone. They'll head to the powder room, where one of them will do the scan, while the other stands guard. They'll return it to me with another brush pass, so that I can put back the phone.

Easy-peasy, right?

We both know better.

The receiving line seemed endless, but making small talk with a woman who only has eyes for my fiancé would have been even harder to endure. And now, to have Hilldale's meanest mommies fawning over her?

I can't wait for this night to be over.

Babette must feel the same way, despite a smug grin that seems set in stone. But I notice the light go out of her eyes when she realizes the Bitches of Hilldale have descended on her. Thus far, only celebrities and other honored guests—politicians and well-heeled party supporters—have been allowed photo ops with the first couple. Babette is a true believer in American politics' pay-to-play structure.

She raises a brow in Narcissa's direction. I take it this is some sort of shorthand between them. I'm right when Zeb sidelines Tiffy, Penelope, and Hayley just long enough for Jack to sweep Babette onto the dance floor as John Legend croons *All of Me.*

From Lee's smile, he's just as amused as I am. "If we follow their lead, we can avoid your new best friends." He holds out his arm.

I take it. "You had me at 'avoid.'"

He's wearing his wedding band. Before the party started, he slipped his iPhone in the left inside breast pocket of his tuxedo—not an ideal location for swiping it. I'd much prefer snatching it off a desk or a table when no one is watching.

It'll be just as tricky putting it back.

In either event, I don't think he'll balk if I put my hands on him.

I guess I'll find out soon enough.

"From what I gather, our significant others are spending a lot of time together—and enjoying it." Lee's declaration isn't angry or sad, just stated as a fact.

As he glides me around the dance floor, his right hand is on the small of my back. My dress is certainly not Babette-approved, which is why I'm sure I've enjoyed so many admiring glances. It has long lace sleeves and a high neck, but it plunges low enough for me to feel his warm hand on the center of my back.

His left hand holds my right one gently. One of the tiny microdots is on the tip of its index finger. If I fail to swipe his phone, I'll place my finger against the flat band of his wedding ring.

As federal crimes go, hacking his phone is bad enough, but it's certainly a much quicker way to deduce if he was in fact the person texting Xia than the microdot's surveillance would give us.

I gaze up at Lee in order to look him straight in the eye, in the hope of distracting him enough so that he doesn't catch on while I pocket his phone. "Does it bother you, the amount of time Babette spends with Jack?"

He shrugs. "No, not at all. Babette loves…I guess the word for it is 'diversions.'"

My back stiffens at the thought that he presumes Jack is that for her. "I'm sure Jack is flattered, and that's all there is to it." My brittle tone isn't all an act.

"Donna, we both know he couldn't care less because he isn't attracted to her." Lee's smile melts into a grimace. "He only has eyes for you."

I untwine my hand from his in order to place it on his chest. This act of intimacy must take him by surprise because his heart seems to have picked up its pace.

Oh, hell—I forgot to palm the duplicate iPhone.

If I snatch his, how long will it be before he realizes it's missing?

I can't think about it now. I've just got to go on the assumption that if I divert his attention long enough, Emma can scan it quickly, and he'll never know it was missing in the first place.

I look him directly in the eye, even as I move my hand toward his inside breast pocket. "You can't say you feel the same way about Babette?"

"When it comes to Babette's fidelity, I've given up the ghost." He sighs. "When I was asked to be Catherine Martin's running mate, I should have passed on the opportunity. I guess my sense of self-importance got the better of me—as if I could truly make the world a better place, being a heartbeat away from the presidency." He shakes his head at what he now sees was his naivety. "I married a beautiful, vain, insecure woman. If you think the Veep's wife lives in a fishbowl with no place to hide, you can only imagine what it's like to be FLOTUS."

"But Babette lives for the spotlight. To have that position, you can't be shy. And being beautiful is always an asset." *He doesn't feel my palm on the broadcloth of his crisp white dress shirt slipping ever closer to the satin pocket holding his cell...*

"Considering her ego, it's all the more reason I should have said no. She approaches it as a privilege, not an honor." There is such sadness in his eyes. "People aren't stupid. The more they know of her, the more they resent her position, and how she misuses the power that comes with it."

"Lee, I think you're blowing this out of proportion," I counter gently. *My thumb and index finger inches closer... closer...until...* "Every first lady has had her detractors."

I've got it: his cell.

My next move may give him the wrong idea, but it's necessary if I'm to accomplish my goal: I lay my head against his broad chest. Sighing, I murmur, "I'm sure that it's warmer in here than it is outside."

"On my way," Emma says into my ear bud.

I see them—Emma and Arnie, waltzing in our direction.

Gently, I lift my hand from his chest…

And put it into my skirt pocket.

But for only a second before placing it back on his chest.

He shrugs. "True. But most first ladies were politicians' wives for most of their lifetimes. Babette and I came out of the private sector. Our public relations training taught us to be daring and flaunt conventions, not kowtow to them. I have a sneaking suspicion that my dear wife's endgame has nothing to do with my historic legacy, and everything to do with her own notorious place in world history."

My ears perk up. "Lee, what do you mean?"

He frowns. "I've never had to paint a picture for you, Donna. My God, you know Babette as well as I do! Everything she does is for personal gain."

I nod. Babette has given me lots of reasons to despise her, whereas Lee has given me none, despite the fact that too many times he's been in the wrong place at the wrong time.

Jack doesn't feel this is coincidence, but I'm still willing to give Lee the benefit of the doubt. Innocent until proven guilty.

Besides, to Lee's credit, once there, he's done the absolute right thing, including undermining Carl. To my mind, that alone proves he's not Quorum.

Arnie bumps into me—too hard.

Naturally, I let go of Lee.

At the same time, I slip the phone into Emma's hand. She pockets it immediately.

"Oh! So sorry," Arnie chatters. He's obviously nervous. "Great song. Great night. Great—"

Lee laughs, unperturbed. "Partners," he answers for Arnie. Then he turns to Emma. "You look beautiful tonight."

Emma murmurs, blushing bright red. "Why…thank you!"

"In fact," Lee adds, grinning at Emma, "may I have this dance?"

Oh.

Hell.

Emma and Arnie stand there, speechless. Finally, Emma turns to me, wide-eyed. "You don't mind…do you?"

"Not at all." I'm grinning like a jack-o-lantern. A part of me wants to cry, while another part of me wants to burst out and guffaw at our predicament.

Not that jail would be any laughing matter, for me, or these two new parents.

I give Lee a kiss on the cheek then I lean into Emma for a hug—

Taking the phone from her hand.

Her face eases into a radiant smile. "Well then…yeah, sure." She takes Lee's hand.

Off they go.

Arnie stares after them. "What the…Did you see that look on her face?"

I squeeze his hand. "No time to be jealous, lover boy. We've got work to do, remember?"

He nods, but he's frowning.

He steps on my feet at least three times before we're out of the ballroom. It doesn't help that he can't seem to keep his eyes off his wife as she glides and giggles with the President of the United States.

"Now I know how Jack feels," Arnie grumbles.

I want to retort, *What the hell do you mean by that?*

But, of course, I already know.

"THIS WAY. I'VE SCOPED OUT THE PERFECT PLACE." ARNIE NODS toward a small hallway leading away from the ballroom's grand foyer.

It's a small sitting room that includes a powder room. "The Secret Service has been ushering guests with tiny bladders toward the lavatories on each side of the ballroom's entrance," he explains. "We should have this one all to ourselves."

Still, just to be on the safe side, as we enter, I shut the sitting room door, and then the powder room door.

Arnie takes the cell phone from me so that he can connect it to the scanner. I don't like the droning beeps emitted. "Damn it! It's got some kind of dual encryption. Let me see if I can break it."

We hear the squeak of a door, then footsteps.

"Hurry," I mutter. "Someone is here." Silently I ease toward the door. As I turn the lock, it clicks so loudly that we both freeze.

I put my ear to the door to check for footsteps.

Instead, I hear giggles. I roll my eyes. "Whoever it is should thank you for disarming the security feed."

He nods as he attaches the cell to the scanner. Immediately, the phone chirps—a good thing, from the way Arnie is fist-pumping the air. I watch as he attaches the scanner.

"How long will this take?" I whisper.

He holds up a hand. As each second ticks away, a finger falls.

Thank God, I think, when he folds his thumb—

Only to raise all five digits again as he starts the process all over again.

"Not funny," I hiss. We hear moaning in the next room. "We've got to hurry! Eventually they'll want to...er, clean up."

Arnie's fingers are falling again. When he gets to the fourth one, we hear another chirp. This time he holds his thumb high.

He's swiping through texts—

His eyes open wide. "Bingo!"

Oh, no. Our target is now confirmed: Lee.

Everything I know about Lee is a sham.

It takes a moment for it to sink in. Memories flood my consciousness. There was the first time I saw him, on Fantasy Island, playing Dominic in Baccarat, then realizing he was Babette's new boyfriend; learning that he'd bid on the right to own me, in order to keep me out of Carl's hands —only to lose. Thank goodness, "Carl" was really Jack, who had come to save me.

Then there was the time Lee divulged to me how he'd been blackmailed by Carl into appointing him as U.S. Director of Intelligence. Together, Lee and I formed an off-the-books alliance to put Carl in jail.

Instead, I killed him.

Now I know it only helped Lee's power play for the Quorum.

My faith in Lee Chiffray has been for naught.

I feel violated.

As gently as possible, I ease open the lock on the door. Not that it matters, what with all the moaning going on out there.

Arnie follows my lead as I inch my way through the bathroom's door and through the room—

Where Jack is kissing Babette.

She is straddling him on a settee, her gold Herve Leger foil-print bandage gown is bunched at her hips. Her back is to us, and her head is angled in such a way that it gives us coverage from Jack's eyes, so I can't tell if they are open or closed.

Not that it matters. His hands roam over her as if they have eyes of their own. To be honest, it doesn't look as if he's on the hunt for her cell phone, unless he feels a full body cavity search will reveal it.

I stop, stunned.

Arnie bumps into me.

Before he can yelp, I put my hand over his mouth.

At the same time, Jack opens his eyes—even wider when he realizes it's me.

I shake my head silently. He knows I mean I won't make a scene.

Not now, anyway.

I tap Arnie's shoulder to break his trance.

I don't know which one of us wants to get out of there faster, him or me.

From the sad look on Jack's face, it may be him.

Arnie holds up the cell and gives Jack a thumbs-up, to indicate that the search is over.

Now that we know Lee is our target, Jack has an excuse to quit groping Babette.

That is, if he wants one.

I tap Emma on the shoulder. "Mind if I cut in?"

When she turns around, I can tell she's truly surprised to see us. Her smile wavers, as if she doesn't want this Cinderella fairy tale moment to end.

Apparently, Lee has worked his charm on her as well.

He relinquishes her to the scowling Arnie. "It was... grand," she murmurs as Arnie tows her away.

Lee grins as he takes me in his arms for yet another dance. "I wish I'd had her as a teacher. I might have been an even better math student."

"Emma? ...Oh, yeah." Good for her for coming up with the profession of teacher as cover, on the QT. It fits, considering her genius skillset at computer science, cyphering, and analysis.

What a different life she might have had if teaching had been her chosen path.

Or, Lee's for that matter. "I would imagine you were a wonderful math student. And businessman. Then, to have combined all of it into morphing Global World Industries into the tech behemoth it's become." Once again, I palm his cell phone, all the while gazing up in mock adoration at the man I now loathe with all my heart.

His eyes lock on mine. Despite his modest shrug, he's

pleased with himself. "I'm just one lucky guy. I was at the right place at the right time, had the right idea, and played it for all it was worth."

In hindsight, he's spot on.

The right place: working with the Quorum.

At the right time: during a management transition. Out with the old (Jonah Breck, thanks to Carl) and in with the new:

Lee Chiffray.

He had the right idea all right: to use the unwitting Babette as his entrée. Yes, I finally agree with Jack: she isn't smart enough to carry it off.

And he played it right: by getting me to buy into his scheme to turn the tables on the competition—Carl.

Then use me to take down Carl.

"Imagine that," I murmur.

While he preens, I rest my hand lightly against his chest and start inching toward his inside jacket pocket.

As he rocks me back and forth to the music, he replies, "Sometimes I wonder what it would be like to go back to the life I had."

"Is that even possible?" I ask innocently.

We both know the answer: a resounding *NO*.

The smile fades from Lee's face. "You've been crying," he says softly.

I nod, though I'll be damned to tell him why.

You lying son of a bitch.

As he wipes an errant tear from my cheek, I slip his phone into his pocket.

"Well, well, don't you two look cozy!" Babette purrs from behind me.

From me, Babette aims for trepidation. Tonight, however, when I turn to her, what I offer is pity:

For the life she must live.

For the lies she must tell.

For the choice she has made.

The sympathy she sees in my gaze causes her to blush hotly. Whereas she came to triumph over me, she too now knows the tables are turned.

Jack and Lee realize something has happened between us, but they can't figure out what, when, or why. Wisely, they pretend otherwise.

When Babette finally collects herself, she taps her husband's arm. "Lee, darling, Narcissa says she left my cell phone with you."

Instinctively, Lee reaches into his inside right breast pocket—

Oh, my God—

As well as his tux's left breast pocket.

The cell phones are identical.

"Which one is mine?" she asks impatiently.

"Jesus, Babette, I don't know. Just give me a moment." He shuffles them from one hand to another as he tries his password on one.

It doesn't work.

He hands it to her. "It must be this one."

But which one was scanned?

Jack notes my confusion. I shake my head, warning not to say anything.

A moment later, Lurch and Zeb are by their sides, ready to shuttle them out of the ballroom. With their help, the guests will soon follow: time to call it a night.

Soon, a cavalcade of limousines, their back seats filled with tonight's tonier guests, will make their way back up to Los Angeles. I'm sure some afterparty has already been planned to keep the festivities going without the rabble around to gawk and point.

As for the Hilldale natives, they'll head off to bed, reliving tonight's memories of hobnobbing with the town's —and the nation's—first family in their blissful dreams.

For Jack and me, it'll be a long night for a very different reason now that we've narrowed down the POI list to two.

ON THE WAY HOME, MY WAY OF IGNORING JACK'S ATTEMPTS TO hold my hand is to hold my hands together in my lap. Finally, Jack speaks first. "At least now I know why I couldn't find her phone."

I shrug. "It wasn't for lack of trying, I'll grant you that."

"Frankly, I was never more relieved than when you gave me the thumbs-up. I thought to myself, 'Finally I can quit sucking up to this bitch.'"

"That is a poor choice of words," I warn him. "From the way it looked, the sucking was next on *her* agenda, not yours."

Jack shudders at the thought. "That should be a point in my favor, don't you think? That I stopped at second base?" He takes his eyes off the road in order to look at me. "Speaking of which, how far did Lee—"

I punch him in the arm so hard that he swerves the car. "How far did Lee get? Let's see...He got me *onto the dance floor*, that's how far."

"Oh." Relieved, Jack chuckles. When he realizes I'm not laughing with him, he adds, "Look at the bright side. It's still a toss-up as to whether Lee is Quorum or not."

I look out the window. "True. But I'm leaning toward your theory: that too many of his actions have been more than pure coincidence, and that Babette is too stupid, vain, and horny to be a criminal mastermind." Finally, I take his hand. "Speaking of horny, let's get home. We both need something to purge the memory of her dry-humping you, and I think I know what that is."

I don't have to ask twice. We pull into the driveway in record time.

11

Pre-Wedding Pampering Pleasures

Planning a wedding is such hard work! All the more reason you should take some "me" time. So you don't stress out over it, here's how to relax, refresh, and renew:

First, find a sanctuary. This can be a posh day spa (preferably with a wonderful masseur), or better yet, a quaint cabin in the woods (preferably without an axe murderer lurking about).

Next, think happy thoughts. This is not the time to worry about the inevitable vulgarity of the best man's speech, the probable intoxication of your least favorite uncle, or the amount of weight you've gained since your wedding dress was altered. Save these worrisome downers for some other day. Trust me, they'll still be there when you get home.

(Unless beastly best man's and horrid uncle's invitations get conveniently lost in the mail; as for your dress: perhaps your getaway day should double as a fasting period. Just a suggestion, no pressure...)

Finally, consider making your pampering pleasure a romantic getaway with your groom. But one caveat: no discussion about the wedding. This is a time to focus on your love, lust, and life not on your choice of appetizers.

Having him there with you has one more advantage. Should an axe murderer indeed appear, you don't have to be able to outrun him—

You just have to run faster than your groom (may he rest in peace).

"PAR-*TAY!*" AUNT PHYLLIS YODELS INTO MY CELL SO LOUD that the whole mission team—right now, camped out in Arnie and Emma's living room—can hear her. "Don't forget! Meet us at the Meat Market, nine sharp tonight!"

"What?" What is she rattling on about? "Where again? And who is 'us?'"

"Really, Donna! How could you forget your bachelorette party?"

Can she hear my groan above all the hubbub? Probably not. "Really, Aunt Phyllis, you don't have to do this—"

Her chortle ricochets through the room, along with the throbbing techno-music that is playing in the background. "'Have to?' Who are you kidding? I *want* to! You'll see when you get here."

"You're there—now? But it's still eight and a half hours until—"

"There are a lot of delicate details to go over with the staff. And you know I've always been a hands-on planner." She giggles raucously. "Be sure you're on time. In fact, I'll tell Evan to drop you off. That way, in case you get tipsy, you won't be driving. You can go back in the limo with Emma,

Mary, and me. Now remember, be here at nine sharp! Don't keep all your girlfriends waiting."

"My girlfriends? What girlfriends?" A little warning sound clicks in my brain. "Wait…did you say Mary is with you? Aunt Phyllis, she's under twenty-one! I won't allow it!"

"She's very mature for her age," my aunt insists.

"No!" In case she's hard of hearing, I shout my answer.

"I am, Mom," Mary pipes up in the background. "You say so all the time. Plus I'm your best girlfriend—*and* your maid of honor. I promise not to drink anything stronger than cola. Can't I just, you know, watch?"

Allowing my daughter watch strange men thrusting, grinding and stripping down to their skivvies won't ease my guilt for agreeing that Babette can be my matron of honor. "I said no—and I mean it!"

I'm so loud that everyone turns to witness the ruckus.

I put my hand over my voice receiver and hiss, "Look, Aunt Phyllis, with all that's going on right now, you really don't have to—"

Suddenly, I hear a crash, followed by a male voice, yelling, "Lady, you've been warned! You can't touch the dancers—"

"So many details, so little time! Gotta go!" Aunt Phyllis's sign-off is an abrupt click.

I look up from my cell phone to find my whole mission team staring at me.

Arnie nudges Emma. "That's it. You're not going." He's still sore that she was so starry-eyed over Lee last night.

"Oh no?" She frowns back. "Who's going to stop me?"

"Me!" Arnie retorts. "And…and little Nicky."

"Wrong! I've already lined up Mary's pal, Babs, to

babysit. If you think you're going to guilt me into staying home while you're out with the boys—"

"Quiet, everyone!" Ryan's eyes roll heavenward. "The fate of the Middle East hangs in the balance, and you're concerned about some bachelorette party?"

Dominic pats Jack's arm. "Not to worry, old boy. Our ladies of the evening will conduct themselves with a little more decorum."

"How is that possible?" I mutter. "You've rented out the Playboy mansion."

"Good God, Donna!" Dominic puffs up like an African white masked owl whose nest is under siege. "You hacked *my* emails?"

"No, Emma did."

Dominic rotates his glare to her.

She shrugs. "An engagement present for Donna. And, by the way, you should check the small print on your party contract. It specifically states that it does not include the grotto."

"Bollocks! Why, Hef promised me!" Dominic whips out his cell and stalks into the kitchen, slamming the door behind him.

Ryan shakes his head. "Are we ready to get to work now?"

"Shouldn't we wait for Dominic?" I ask sweetly.

"I don't have all afternoon, and neither do you," he growls. "Speaking of which, will Babette be at your bachelorette party?"

Shaking my head, I declare, "Good God, I hope not! Although, knowing her taste in men...Oops! Sorry, Jack! No offense."

"None taken." From his frown, I know he's lying.

Ryan leans over so that we're nose-to-nose. "Invite her."

"It wouldn't be appropriate for a first lady," I insist. "And besides, it's too late."

"You can tell her the invitation got lost in the mail or something. Just make it happen."

"Right." I shake my head at the thought. "And while she's stuffing twenties in some dude's G-string, I can grab her cell phone—"

"Sounds like a plan." Ryan leans back, all smiles again. Okay, maybe that's an exaggeration. Let me put it this way: at least he's not frowning. "The sooner we figure out which of them is our target, the sooner we can take him or her down. Besides, we have an added incentive." The thought is sour enough that he purses his lips. "Tell her, Emma."

"Like all devices assigned to White House personnel—POTUS and FLOTUS included—the cell phone that sent Xia the texts is equipped with sophisticated encryption technology. So, please excuse our team for taking so long to crack it." She smiles modestly. "Breaking the encryption allowed us to follow various trails: digital breadcrumbs, as it were. Our big find? Well, besides the correspondence with Xia, the cell's text archive shows that the messages were blind-copied to another cell phone."

Jack whistles in surprise.

"We can't tell if it was one of the White House's dark devices," Emma continues, "but we're working under the presumption that it is. If so, obviously this person was also integral in Catherine's assassination."

"Emma will text you with the cell's MEID—that is, the Mobile Equipment Identifier number. That way you can call

Todd Courtland with it. If it was, in fact, White House issue, he should be able to tell you who was assigned that particular cell phone."

Nodding, I hit Todd's number on my cell.

He picks up in three rings. "Mrs. Stone, a pleasure to hear from you." The warmth in his voice surprises me.

"Why, thank you, Todd. And we greatly appreciated the very comprehensive list you sent over," I assure him. "I have another request. If I give you the Mobile Equipment Identifier for a White House-issued cell phone, can you give us the name of the person to whom it was assigned?"

He hesitates a moment, but finally murmurs, "Of course. Let me grab a pen." I hear rustling. A moment later, he's back on the line. "Shoot."

I read him the fifteen-digit number.

"I'll check it out and get back to you. Hey listen, I'll be in town soon—a few days before the wedding, in fact."

I laugh. "If you're hinting around for an invitation, no need to worry. I'll add you to the guest list." Sure, why the hell not? Everyone else in the world is on it.

"Oh! Gee, thanks. But, yes, I'm already on it, as part of POTUS's entourage."

No surprise there.

"Got to run now," Todd adds. "There's a bill on Capitol Hill that needs some arm twisting. My best to Jack."

I click off to find the man in question scrutinizing me.

Jack is scowling. "Another admirer? Will he stand up to object the declaration of us as man and wife?"

"I'm sure Babette will beat him to the punch," I counter coolly.

Ryan drills me with his eyes. "Speaking of our illustrious

first lady, invite her to your bachelorette party—right now. This isn't a request; it's an order."

"Go ahead, I dare you," Jack mutters under his breath.

"Okay, you're on." I stick out my tongue at him. "Odds are, she'll say no, anyway."

"Good. Call her now." Ryan motions to my cell phone. "But do it through the White House switchboard. Although Lee knows we have his number, can't let Babette in on the fact that we've got hers too."

Jack frowns at the implication: that Lee specifically gave me his private cell number, so that we could coordinate our rendezvous while plotting against Carl.

I nod, then punch in the preferred number. When the phone is answered, I give my name and ask for Babette.

Narcissa picks up. "Donna! What a surprise! Why, Mrs. Chiffray and I were just talking about you!"

"Really?" Ouch. What now? "Babette's ears must be burning as well." Given half a chance, I'd light the match myself. "I am *so, so, sorry,* but somehow Babette got left off the invitation list for my bachelorette party."

"No, she did not," Narcissa declares sternly.

"Oh…" I look helplessly at Ryan. "It was unintentional—I swear! Just a silly little oversight! I hope she doesn't assume otherwise—"

"Donna, please!" Narcissa's cutoff is curt. "We know it wasn't an oversight because the invitation arrived. Late, granted, but mail that is sent via the White House takes an extra day or two by courier—so you're forgiven."

Whew. "Oh. Thanks." I guess.

"But, unfortunately, Mrs. Chiffray will have to pass on the honor of attending"—I hear papers being shuffled

—"quote, Donna Stone's Bachelorette Bash Extravaganza at the Meat Market Lounge, where you will partake in private dances from such illustrious hot bods as Luscious Louie, Take-It-All-Off Artie, and Built-Like-A-Brickhouse Benny, along with swag bags that include milk chocolate dongs, Gummy balls, fuzzy cuffs, and edible manties, endquote."

Ryan slaps his head in frustration. *Now that I know what's in store for me, I know how he feels.*

"Yes, well, I thoroughly understand that it's not quite Babette's thing." *In a different setting, perhaps Luscious Louie would have fit the bill, but I'll never get Narcissa to admit that.*

"However," she continues, "as your matron of honor, Babette feels somewhat remiss that she hasn't been able to attend to you in the traditional manner. She asks that you join her later this afternoon at the Hotel Bel-Air's Spa La Prairie, where she's arranged for facials, mani-pedis, deep-tissue massages, and a steam."

"Really? Wow! That's, well, quite sweet of her."

Ryan tosses his hands up to the heavens in silent prayer.

"Two o'clock, then. The first lady looks forward to bonding with you. Sisters from another mother, as it were." *I haven't heard such enthusiasm since the last funeral I attended.*

"Certainly, I'll be there. Please thank her—"

Click.

"—for me." I stare down at my disconnected cell phone.

Ryan turns to Jack. "Did you invite Lee to join us?"

"What? No! I was hoping it would be just us guys, as opposed to us guys and POTUS's Secret Service detail, watching our every move."

"You've got a point," Ryan concedes.

"Why does he have a point, and yet I don't?" I ask.

"You're lucky it all worked out," he reminds me. "The Secret Service won't be allowed into the spa's locker room. So, while she's getting her massage or takes her sauna or whatever, you can grab her cell phone and scan it. That way, we'll know for sure if the cell that was used to contact Xia was hers or Lee's." He grimaces at the thought that it might be POTUS's.

I can't say that I blame him. At the same time, I'm now willing to accept it.

It's not like I have a choice.

Dominic sticks his head back into the room. "Jack, we can have the grotto as well if we move the event to tomorrow night instead. What do you say, old boy?"

I bat my lashes at Jack. "Yes, old boy, what do you say?"

"Sure, whatever."

My cell phone buzzes. The Caller ID shows that it's Lee.

I hesitate long enough that Ryan's eyebrow goes up.

Of course, I answer it. "Hi, Lee, what's up?" I'm trying to keep the quiver out of my voice, especially since every tick and whisper can be heard by the rest of my Acme team through their ear buds.

Hearing that it's POTUS, Emma sighs longingly.

Arnie slams his hand on the table.

Ryan snaps his fingers for Arnie to behave.

"With Jack away at his bachelor party, I was wondering if you'd be free for drinks tomorrow evening."

"Um…"

Ryan nods vigorously.

On the other hand, Jack sits stone-faced. I wonder if he's

having second thoughts about cutting Lee from his bachelor party guest list.

"Sure, okay. There, at Lion's Lair?"

"No. Babette will be entertaining here." He sounds so sad. "Besides, I'm getting cabin fever. This gives me an excuse to get out."

"Where then?"

"Balboa Island. I have a private home at my disposal, on South Bay Front, at the corner of Sapphire. Shall we say eight?"

"Yes, okay." I hesitate before adding, "Lee, how did you know about Jack's party?"

He laughs. "Abu is in the wedding party, remember? He texted for Lurch's approval to get the night off. "

Abu winces and shrugs, *Sorry.*

I roll my eyes at him. "You know, Jack would be thrilled if you joined them tomorrow evening."

"*Thrilled?* What the hell, Donna?" Jack mutters.

I hold my finger to my lips to shush him.

Lee laughs uproariously. Did he hear Jack?

In any regard he says, "As the leader of the free world, my days hanging at the Playboy Mansion are over. Besides, you're a hell of a lot more fun to hang out with, than any Bunny."

It's my turn to laugh. "Thank you for that. I'll see you then. Goodbye."

Always the gentleman, he waits until I hang up first.

"Well, that's a lucky break!" Ryan exclaims.

Jack must not think so, because he leaves the room.

∾

"What's that smell?" I ask my facialist. I lay as limp as a rag doll after the pummeling by a masseuse who must get off on the phrase, Ouch, ouch, *ouch!*

"It's a bit strong," the facialist admits. "It's the astringent we use on your face before putting on the finishing touches. Works miracles."

I can't see because of the cucumber slices on my eyes, but I can certainly smell it. "Wait…Is it…*bird crap?*"

"Well, yes. Nightingale droppings, to be exact. But don't worry, it's been sanitized with UV rays. It's filled with protein and you'll immediately see a luster to your skin. *Soooo* worthwhile!"

"I guess if it makes you barf, you can think of it as a weight-loss inducer too," I retort dryly.

"I never thought of that, but I guess you're right!" She giggles. She sponges off the bird poop in order to slather on some thick white goop.

"My friend—is she here yet?" It's been over two hours since Babette had a note sent to my spa suite, informing me that she was running late from her shopping spree on Rodeo Drive.

"Oh, yes," the facialist assures me. "She should be done with her massage by now. She had an aromatherapy steam bath set up for her as well, so your friend may be tied up for quite some time. Her room, the Presidential Suite, has its own sauna."

"Ah! Good to know." If that's the case, there's no time like now to get her cell phone.

The facialist looks further down Babette's checklist. "Oh! And, after the steam, she's booked a Vampire facial lift."

I frown. "What exactly is that?"

"All the stars do it. The doctor takes your blood, then re-injects it into your face. The new stem cells reinvigorate the growth of collagen, fatty tissues, and blood cells. You're practically a new person!"

"I'm sure she'll be singing its praises," I murmur. Anything that would make Babette more human is worth a try. Then again, she may be disappointed when they won't let her drink it. "Would you excuse me? I think I'd like to take a nap."

"Sure, no problem. We have to let this protein cocktail set for a while, anyway." The woman looks at her watch. "I'll be back in forty minutes."

"Perfect," I murmur. I try to smile, but whatever she's put on my face is already hardening.

Just as she heads out the door, my cell buzzes. It's Todd.

"Got anything for me?" I'm barely moving my lips because the goop on my face is hardening.

"Yes…and no. The cell is assigned to one of the cleaning crew. This person had limited access to both POTUS's office, and the first family's personal quarters." He sighs. "However, he is no longer with us."

Interesting. "As in, quit?"

"As in, dead. His name was Bradley Kazinsky. He was killed by a hit-and-run driver as he was crossing Constitution Avenue after one of his shifts. Sorry, Donna. I wish I could have been of more help to you."

"Me too, Todd. Have a good night." Drat.

My facial cream has hardened enough that it's now a glistening, albeit featureless mask. Not that it matters. By the time I wrap my hair in a towel and tighten the sash of my plush robe, Arnie has disengaged the hotel's security webcam so that I can take care of business.

I slip off into the direction of the Presidential Suite.

ZEB IS GUARDING THE ENTRANCE TO BABETTE'S ROOM. HE doesn't look happy. Two other agents in his detail have positioned themselves strategically within fifty feet of the path to her private cottage. My only way in is to pick the lock on the wrought iron gate on the stucco wall of the cottage's courtyard, which for some odd reason, isn't being watched.

It opens just in time. One of Babette's toy soldiers is headed this way. The way he's adjusting himself, I guess he doesn't have a hollow leg.

As I suspected, Babette has left the cottage's French doors wide open on this warm, breezy day.

The bed is rumpled. Apparently, the masseur gave her quite a workover. There is a hissing sound coming from a room on the far side of the bathroom. I assume it's why she's moaning so loud in the sauna.

Or else it has something to do with the very expensive man's suit folded nicely on the desk chair.

Damn that Babette! She used our little gal pal excursion to slip away for a hookup!

Why am I not surprised?

I recognize the cell phone from the other night—or perhaps its twin. In any case, it's White House standard issue.

I pull out the scanner and attach it to Babette's phone. I muffle the first buzz that gets me through the passcode. A moment later, I have to do the same with the second buzz because I hear rustling on the other side of the door.

I've just laid the cell phone back on the desk when I notice something else on the night table: a ring with the large black crest and the number thirteen.

Babette's lover, the Quorum operative, is here now with her.

Frantically, I rummage through the pockets of his suit jacket. No phone.

I've just reached for his pants when the sauna door opens. Babette, naked and skin mist-dampened, is being kissed, as her tall, dark, and handsome lover carries her into the room.

I duck and roll—

Under the bed.

The bed's frame sinks as they land on top of it.

From the full-length closet mirror, I watch as Babette positions herself over him, her face pointing toward his feet, in order to take him between her lips. The mattress's squeals, from her bobbing and his thrusting, are drowned out by the lovers' grunts and groans.

But, just at the moment of his climax, she releases him—

So that he comes on her cheek.

After patting it all over her face, she licks her palm.

Yuck.

Satisfied, she flops down beside him.

They lay so silent that I wonder if they can hear me breathing.

Finally, Babette laughs. "I was a very bad girl. I didn't drink it."

"Yes, you were," he murmurs. "Do you remember what I told you would happen, if you did that again?"

She says nothing.

The sound of a slap cracks the silence.

"Harder," she begs. "With the buckle. *Please.*"

He accommodates. The smacks are slow at first, but build to a furious crescendo, along with her moans.

Their love play gives me cover to roll back out from under the bed. I crawl on my hands and knees until I get to the courtyard.

Unfortunately, the Secret Service agent is still guarding the door. How did Babette's lover get in? Do Zeb and his team know about him, but keep their mouths shut?

No wonder Zeb can't wait to retire.

Since I can't just waltz out the gate, I climb over the bougainvillea trellis and over the stucco wall—

Only to topple over it, onto a row of azalea bushes.

Damn it, by the time I climb out, I'm scratched and bloody.

The other hotel guests stare as I limp back to my suite. I can only imagine that my facial has hardened into a kabuki mask by now.

I arrive with just two minutes to spare before my facialist walks in. Noting my scraped knees, she asks, "Oh, my goodness! What happened to you?"

I shrug. "Rough skin. I inherited it from my father."

She picks up the jar holding my facial cream. "I'd rub this into it, but I'd get in trouble because it's so expensive."

"Really? What is it, exactly?"

"Spermine." She smiles benignly.

"As in…cum?"

The woman nods apologetically.

Well, at least that's one spa treatment that Babette didn't have to pay for.

I LIMP THROUGH THE LOCKLEARS' FRONT DOOR, TOWARD THE couch, where Arnie is sitting, computer on his lap. When he looks up, I toss him the scanner.

Seeing me, Jack meanders over. "What the hell happened to you? Most women look refreshed after a spa day."

"I got a workout instead," I retort. "Oh, and so did your girlfriend. Her mystery lover joined her in the Presidential Suite."

Jack sits up straight. "The guy with the ring?"

"Yep, one and the same. Why, are you jealous?"

He greets my jibe with a roll of his eyes. "By any chance, did you happen to scan his cell phone too?"

"I tried, but they were coming out of the sauna."

Frustrated, he shakes his head.

"Still, I guess we have our answer," I point out. "She's in bed with the Quorum. Ergo, she's our target."

"Wrong," Arnie says. He holds up the scanner. "As far as texts to Xia, her phone is clean."

Shit.

"Could it have been scrubbed?" Jack asks.

Arnie shakes his head. "From the back-end coding, my guess is no. The archive is original, and complete."

"Well, there goes my excuse for bowing out of drinks with Lee," I mutter.

"Really? You were looking for an excuse?" From Jack's tone, I can tell he doesn't believe me.

"I had one when you had your chance to invite him to hang out with you," I counter.

Jack frowns. "We all heard the man. He'd much rather be with you."

I don't have time for his sulking. I grab my purse and leave.

12

Your Bachelorette Party

Ah, your bachelorette party! Time to kick back with your gal pals for one last night of carefree, salacious singledom!

To ensure you survive it without regrets—or for that matter, a perp walk of shame—remember these caveats:

First, don't drink so much that you don't remember anything. A blinding hangover makes for a really funny movie, but if you show up at the wrong time and the wrong place for your nuptials, the last laugh will be on you.

Next, go for real thrills, not cheap ones. Bungee-jumping, zip-lining, parasailing or whitewater rafting will net lifelong memories. Hiring an instructor to demonstrate the art of putting a whole banana in your mouth is not the kind of pre-wedding memory you'll want to share when it's time for your daughter's big day.

And, finally, don't worry about what he did during his bachelor party. What happens that night should be allowed to reside in the dark recesses of his memories—filed under "Stupid Things I Did as a Single Guy."

However, should he insist on confessing, remind him what a great shot you are, with a trip to the shooting range. A stray bullet whizzing past his ear will keep his lips zipped for good.

THIS IS *SO* NOT MY SCENE.

Evan, too, is pop-eyed at the view before us: women—hair fussed to a frenzy, bodies trussed in tight spandex, feet hobbled within pointy sky-high stilettos—who are lined up behind the Meat Market Lounge's red-velvet rope.

The former furniture store that now houses Los Angeles's hottest male strip club throbs to the pulsating percussion of Marco Bailey's *Injection*. The song's title aptly reflects their ideal fantasies.

Mary—anxious, her cheeks flushed—waits for me by the front door between two slabs of beefcake, who are the club's bouncers. She waves frantically until I'm at her side, then hugs me tightly, as if she never wants to let me go. "Mom, these women are—crazy!"

I have to laugh. "What, exactly, did you expect?"

"I don't know. I guess…well, I guess I expected Channing Tatum." She blushes at the thought.

I pat her hand. "I know, honey. Sorry you're disappointed. But the sooner you learn that real life is nothing like the movies, the happier you'll be." I look toward Evan, who has idled the car in order to gawk at women gone wild. "Listen, Mary, if you don't want to stay—"

Before I can get another word out, she showers me with grateful kisses and leaps into the passenger seat next to Evan.

I wonder if he'll have the same reaction if he's allowed to step foot into the Playboy Mansion. My guess is no.

Ah, men.

The bouncers nod to me. Another slab of buffed man meat, wearing nothing but a bowtie and tights, takes my elbow in order to ferry me through the panting crowd. Apparently, Aunt Phyllis has already greased palms—among other things, if my guess is right.

I shudder at the thought.

It's going to be a long night.

THE CLUB IS DARK, EXCEPT FOR MEANDERING STROBE LIGHTS, which flash for a mere second on a face here and there throughout the crowd.

I'm led to the "party playpen" that has been secured for us. It is snuggled next to the stage, allowing me and my guests to be up close and personal to the action, which at the moment is three of the club's male strippers dancing around the woman who sits on a chair in the middle of the stage to Dire Straits' *Single-Handed Sailor*. They've shed their sailor whites from their torsos. In unison, with one hand they rip their flare-legged pants from their legs. What they do with the other hand has the woman spellbound, even as she stuffs their G-strings with fivers.

The women in my party hoot and holler and entice with bills of their own.

Except for Emma and my aunt, I don't recognize any of them.

But when my escort opens the red rope to the playpen so

that I may enter, these strange women rush me in order to squeeze me with hugs.

The last one, a comely brunette with deep dimples on either side of a cupid-bow mouth, declares, "Oh, my God! Finally, we meet!"

I detect a posh British accent. "Excuse me, who are you again?"

"Lady Daniela Braxdale-Cuthbert, my dear! But, please, call me Dannie! All my friends do."

Before she can pull me down onto the playpen's curved and cushioned bench, another woman does so, but with such gentility that I feel as if I should know her. And, yet, for the life of me I can't place her.

She air-kisses me in close proximity of each cheek as she proclaims, "*Ma cherie*, what a lucky bride you are! *Voici la belle vie!*"

Dannie hands me a champagne glass, while lifting another flute of bubbly toward the other women—the Frenchwoman, Aunt Phyllis, Emma, and three others: a much-too-buxom blonde with a Southern drawl, a sultry Latina, and an ebony-skinned beauty, who is so tall and exquisitely beautiful that she must be a supermodel. They all chatter at once, but with the blaring music and the buzz of the crowd, I can't hear a damn thing.

To cover my ignorance, I nod and smile benignly, as I inch my way toward my aunt. I grab her wrist just as she's about to slip a bill into the banana hammock of the dude giving Emma a lap dance.

"What the hell, Donna?" she declares, but I don't let go.

In fact, I take both of her hands and hold them in her lap

until she looks me in the eye. "Aunt Phyllis, who are these women?"

"What do you mean, who are they? I got them out of your cell phone's contact book!" She shrugs. "Sorry the gang is small, but these VIP lounges don't come cheap! I had to promise the club a minimum of a hundred dollars per person, so I only chose women you earmarked with plus signs."

Horrified, my jaw drops. "My point exactly: *I don't know any of them.*" A strange thought dawns on me. "Which cell phone?"

"The gray one. It was on the kitchen counter." She giggles, "I guessed at the password: your initials, then each of the kids', then the year you and Jack met."

"You opened Jack's cell. Mine is red." Oh, hell. For some reason, Jack held on to these women's digits.

At the same time, the thought sinks into Phyllis's pea brain. She goes white under her tan. "Donna, I am so sorry! Had I known he was playing off on you—"

"Is that what you think—that he's…?" Tears cloud my eyes.

"Nah!" she chortles. "*Gotcha!*" She sweeps her hand toward the others. "Hey, put it in perspective! Who better to tell you what you're getting into than women who share a mutual respect for the man you're about to marry?"

"'A mutual respect?' Please, don't sanitize the situation. He still has their contact information for a very obvious reason."

"Oh, really?" Aunt Phyllis's smile fades. "And what would that be, missy?"

I feel my right brow inching up. "Look at them. They're all gorgeous! Do I really have to paint a picture for you?"

Disgusted, Aunt Phyllis shakes her head. "Oh, ye of little faith!" She puts her fingers to her lips and lets loose with a whistle that should summon every cab from here to Carson City.

My guests' heads turn in our direction, surprised.

Aunt Phyllis points at the supermodel. "Umma, how long have you known Jack?"

The young woman thinks for a moment. Then, softly, she says, "Practically all my life. I consider him"—she blushes —"*baba*."

I shake my head. "I don't know the term."

"In Kiswahili, it means 'father.'"

My heart sinks to my stomach. How could Jack have a grown daughter? "You mean, he and your mother—"

"No! ...Oh, no, no, no!" The thought elicits a giggle from her. But, when her smile disappears, sadness deepens in her eyes. "My mother was killed when I was five, by militants. I was sold into slavery. Jack Craig stopped the convoy that would have taken me to my fate. He arranged to have me sent to England, where I was schooled." The memory clears the anguish from her brow. "I owe him my life! I came to celebrate his happiness with you." She takes a sip of her champagne. "And to enjoy the eye candy." Everyone laughs. She raises her glass. "To Jack!"

"To Jack!" the women shout.

I turn to the Frenchwoman. "And how do you know him?"

"Jacque and I were lovers." The statement comes with a naughty smile. "Surely he has mentioned Coquette Rambert, has he not, *mon amie?*" Noting my blank stare, she shrugs. "But, of course not. It was a mere moment in time, I assure you. Just long enough for him to convince me that it was worth risking my life by spying on my lover—a Russian general who thought nothing of murdering innocent women and children in Latvia. When the pig discovered my duplicity, Jacque risked his life to smuggle me out of the country." She raises her glass, "To the health and happiness of a man who gave me purpose"—she smiles slyly at me—"and was one of the best lovers I never had."

Everyone laughs. Everyone drinks. And, apparently, everyone has a story.

The adorable Texan reaches over to squeeze my hand. "Oh, mah *Gawd*—on that note, I've got to go next!" She waits for my nod, then shakes my hand vigorously. "I'm Katy May Cuthbert. I worked a pole at the Hanky-Panky in Waco. It was a biker hangout, y'all." She bats her eyes. "Turns out, one of the skinheads—their leader, truth be told—was sweet on me. I'll admit it, I played up to him 'cause he tipped well. He was always conducting business in the club, so the tips came regular, not just from him but all of his boys—that is, until word got out that I was his girl. Soon, none of the other patrons would ask me to dance for them 'cause they was all scared of him." She blinks back her tears. "He was rough trade, if you catch my drift. Some nights, he'd whale on me until I was black and blue!" Katy May shakes her head sadly. "When he got picked up by the Feds, Jack was sent to interview me. He realized I was in the catbird seat to hear and see a lot of the skinhead's shenanigans, maybe even some things I wasn't supposed to, right?" She shrugs. "It ain't like I was just a piece of furniture or something, although the other Feds treated me that way.

Not Jack. At first, I was afraid to talk. But he convinced me to turn state's evidence, and made sure I was placed in Witness Protection." She wipes away a tear. "I was able to start new. I went back to school and got my teaching degree. And now I'm married to a good man." She holds up her hand so that I see the simple band of gold on her ring finger.

The audience's hoots and hollers are so loud now that they get her attention. Her head turns toward the stage, where the sole dancer gyrates in full Native American head-dress and nothing else. She smiles slyly.

Of course, I'm wondering: Did he sleep with her?

As if reading my mind, Katy May shakes her head. "Your Jack is one hot piece of lead. And don't think I wouldn't have done been his gal if he'd asked." She sighs. "Maybe it's for the best. Jack would have been a temporary detour. When I met Franklin, my heart knew it had found its home." Her eyes drift to the dancer on the stage. "My Franklin doesn't look anything like that man. He's got a potbelly and bad teeth. But he brings me flowers once a week, and built me a cabin in the woods, far away from Waco. I would never have found him if it hadn't been for Jack." She raises a champagne bottle. Pouring a little in everyone's glass, she proclaims, "This one's for your Mr. Craig."

My Mr. Craig. I like the sound of that—so much so that I down mine along with everyone else.

"*Ay, Dios mio!*" The Latin beauty purrs. "Gringas, you are much too sentimental! Donita, I am Maria Dolores Sostré Colón." She nods, but doesn't offer her hand in greeting. "And, to be honest with you, I am here for… *cómo se dice?* Ah, yes"—her smile flatlines—"payback."

Oh, no. And, wouldn't you know it? Tonight I'm not packing heat.

Her right hand moves into the folds of her shawl.

Is she reaching for a gun? My thoughts are how to deflect her aim. I'd never forgive myself if her bullet hit my dear Aunt Phyllis.

Or, for that matter, Emma.

Outside of Jack and my family, she is my dearest friend. It's funny how the experiences we share with others bind us deeper to their fates.

In the time it takes Maria to remove her hand from below the shawl, I've shaken the champagne bottle—

And spritzed it directly into her face.

"*Caramba!*" she sputters. "Why did you do this?"

Her hand goes up to deflect the fuzzy liquid and to wipe her face. That's when I see what she's holding: a beautiful card.

"Because you said 'payback,' I thought you meant, well…a hit."

Droplets of champagne in her hair are flung off as she shakes her head *no*. At least she's laughing—uproariously, in fact. Slowly, she holds out the card to me. When I take it, she leans back, as if to prove that she means no harm.

I look down at the card with one eye, but keep the other glued to her.

"What does it say?" Emma asks.

"Read it out loud," Aunt Phyllis insists.

"It's…very sweet," I concede. "'Jack, *mi amigo*, I will always remember your kindness during a tough time. Please know that, when needed, I will return the favor, no questions asked. *Con amor*, Maria Dolores.'" I close the card. "What does it mean?"

"We faced off in Rio," she begins. "My target was an Argentinian contractor, who was handing over the design for a new U.S. long-range missile to a Russian diplomat. Jack was after the Russian." She shrugs. "He got his man, but mine ducked out of the way." She smiles slyly. "Later that night, he made it up to me."

"Oh, I see." My tone should give her frostbite. Is that why she's here, to rub my nose into the fact that Jack had a life before me?

If she insists on taunting me, she'll regret it. I'm tipsy, and still upset at what might yet need to take place between him and Babette. All it would take is one good hit at a strategic angle for the champagne bottle in my hand to crack perfectly against the ice bucket, leaving me with a shard sharp enough to cut her jugular. The club's crowd is so frantic that maybe no one will notice.

Maria, for one, is quite aware of the bottle I hold in my hand. "No, no, no, *hermosa*! He didn't 'make it up' *that* way! I mean, yes, he bought me a drink. *Ha*! As if that would replace the money I lost on the hit." Her chortle is deep and throaty. "Two days later, the bounty is wired into my bank account. An hour goes by, and I receive an encrypted file containing a photo of my target, shot through the head."

"Jack did the hit so that you'd earn the scalp?" Lady Daniela shakes her head in admiration. "Now, that's a gentleman!"

"*Sí!*" Maria nods enthusiastically.

What a guy. A regular Saint Dexter.

I empty the bottle into my glass. Hate to see good bubbly go to waste.

I know she means well. Still, I'm somewhat taken aback by his chivalry. We are not in a nice business. Ergo, we are not nice people. But each of us makes his or her own peace with the devil in our own way.

Which brings us to Lady Daniela. I take another swig of champagne in order to get up the gumption to ask, "So, tell me about your Jack attack."

"It may just be the cutest meet of the night," she gushes.

"Cuter than human trafficking, biker skinheads, a bonus hit, and the proverbial whore with a heart of gold? I'm all ears."

My guests laugh so hard that tears are rolling down their cheeks—proof positive that I'm wittier when I'm soused.

Dannie's laugh trills through the air with the greatest of ease. "My role in her Majesty's Secret Service is to divert any and all unpleasantness that may befall members of the Royal family." She shrugs. "As you can imagine, the low-hanging twigs on the family tree are particularly susceptible."

"Why is that?" Emma wonders aloud. "I mean, you'd think they'd enjoy having the bennies without the glare of the spotlight."

"To the contrary, some of them live on tight budgets, and resent their lack of prominence in comparison to those closest to the throne. They too want to make their marks, if not in history, then in commerce." She rolls her eyes. "Sadly, business savvy does not flow, but trickles into the Windsor gene pool, as was the case with a certain duke who shall remain nameless. Usually such schemes are a bust. They break even at best. In this particular case, it came close to taking down the monarchy."

"How?" I ask.

"Let's just say that the duke's investment in a little-known Internet start-up allowed those running the venture access to the monarchy's secure server, and subsequently the British government's most precious databases as well. Had word gotten out that the duke was the Trojan horse, public outrage might have ended the monarchy."

"How does Jack fit in?"

"When I reached across the pond to the cousins, he responded. He'd been researching the holding company for the start-up firm. It was something called Romanov Corporation, and it's owned by one of Putin's closest mates. Because of Jack's intel, we were able to mitigate the hack with counterintelligence."

"So you've never actually met Jack?" Did I sound too hopeful?

"I didn't say that," she chuckles slyly.

When she notices I'm not laughing with her, she adds, "I presume you're wondering how closely we worked together. Not to worry, love. By then he'd fallen in love with you— apparently from afar! Surveillance makes the heart grow fonder, does it not?" She sighs. "But, I can tell you in all honesty that I tried my damnedest to break your spell on him."

Daniela is not only astoundingly beautiful, but smart, lethal, and on the right side. In other words, a perfect match for Jack.

And yet, he spurned her for me.

Because he loves me, and me alone.

So then, why am I here?

Aunt Phyllis thinks she's being cute by coercing two of the dancers to manwich me between them. I pay them a hundred each to bother her instead. But before they make their move on her, I kiss her plump cheek and whisper, "Thank you, for the best gift ever!"

She wags a finger at me. "I don't think you're allowed to take the boys home with you!"

Ha! Never in a million years. To paraphrase Katy May, my heart wants to go home—

To Jack.

I COME HOME TO FIND TRISHA ALREADY SNUG IN HER BED. THE other kids are binging on *Game of Thrones* episodes. I've yet to break the news to them that by being kicked off the guest list of my engagement party, they missed seeing their favorite actors from the show in person: Peter Dinklage and Maisie Williams.

I wish I could have done the same.

Jack is not upstairs, but, from our bedroom window, I notice a dark figure out back, on one of the terrace chaises. He has it reclined almost all the way back, so that he can look up at the stars.

His head turns when he hears the back door open. When he sees that I'm the interloper, he smiles and sits up. "I wasn't expecting you back so early."

"Aunt Phyllis's idea of a good time and mine are definitely two different things," I assure him, as I ease down onto his lap. "Your ears must be burning, what with all the tributes you've gotten tonight."

His lips feel warm on my forehead. "Oh, yeah? From whom?"

"Apparently every woman who's ever set eyes on you: Umma, Katy May, Lady Dannie, Maria Dolores, Coquette—"

His jaw drops open. "What the hell? How did they—"

"In her attempt to plan my bachelorette party, Aunt Phyllis got ahold of the wrong little black book—*yours*."

"Oh." A second later, the seriousness of this sinks in. "But how did she hack it?"

"Your iPhone's password isn't all that hard to figure out. Ha! And when I think of all the times I wanted to read your texts, just to check up on crushes from any former girl-friends"—I lean back onto his chest—"well, it's nice to know all those worries are for naught."

He wraps his arms around me. "Oh, yeah? You mean, you're not at all concerned about what may happen at my bachelor party at the Playboy Mansion tomorrow night?"

"After tonight, not in the least. Just do me a favor and delete any contact info a Bunny or two is bound to give you. I'd hate for Aunt Phyllis to invite them to some surprise anniversary party. The tributes for your chivalry are sure to make you blush."

"I guess my title as Undercover Lover is retired, once and for all." His laugh dissolves into a shrug. "More than likely, I'll spend the whole night thinking about you…and Lee."

"Let me give you something to think about instead." I tilt my head up in order to find his lips with mine.

Yes, he is ready for me.

____

13

What Your Invitations Say
About You

____

Your wedding invitations are not just a reflection of your event's theme, but the whole of your personality. Even more to the point, they are a statement of your mutually shared love. Here are a few don'ts:

- *Don't choose a crazy font. Or include emojis. Or for that matter, zany photos of you in silly costumes. You may find these ideas cute, but they'll make the wrong statement to your guests. We're marrying on a whim.*
- *Don't choose a paper stock of any hue that might be encountered on an acid trip. The goal is that the invitation is readable—that is, if you truly want the recipient to show up. (But if you'd really prefer they skip the event, by all means, make it something that can easily pass for junk mail.)*
- *Don't include pop culture references in your invitation. Ten years hence, you'll wonder, "What was I thinking?" or worse yet, "What the hell does that even*

mean?" Also, stay away from jokes. Phrases like, "After the vows, we'll proceed to the elimination round," and "Children welcomed, as long as they know how to mix a mean martini," may make you giggle, but they also give the impression that your marriage is a joke.

In that regard, only time will tell.

I DON'T MISS HIGH SCHOOL IN THE LEAST.

I'm struck with this thought as I walk the halls of Hilldale High in search of Mary's fourth-period French class. High school hasn't exactly been easy on Mary, considering all the family drama in her life during her two years here. And let's not forget that she keenly felt Carl's desertion from the time she was in the third grade.

When I reach the right door, I wave to Mademoiselle Lynch, then point to my eldest child.

Mary looks up as her name is called. She follows her teacher's glance in my direction. Her surprised stare is quickly replaced by a curious grin when I beckon her forward with a smile.

She grabs her books and heads to the door.

I have the perfect reason to coerce my daughter into playing hooky:

I need her help in picking out my wedding gown.

While we're at it, we'll choose her dress too.

Afterward, I'll explain why I have to allow Babette to take Mary's place as my matron of honor.

"What's up?" she asks.

"We're going shopping." I announce grandly. "Dresses for the wedding."

"But I thought Chantal had something in mind for you—and me too, for that matter." She winces at the thought. Can't say I blame her.

"I don't think it's a decision she should make for us. Do you agree?"

"Heck, yeah!" Realizing she may have said it too loud, she looks furtively behind her. Thank goodness, Mademoiselle Lynch is too busy writing common phrases on the blackboard to hear her.

"Good. And afterward, we'll pick up pizza for dinner."

She shakes her head. "No way! From now until the wedding, we're eating rabbit food and that's it."

That's my girl. Always practical.

We giggle as we run down the hall.

I don't believe for one moment that it will mitigate her disappointment in being replaced by Babette as my matron of honor, but at this point I'm looking for shared memories.

Let this be the next of many to come.

"Oh, Mom." Mary's voice is barely a whisper. "It's *the one.*"

My eyes have been on her since I summoned her into my dressing room at the Hilldale Bridal Shoppe; I follow her eyes to my image in the full-length mirror.

The dress is sleeveless, with a sheer back and scoop neckline made of illusion attached to a strapless silk silhouette that encases my body like a glove. The gown flares out to a trumpet hem and a short train.

Simple. Elegant.

"Perfect," Mary declares, as if she's read my mind.

"You haven't done so badly yourself," I point out.

She nods, still in awe that I've approved the dress she has chosen: a tea-length Rebecca Taylor ball gown. Strapless, with a smock-waist and a peekaboo black tulle hem, its silver brocade bodice is overprinted with flowers of fuchsia, pink, and black, like a Monet watercolor come to life.

"I'm glad you like it, Mom. I had Emma text me the gown she chose. I loved it so much that I asked her if she didn't mind if I got it too. She said 'Go for it, Chantal can be mad at both of us.'" Mary laughs as she does a full turn in front of the mirror. Her head shifts to watch its flow from all angles. "The only difference is that the background of her dress is fuchsia. That way, the guests can tell that I'm clearly the maid of honor."

At the mention of Chantal, I look down to the ground. Babette will throw a hissy fit when she sees we've all chosen our gowns without her approval. Whereas I couldn't care less, I still have to come clean with Mary about Babette. "We better change and get the sales clerk to ring these up."

After she unzips me, she kisses my cheek. "For once, I feel as if our family is normal."

If only it were true.

"AFTER DINNER, LET'S PLAY DRESS-UP!" A MOUTHFUL OF PIZZA won't deter Trisha from making her case as to how we should spend the rest of the evening. "We can all wear our wedding dresses! We can have a wedding fashion show!"

"I'm not playing," Aunt Phyllis pouts. "Fräulein Stormtrooper—a.k.a., Chantal—did a bait and switch on me!" She holds up a drab gray chiffon gown—nothing at all like the bright red Bob Mackie knock-off in the wedding planner's PowerPoint presentation. "It makes me look washed out," Aunt Phyllis opines. "I'll look like my grandmother at her wake!"

I put down my forkful of salad. "I grant you permission to choose any dress you like." Sure, why the hell not? Freedom from tyranny is what this country was founded on.

"I'll help you pick it out," Trisha offers. "The stores stay open until nine. Why don't we go right after we finish dinner, since the boys are at the Bunny House."

"Hey, pipsqueak!" Jeff shouts from the great room. "We're not boys. We're men. I'm a man too, remember? And I'm *right here.*"

I reply, "Are you upset because you couldn't go?"

He walks over to the doorway. "Nah. I'm not attracted to bimbos anyway. Besides, I hacked the mansion's security cam. It's just as good as being there." He wiggles his brows mischievously.

"That's my boy." I will, of course, be monitoring his monitoring—you know, for errant nip slips. On a screen the size of his computer, I imagine it would resemble the release of the Hindenburg. *Oh, the womanity.*

Darn it, I'll have to pass. In thirty minutes, I have a date with destiny.

Well, with Lee. And it's not really a date…

At least, I don't think it is.

Oh. Hell.

"I'll go too," Mary pipes up. "Besides, you can help me with the bridesmaids' presents."

"Just the bridesmaids get presents?" Trisha asks. "Can't I get a present too?"

"Sure." Mary tousles her younger sister's hair. "You're part of the bridal party, aren't you, silly?"

"But Mommy's the bride. Shouldn't she pick them out?"

"She's too busy between now and the wedding. Besides, that's the job of her maid of honor, so I get to do it."

Trisha shakes her head adamantly. "No you're not. Mrs. Chiffray is Mommy's maid of honor."

First, Mary laughs at the thought of that. But, when she sees the sullen look on my face, she stops cold. "Is it true?"

"Yes." The frustration of it all has me shaking my head. "She insisted. And considering all that has to be done between now and then, I thought it would be foolish to look a gift horse in the mouth."

"But...you asked me first!" Mary's bottom lip trembles from her anger.

"I know, Mary. But you see, Babette has been so instrumental in the planning—"

"She's not important to you. I am!" Tears glisten in her eyes. "At least, that's what you told me."

"And you are. It's just that—"

"Look, I get it. She's the queen bee. No matter how mean she is, or how selfish, all she has to do is snap her fingers, and everyone is at her beck and call—even you." Her eyes open wide. "My God—it's just like high school!"

Disgusted at the thought, she bolts up the stairs.

Trisha stares after her. "Does that mean there's no fashion show?"

Aunt Phyllis shapes her mouth into a hard smile. "No, but there's ice cream. Ben & Jerry's Cherry Garcia." She takes my youngest's hand in order to guide her toward the kitchen.

When they pass me, Phyllis hisses, "Fix this."

I tread up the stairs to Mary's bedroom door.

No matter how hard I knock, or how much I plea, the only thing she has to say to me is, "Go away!"

I don't want to leave, and really, I shouldn't leave. But I've just been texted from Lee:

A car is waiting outside for you.

There's a definite upside to proving that either POTUS or FLOTUS are part of a vast web of terrorism: both will be detained at Club Fed, and therefore unable to attend my wedding.

I grab my purse and go.

My trail of tears will dry in the thirty or so minutes it takes to get to Balboa Island.

I hope.

14

Tossing the Wedding Garter

In the history of weddings and marriage, the "garter toss" is a centuries-old tradition. When given to witnesses, it signified the consummation of the marriage.

In most cases, the hope was that the bride was a virgin. (During the Middle Ages, this was assured by a metal contraption known as a "chastity belt," to which only a father or husband held the key. Today, even non-virgins wear them as well. They are no longer made of metal, but spandex, and go by the name of "Spanx.")

If today's bride (virgin or not) tosses a garter, it takes place sometime during the wedding reception. Usually she's a bit tipsy, which is why she giggles, as opposed to blushes, when her new husband scurries under her dress in search of it, only to emerge victorious, the garter between his teeth.

Despite the fact that it's easier than apple bobbing, and much more fun (for the groom, at least), over time, the tradition has lost its luster. Maybe it has something to do with the fact that today's bride isn't so keen about being mauled under her very expensive designer gown. Go figure.

Besides, if the groom is going to sink his teeth into anything, perhaps he should wait until their honeymoon night. That way they avoid shocking their guests—including the bride's very protective father and brothers.

Especially if the invitations read "Concealed carry optional. Judicious marksmanship appreciated."

MY RIDE IS IN A BLACK LEXUS SEDAN. EXCEPT FOR THE darkened windows and windshield, it is an unobtrusive vehicle in Orange County.

It's after rush hour, and now that the county's elementary and middle schools are out for the summer, you wouldn't think that it should take close to an hour to get to Balboa Island, but it does. Part of the problem is the number of tourists trying to hit the beach before sunset.

To double our trouble, we've picked up a shadow: in this case, a short balding dude in an innocuous white Prius. My guess is that our tail is actually CIA, at the behest of the Secret Service. Am I friend or foe? Is this business or pleasure? In any event, POTUS's protection must never be compromised, despite the compromising positions those closest to him may find themselves in.

If only they were as watchful of Babette. In that regard, the lead agent in her Secret Service detail, Zeb, has convinced POTUS that he has her covered.

Perhaps he should take an early retirement.

Our shadow stays with us until we hit the Jamboree

Road exit. There, he is replaced by a woman in a black Mini-Cooper. She hangs in until we cross the Balboa Island Bridge, where a bearded dude in a pick-up truck follows us.

No doubt my tails have already verified that we weren't followed.

South Bay Street is the last cross street off the island's main drag, Marine Street. When we get to it, we turn right. When the Lexus hits Sapphire, it rolls a house or two beyond it: our final destination.

Lee is secured in a three-story gray clapboard. Like all the other houses, it runs the full length of the block, between South Bay and the boardwalk facing Newport Bay, and just beyond it, the seaside town of Newport.

I count three Secret Service sentries, strategically stationed on the outdoor decks and terraces throughout the expansive home. They wear chinos, baseball caps, and golf shirts under windbreakers that easily cover all concealed weapons. If you didn't know better, you'd think they were retired good ol' boys, catching the setting sun's last rays as it sets in the distance over Newport Beach.

When we are within ten feet of the driveway, the garage opens, then immediately closes behind us.

A second later, Lurch is walking out of the door leading into the spacious bayside villa. "Mrs. Stone, good to see you." He smiles, but because he's wearing dark shades, I can't see his eyes. Still, I know they're scanning me for anything that may be a breach of security.

To assure him I've got nothing to hide, I'm dressed in a manner that leaves little to the imagination: a white tank top, a white lace shawl, a simple cotton handkerchief-point skirt, and flat sandals.

As proof, he motions toward my tiny straw clutch bag. "May I?"

I hand it over. "Be my guest."

When he's satisfied that it holds only my key, my ID, and a change purse—not even a cell phone, he hands it back.

If I wanted to hurt Lee, I would use something already inside the house. We both know it.

What he doesn't know and wouldn't guess in a million years is that the cell phone scanner is attached to my hair barrette. Two of the microdots are under the nail of each of my hands' ring fingers.

I'd say I'm ready. For what, I don't know.

LURCH OPENS THE DOOR SO THAT I MAY WALK THROUGH BEFORE shutting it behind me.

In other words, now it's just Lee and me.

There is a short hallway between the garage and the only room on the main floor: a living room-dining room combination, with a spacious kitchen.

Its two-story window runs the full length of the home's view of the boardwalk. A large yacht—almost a hundred feet in length, and topped with a helipad—is tied to the pier directly out front. The name on the stern proclaims:

Sweet Irony

The harbor faces directly west. It's late enough that already the sun has vanished from the horizon. The channel between Newport Beach and the Pacific Ocean has changed to a brilliant absinthe hue.

The home sits high enough that strollers along the boardwalk couldn't look in if they tried. To assure this is the case, a thick drape of bougainvillea hangs on the wrought iron fence that encircles the property.

I can't see Lee's face from where I stand—he's sitting on the L-shaped couch, in front of a mammoth coffee table that faces a fireplace, where crushed glass sparkles from a gas flame. However, I can see his reflection in the floor-to-ceiling dining room mirror.

Through it, I see his cell phone too: sitting on the foyer table by the front door.

I'm resigned to the realization that this man, whom I thought I knew well and trusted, did in fact order the hit on Catherine and is yet another Quorum foe.

Now, to prove it, I must take his phone and hack it—no matter what it takes.

It should make for an interesting night.

"You're just in time for the final moments of sunset." He rises and walks over. He is tanner than when we saw him in Washington, and certainly more relaxed.

His congratulatory kiss in the Oval Office has made him bold enough to try it again. I presume he thinks, *Jack isn't around to bristle, so why not?*

He pulls me close. Our lips touch. The gentleness of it all is emphasized by the fact that he keeps his eyes closed. It's a while before he opens them, at which point he scrutinizes my face for a sign that he's gone too far.

He has, but I can't let him think that. At least, not until I have what I need: the proof that he is Quorum.

Instead, I rub the two-day stubble on his cheek. "I'm surprised that Babette lets you walk around with this."

"She hasn't seen it," he retorts dryly.

No better time than now to change the subject. "This place is very nice. Is it yours?"

He laughs. "Nothing belongs to me. It's all part of GWI, for obvious reasons."

I scold him with a wagging finger. "If anyone is in the position to simplify the tax laws, it's you."

"Guilty as charged." He shrugs. "Are you up for a drink?"

"Sure." I look at the tumbler in his hand. "What are you having?"

"Whiskey sour, but we aim to please." He points to the liquor caddy in the dining area.

"Red wine, perhaps?"

"I think I can handle that." He walks over to a wine rack. As he peruses the bottles, I meander toward the foyer table, where I pretend to check my hair in the mirror hanging over it. He's too busy wrestling with the bottle's cork to see me pocket the cell phone.

Or, to attach it to the scanner.

I then walk toward the open sliding door and onto the deck, so that he can't see it when I connect both devices and place them in my clutch.

A weathered teak table commands the deck outside the sliding glass doors. It is set with a white linen tablecloth held down by a couple of hurricane lamps.

I gaze beyond the deck to the pier. "Does the yacht belong to GWI too?"

He walks over with my glass in one hand and his drink

in the other. "Yes, but not for long. I have a buyer for it. He's picking it up this weekend, in fact."

"Is he aware of the historical significance?" We clink glasses. I savor a sip.

His is gone in a gulp. "Of course! How else could I sell it for ten times what it's worth? Sucker." He shakes his head in mock shock.

I laugh along with him. We stand side by side, for a long, long while.

Long enough that the outside air has now turned chilly and the veneer of the sun's now red rays have coated the cobalt sky, turning it a deep plum. Long enough for a fine mist to thicken, hiding the boats in the channel from view.

But not long enough for me to feel comfortable when Lee puts his arm around my shoulder, and leans his head against mine—

Or when he kisses me on the forehead—first. Finding no resistance, his lips find their way to mine.

My mind forces my body to respond with all the right signals. My lips part. I melt into his arms.

I don't recoil when I feel him harden.

But, I nearly jump out of my skin when I hear the slight buzz of the scanner telling me that it's done its job.

"You're shivering," he murmurs. "We should go inside."

Nodding gives me a chance to move away from him.

And it gives me the courage to ask, "Lee, why am I here?"

It is now dark enough that I cannot read his eyes. But I can certainly hear the wistfulness in his voice: "I think you know why." He takes my hand and walks toward the door.

It's time to pay for my theft.

LEE WALKS OVER TO THE BAR TO REFILL HIS DRINK. HE POURS himself a double.

I'm just as nervous, but the last thing I need is more wine.

He takes a seat on the couch and motions for me to join him.

Any other time, I'd choose the opposite side of the sectional. However, tonight is not any other time. This time, I must do something that breaks the bond between my heart and that of my betrothed's.

I can't—I *won't*—lie to Jack and say it didn't happen.

I sit next to Lee, close enough that should he lean into me, we'll be thigh to thigh.

He does just that: shifts toward me. His mouth opens.

I expect a kiss. I brace myself but lean in—

"Donna, my guess is that your investigation will lead you to Babette."

Oooh. Okay, curve ball—

And no way to hit this one out of the park.

Certainly not by letting on that he's Numero Uno in the suspect department.

First, I take a deep breath. Next, I furrow a brow to indicate concern. "And why would you suspect that?"

"I've mentioned her stress over her position, and that her form of release is trying for both of us—taking a lover." His hand finds mine. His index finger moves down my wrist.

Does he feel the goose bumps rising beneath his touch? I wish I could pull away, but for the sake of this mission, I must play along. "What does her indiscretion have to do with our investigation?"

His finger stops mid-point on my wrist. This lack of motion is enough to draw my eyes to his. "It may not. But taking a lover has been just one of the ways in which the pressure of being first lady has gotten to her. Her pattern of recklessness leaves her open to dangerous vulnerabilities."

"Like blackmail?"

"Perhaps."

Why, the heartless son of a bitch! He's setting her up to take the fall.

Play it cool. "What are you asking of me, Lee?"

He lifts my hand to his lips. The kiss he places there is gentle. "That you…that you let me deal with it in my own way."

"And what would that be?"

He says nothing, but he doesn't shift his gaze from me. Finally, he sighs. "I'll make sure that the traitor will pay."

"By that, you mean Babette?"

"What *about* 'Babette?'" At the sound of her voice, we turn toward the hall.

Oh, hell.

Babette stands in the doorway of the hall leading from the garage.

Unlike the man standing behind her, she is not smiling.

He is tall, broad-shouldered, and has a swarthy complexion. Sharp cheekbones flank a high-bridged nose, recessing further his already deep-set eyes.

His perfectly erect stance would look odd in anything less formal than the nine-thousand-dollar gray linen Gieves

& Hawkes suit he wears so casually over a black collared cashmere polo shirt.

But it is his pinky ring—its crest gilded in gold with the number *13*—that defines him best.

Lee gives me the incentive I need in order to tear my eyes away as he stands and reaches forward to shake the man's hand. "Salem, good to see you've made it into town a few days early after all." He nods to me. "Salem Rahmin al-Sadah, let me present one of my security consultants, Donna Stone—although soon to be Donna Craig. She gets married in a couple of days."

When I hold out my hand, he bows in order to brush it with his lips, then murmurs, "My congratulations to you, Ms. Stone."

"In fact, I was just telling Donna how much I've enjoyed seeing at least one of the two wonderful ladies in my life consumed by Donna's pending nuptials." Lee's smile, solid and wide, is devoid of any guilt.

I hope I can say the same for mine. "Which is why I asked if he meant you, Babette." I add, "And I was about to tell him how guilty I feel about it, what with all you have on your plate in the coming week." *Broad hint: it's okay to drop my wedding from your agenda…*

Still suspicious, Babette's eyes narrow, honing in on mine like a hawk in flight that has spotted easy prey. "Is that so? Who else might he have been referring to?"

"Janie, of course. She's just as excited about this wedding as you. But because you've so generously offered to help Donna plan it, certainly it's taken more of your time than anyone else's." Lee's tone makes it clear that he sees no need to quell his irritation.

Babette's scrutiny of me falters under its heat. "Janie? ...Yes, of course." She shrugs. "You're right. The whole affair has exhausted me. I don't know how I ever let you rope me into it, Donna." She tosses her head at the thought of this fantasized impudence. "But at least we had our little gal pal getaway to take the edge off. What do you think, Donna? Was it as good for you as it was for me?" Her frosty smile taunts me to rat out the fact that she stood me up.

Don't dare me, lady. As it is, you're hanging by a thread.

In an attempt to deflect her wrath from me, Lee declares, "You're four hours late, darling. I'd about given up on you and Salem. The whole purpose of coming out here was to allow him to tour the *Sweet Irony* while it was still daylight."

Babette's cheeks darken at the implication. "Traffic was a bitch. I doubt you minded much, what with Donna to keep you company."

"She just arrived," Lee responds. "Funny, she didn't mention any delays—did you Donna?"

To get Babette off the hot seat, Salem dismisses the thought with a shrug. "Not to worry. My fleet captain will determine its worthiness, just as my interior designer will see to its creature comforts." Noting Lee's smirk, he adds condescendingly, "I'm sure it's more than up to snuff."

As fun as it is to listen in on the lifestyles of the rich and famous, I figure there's no time better than now to slowly inch my way over to the foyer table in order to put Lee's phone back where it belongs.

"Not its interior, at any rate!" Babette pouts. "I chose every piece of furniture and fabric myself! And you've always complimented my taste, Salem."

I'm halfway there...

"Not to worry, Babette, I won't change a thing—not even a cushion." He smirks knowingly at Lee. "My designer suggest I leave everything as is. The original furnishings on an American president's yacht might actually quadruple its value."

I'm just a few feet from the foyer when Lee catches my eye, as if to say, *I told you so.*

I acknowledge him with a sympathetic shrug—

Then wait until he turns back to Babette and Salem.

"Well then, I guess this trek was for nothing," Babette snaps.

Just a few more steps…

"It's not a complete waste." Lee takes hold of her hand. "Janie is with Frannie. We can stay here tonight, just the two of us."

There, the phone is back where it belongs…

"You've completed your business with Donna?" Babette's sarcasm is not lost on anyone.

Just hearing my name rattles me enough to knock over one of the candlesticks on the foyer table. I straighten it before flipping back around to face my hosts.

"She's up to speed on the issues at hand." Lee turns toward me in order to nod in my direction. "She's always been a fast learner."

I nod, even as I once again clip the scanner onto my hair.

"I'll bet." Babette's head nearly twists one-hundred and eighty degrees in order to glower at me. "The al-Sadahs have just arrived at Lion's Lair. As their hostess, I should make sure they have everything they need."

One, in particular, from the look of longing she gives Salem.

"Narcissa will take them in hand." Lee's tone says it all: *the matter is settled.*

"The president is right. Take the time to enjoy a romantic evening by the shore," Salem insists. "With Narcissa's help, my wives and daughters will be comfortably settled in their quarters at Lion's Lair."

She shrugs angrily. "Lee, where is your cell? I want to give Narcissa instructions on which rooms to place our guests."

"On the table there." He points to where I'm standing.

But by now, I'm staring out at the ocean, my arms folded at my waist.

As Lee shakes Salem's hand, a thought strikes him. "May I ask a favor of you, Salem?"

"By all means."

"Perhaps you can drop Donna at her home? It's just a few blocks from Lion's Lair."

Salem's eyes shift in my direction. "But, of course! It would be my honor."

His sly grin is not lost on Babette.

Nor on Lee.

Trust me, I'm not so excited about it either. If I had my druthers, I'd run in the other direction, and fast.

Unfortunately, if I did, Ryan would yank out the last of his hair in frustration. The chance to position a microdot on Salem would make his week.

Or better yet, scanning his cell phone.

I wonder if Lee knows he's done me a big favor. From the look on Salem's face, I'd guess he's thinking the same thing.

15

Writing, and Honoring, Your Vows

Many betrothed couples prefer to write out vows, as opposed to having an officiant ask the questions that lead to their binding (one would hope) proclamations of commitment. Should you choose this route, please avoid the following:

- *Vow No-No Number 1: Whereas some creativity in customizing your vows may indeed be refreshing, seeking inspiration from Dr. Seuss, despite having read all of his books, the Tao of Theodor Geisel does not make for a mature view on marriage. To wit:*

Will you love him good or bad?
When he's happy, even though you're sad?
Yes, I'll take her for my wife!
Yes, I'll love her all my life!

- *Vow No-No Number 2: Stay away from single-syllable responses. Let's face it: you're the entertainment at your own wedding. Unless your marriage is doomed from the outset, you may not get a second chance to razzle-dazzle them. So go ahead and give it all you've got, both in a few well-chosen words and with heartfelt emotions.*

- *Vow No-No Number 3: Don't wing it. A course or two of Improv in college cannot prepare you for the rush of emotions that takes place when you stand, face to face, with the one person who is willing to spend the rest of his life with you. Riffing just won't do.*

Write something down. Take the time to memorize it, verbatim. That way, you'll breathe easy until the point which you both say, "I do."

At that point, if he refuses to speak those two last words, any profanities coming out of your gaping maw are understandably forgiven.

"H OW LONG HAVE YOU KNOWN L EE AND B ABETTE?" I ASK, NOT just for reconnaissance purposes, but to engage Salem in any way that breaks his smoldering Blue Steel gaze. To top it off, he sits practically on top of me, despite the length and depth of his limo.

It doesn't help that, when the limo slides from one lane to another, it tosses me into his lap.

And he certainly doesn't mind it when the glasses of champagne he insists on pouring us slosh onto us, like tidal waves spilling over a New Orleans Parish floodwall during a hurricane.

The question takes him off guard. He leans back and his

eyes narrow as he considers the question. "Lee and I were at Columbia Graduate School together." He chuckles. "Without him, I don't think I would have made it through."

Hearing this, my heart sinks. If the two men are that close and have known each other for that long, then perhaps Lee really is our target. Was Babette put on Graffias' board as Lee's surrogate?

In mock dismay, I playfully circle the rim of my champagne glass with my index finger. "How did he save you? Did he take your exams for you or something?"

"No, nothing like that. Although I was the party animal of our dynamic duo." He raises a brow. "It's an occupational hazard for men like me."

I take a sip from my glass. "Oh? What kind of man is that?"

"One whose wealth is larger than most European countries. One who is easily bored with virgin wives, no matter how many he takes."

I guess that's where Babette comes in.

And by the way his hand slips up my skirt, me too.

I shove it away. "Sorry, not interested. I'm two days away from getting married, remember?"

"Isn't that the time a woman is tempted to have one last fling?" He pulls me into his lap.

"Depends on the woman." To make the point that I'm not one of them, I leap up.

Gravity has other plans for me. A fast turn around a corner sends me toppling back down, right on his lap.

He shoves his tongue deep into my throat. Okay, I'll play —for as long as it takes me to swipe his cell. While he paws at my breasts under my tank top, my hands sift through his jacket pockets. *Damn it, where is his phone?*

When he comes up for air, he's smiling. "You're good at faking your virtue." He hefts a breast, as if weighing its value.

I slap his hand away. "Who says I'm faking?"

"Babette."

I sit down on the seat opposite him. "Oh, yeah? How would she know?"

"The dalliance between her husband and her best friend drives her up a wall."

I'm the best she can do for a friend? That's her first mistake.

I pout coyly at him. "And into your arms, I suppose?"

He shrugs. "What Lee doesn't know won't hurt him."

I look him right in the eye. "What makes you think he doesn't?"

He frowns. "He would have said something to me. We are that close."

"Since when do true friends bed each other's wives?"

"The stronger man always takes, even if the prize is another's wife. The weaker man accepts this. They are subjugated to their proper roles—either ally, or slave. It's how wars are won."

What a pompous ass. "Have you ever wondered if Lee has fucked any of your wives? He is the leader of the free world, after all, which makes him a much more powerful man than a mere supplicant to the Arab princes."

Anger darkens Salem's eyes. He jerks me toward him, then hisses, "I'm a supplicant to no one!" Seeing the taunt in my eye, he smiles. "And my wives are too obedient. They've learned the hard way that I don't spare the rod."

My stare doesn't waver. His does, however, when I whisper, "How about Babette? Has she too learned this"—I lick my lips—"the *hard* way?"

He chuckles. His hand eases off my arm. "By their nature, all women are submissive. Allah deems it so."

I throw my legs over his lap. Leaning down on one elbow, I declare, "Strong men need challenges or they get bored."

He takes this as his cue to heave himself over me. His fondling of my breasts is rewarded with fervent kisses and my own roaming hands—over his back pockets—

But, still no cell, damn it.

The car slides to a stop. We must be in front of my home.

Time for Plan B: My right hand roams over his head, neck, face, and ears before I clench his hand with my left. With one gentle tap, a microdot adheres to the crest of the pinky ring on Salem's right finger.

Finally, our lips part. He too realizes the party is over. Before righting himself on the back seat, he flips my top down over my breasts. "I want you as my conquest, Mrs. Stone. Imagine, taking a bride before her wedding night! Slip away tomorrow, at noon. I have the penthouse suite at the Beverly Wilshire."

Plan C has just presented itself.

No. Enough.

"Sorry, Salem, but playtime is over." I grab my clutch and reach for the door.

He grabs hold of my wrist. "Your loyalty to Lee is intoxicating. Sadly, it is also misplaced."

I wrench my hand away. "Says who? You?"

"I don't have to say it. Lee shows it in his actions. He's released you to me."

"He did nothing of the sort!"

"Don't kid yourself. Because of my attentions, he lusts for Babette again. He knows I've taught her a few new tricks." He laughs. "I'm sure Babette is ecstatic. She's always been so jealous of his trysts with you."

"Babette was wrong," I retort. "You see, Lee never had me to begin with."

"All the more reason for you to submit to me." His grin widens at the thought. "Yes, I should have you first. Lee will be angry at first, but then he will thank me for breaking you in for him."

"Fuck off." I reach for the door.

The force of his hand against my cheek sends my head reeling into the limo's back seat.

He straddles me. After pinning me down across my chest, he hisses, "I have so many fun little toys at my disposal to help me break you of your of vanity. When I am done, you will plead for mercy. And yet, *you will beg for more*." He squeezes my mouth into a pout so that he can kiss me.

There is nothing I can do to stop him.

He finishes by licking my lips. Seeing the shock on my face, he laughs. "Consider our liaison my wedding gift to you."

A better present would be his head on a platter.

I could start by severing his jugular vein with the broken stem of my champagne glass—

But no. It would defeat the purpose of watching him be

tortured for all the terrorist acts he committed in the name of the almighty dollar.

He slides onto the backseat. My heavy breathing earns no sympathy from him, only a chuckle.

He raps once on the chauffeur's window. The door flings open. Strong arms grab me and pull me out.

I STUMBLE INTO THE HOUSE. I'M STILL BREATHING HEAVY FROM the weight of that oaf on my chest.

Jeff doesn't look up even as he waves me over to his computer. "Yo, Mom, you've got to see the feed on the bachelor party! It's a hoot! Evan didn't get in, but two Bunnies brought him food and sat with him in the limo. One was last year's Playmate of the Year! She even wrote her telephone number on his wrist! I bet he never washes it again." He clicks onto another screen. His eyes open wide at what he sees. "Oh my God! Who knew Dominic was such a horn dog?"

Aunt Phyllis sighs. "Everyone knew, dearie. Welcome to Planet Earth."

I start toward the great room, but as I pass the foyer mirror, the red handprint impression on my face stops me cold. "Um...I'm tired. I'm going upstairs to take a bath." I curse myself for the quiver in my voice.

"Donna, if you're worried about Jack, don't." Phyllis says, as she looks up at me. "No matter how many Bunnies shake their cottontails in his face, he's been a perfect gentleman."

I hope I turned quick enough that she missed my bruise.

"I'm sure it's just good clean fun. See you in the morning." I run up the stairs.

I pass Mary's door on the way to my bedroom. It is still closed.

Trisha's is too, so at least I know she's in bed, and not shocked by all the men behaving badly.

I turn on my shower and jump in fully clothed.

I see no reason to strip down. Salem has done that for me.

Right now, I just want to scrub the thought of his touch from my memory.

I'M IN BED WHEN JACK GETS HOME. I FAKE SLEEP, BUT HE'S NOT having it. He flips on my nightstand light. I'm so startled that it takes me a minute to get my bearings and pull the sheet over my head.

Too late. I know that Jack has seen the bruise because he jerks down the sheet in order to get a closer look. "Aunt Phyllis said she saw this."

He touches it gently with his fingers. At first, he says nothing. Then: "Why—that son of a bitch!" He throws the book that lies on my nightstand against the wall. "I'll kill him!"

I leap out of bed toward the door, in order to block it. "No—you can't!"

In three strides, we're facing off. He shoves me away from the door. "The hell I can't! I don't care if he is the President of the United States—"

"Who...*Lee*? You think Lee did this to me?"

He stops in his tracks. "But…if not him…who?"

I take a breath before muttering, "Salem."

"*Salem?*" He paces the room. "You mean, Lee set up some sort of…*threesome?*"

"Are you crazy? No! Salem showed up *with Babette—*"

"A *foursome?* Oh, my God…" He stares at the ceiling, as if that's where he'll find the comprehension he seeks.

"Jack, please! Get your mind out of the gutter—at least, until I finish talking."

He folds his arms across his chest. "Sure. Go for it."

"The reason Lee asked me to meet with him was to warn me that most likely our trail will lead to Babette."

"I presume you didn't tell him we've already ruled her out, and that he's our number one suspect," he smirks.

"Of course not. In fact, while he was making drinks, I hacked his phone with the scanner."

"Good girl." For once, Jack has a reason to smile. "I can imagine he was fine with throwing her under the bus? What a guy."

"As it turns out, Lee was in the middle of his riff as to why Babette would turn out to be our suspect when the lady herself walked in with Salem. He's interested in buying the Chiffrays' yacht, and was there to tour it."

"When did he slap you, and why?"

"Babette and Lee decided to spend the night on the island. I came back to Hilldale with Salem."

"And knowing Salem, he made a pass—and you rejected it."

Very gently, I rub my cheek. "You could say that."

"Were you able to scan his phone too?"

"Unfortunately, no. I was somewhat preoccupied." I sigh. "But I planted a microdot."

"Nice. Where?"

"On the crest of his ring." I run over to the closet and pull out a sundress. "In fact, we should have Ryan and Arnie meet us at the office. The sooner we see what's on the scanner for Lee's phone, the better."

"By the way, who suggested that you hitch home with Salem?"

I think a moment. "Lee. You see, Salem gave Babette a lift from Hilldale. He and his family are staying at Lion's Lair, so it made sense."

"Not necessarily. For that matter, Lee could have had one of his Secret Service agents take you home." He lets that sink in. Seeing my frown, he adds, "Admit it, Donna. He set you up."

I stop zipping mid-back in order to face him. "Which is it, Jack? Is Lee gaga over me, or is he using me to service his friends?"

"Maybe both. In any event, we'll know as soon as Arnie downloads the scanner intel." He kisses my forehead. "I hope you're prepared for the worst."

"You'll be happy to hear that I am." I walk out the door first, so that he can't see the disappointment in my eyes.

When Arnie answers the door, he doesn't look too happy. "Emma threw me out of the bedroom," he mutters.

Jack frowns. "How come?"

"Jeff hacked the Playboy Mansion's webcam. He copied

footage of a Bunny begging me to go into the grotto with her."

Jack furrows his brow. "If I remember, you passed on the honor."

Arnie turns to me to plead his case. "I did! I swear! But Jeff somehow edited it so that it looks like I entered. It's so dark in there that you can't see anything, but you can hear some girl screaming, 'Yes! Yes! Yes!'"

He shouts with such verve that I have to hold my hand over his mouth. "Okay, I get the picture. I'll have a talk with him the moment I get home."

Arnie wipes away some flop sweat. "Thanks, Donna. I mean, I know he's always had a crush on Emma, but this is going too far."

Knowing Emma, she's also in on Jeff's joke. In fact, I wouldn't be surprised if she put my son up to it.

Frankly, I wish I'd thought of it. Jack and I could use a laugh tonight.

Ryan pokes his head out the door. "Are you going to stand out there all night, boohooing?" he grouses.

Arnie and I hurry in after Jack.

"IT AIN'T HIM." ARNIE TOSSES ME THE SCANNER.

I stare at him. "What are you saying?"

"Lee didn't send the texts to Xia. At least, not with the cell phone containing this text archive."

Jack sits up straight in his chair. "Are you sure?"

"Positive." Arnie's apology is a shrug.

"So, *both* Lee and Babette are eliminated?" Ryan asks. "I guess that's good news."

"But…how can that be?" I ask. "It's the only cell phone he carries! And we know for a fact that one of the two phones Lee had on him during our engagement party was used to contact Xia!"

"Remember, our POI was on to the fact that you were subbing for Xia on the night of their rendezvous," Ryan reminds me. "If he, or she, has access to the first couple, maybe it was planted on one of them that night in order to implicate him or her."

"Or, perhaps Lee or Babette got a new phone in the meantime," Jack counters. "In any regard, there goes any evidence against the first couple."

Suddenly, a thought hits me. "According to Todd, the person assigned to the phone—Bradley Kazinsky—is dead. It doesn't mean he died with his phone on him. If the phone's signal is still live—"

"Then it would stand to reason that it's in the hands of our top suspect," Jack says.

"The other person who was blind-copied on Xia's text correspondence regarding Catherine's assassination is just as important to us," I add.

Ryan frowns. "We've got no leads on either. We're back to square one."

"Not necessarily," Arnie counters. "If the contact cell is still in use, we can intercept its signal if we're in the right place at the right time."

It hits me. "Lion's Lair."

"Exactly." Arnie is now so excited that he's pacing through the dining room.

"But, how?" Jack asks.

"We activate a phony cell tower, which acts as an 'interceptor' for all cellular data going in and out of Lion's Lair," Arnie explains. "It'll allow us to retrieve archived data, and identify what phone it was retrieved from. We'll even be able to trace it via its GPS signal." He snaps his fingers. "In fact, we'll be able to actively control the phone's incoming and outgoing messages as well."

"And when the time comes, we can spoof the cell with any text message we want to send," Ryan replies.

"You've got it." Arnie lifts his hand for a high five. It hangs there uncomfortably until he realizes Ryan isn't playing.

I punch him in the arm. "Why didn't you mention this before now? I could have avoided being mauled by Salem."

"I thought about it," he concedes, "but had we begun monitoring in D.C., odds are we would have gotten caught and it would have been for naught. In the first place, the NSA is on the lookout for phony cell towers. The Chinese and Russians are notorious for putting them up all over the town."

Jack shrugs. "Figures."

"Not only that, the other issue we would have faced is monitoring the massive amount of intel," Arnie adds. "Considering all the cell phones used at the White House, it would have been like looking for a needle in a haystack."

"Whereas, at Lion's Lair, there are a finite number of cell phones to monitor. Even with the Secret Service detail, the staff is less than sixty people."

"It doesn't sound easy to erect without notice," Ryan points out.

"Frankly, the latest models of the StingRay—it's a specific brand of cell-site simulator—are as small as a handheld device. The trick is mounting them on a pole, or a tree, or somewhere else, as high as possible."

"What about one of the turrets at Lion's Lair?" I ask.

Arnie nods. "Sure, but how will you get access to it?"

"Janie's suite is located in one of them. It has a balcony and everything. Trisha will be over there tomorrow evening for a sleepover. Janie is screening the latest Pixar animation for my daughter and two of Salem's daughters as well."

"That'll do it," Arnie says. "Hey, here's a brilliant idea—I'll camouflage it as a birdhouse!" He leaps up, excited. "The pole will be the signal tower, and the signal scanner itself will be buried in a false bottom of the house."

"Beautiful. I'll drop it by as a thank-you gift for Janie," Jack suggests. "For participating in the wedding. I'll even offer to install it on the balcony."

I smile. "The kids will enjoy that. And when this is over, we'll replace it. No one will be the wiser." A revelation hits me. I bolt straight up in my seat. "Now that we've confirmed our target is not Lee, the person who contracted Xia may not know she's dead! Granted, the target saw me, that is, 'Xia', enter the Georgetown mansion, and the four-alarm fire that followed, but there's been no verification that she died inside the inferno."

"That certainly works in our favor," Jack replies. "When the time comes, perhaps we should resurrect her ghost via text, and haunt her double-crossing client."

I turn to Ryan. "Speaking of Salem. I planted a microdot on his ring."

Ryan smiles. "Arnie, has the signal come in yet?"

Arnie opens another screen on his computer. "The signal is live…but…"

I roll my eyes heavenward. "But what?"

"The audio works fine. But you must have adhered the camera facing into the crest, because the video is static. I'm reading some text or something."

I frown. "How could that be? The crest is onyx."

Arnie takes a closer look. "No, apparently it's colored glass…and there's a microdot behind it! Just like—"

In unison, Arnie, Jack, and Ryan exclaim, "Pinky Ring's!"

I stare from one to another. "What?"

"Not what, but who," Ryan explains. "A couple of years back, Jack chased down a Quorum operative wearing a duplicate of the ring."

I nod. "I know. He mentioned it."

"What I forgot to mention was that the guy's ring had a hidden compartment within the crest," Jack adds. "It contained a phone memory card holding steganography. Arnie cracked the encryption. It was how we knew Carl had been turned by the Quorum."

"I see. And whatever is in Salem's ring may also contain valuable intel," I murmur. "So I have to meet with him after all."

Ryan looks at me sharply. "He asked for another liaison?"

"Asked?" I shudder. "It was a command."

Ryan shrugs. "Great. Then you'll go."

"No, she won't." Jack shakes his head adamantly. "He's a sadist. Look at her face, damn it! And that was from being in the back of a limo with him for half an hour!"

Ryan waits a good minute after Jack's rant. Then, very quietly, he says, "It's what she does."

There is nothing Jack can say to that.

So, he doesn't. Instead, he walks out of the room. And out of the cottage.

Ryan turns to me. "I'm sorry, Donna. If we want to put a knife in the eye of the Quorum once and for all, we need Salem's microdot. At the same time, if you can keep ours intact, all the better." He pauses, then looks away before adding, "Do whatever it takes. You'll report directly to me with your reconnaissance."

It's called taking one for the team. Not that Jack needs to know that.

I run out after Jack.

WE'VE PULLED UP TO THE DRIVEWAY BEFORE JACK SAYS A WORD. Make that four: "You don't have to."

"I do. We both know it." I stroke his arm. "Jack, I won't let him touch me. He won't have time. I'll hit him with a Roofie—over and out! Then I'll open the ring, take the intel, and I'm outta of there. Easy-peasy."

"Sure. Whatever."

"You sound like a sullen teenager."

"Speaking of which, Mary is sitting on the front stoop." He nods in her direction.

"Oh…yeah. We…she found out that Babette has deemed herself my maid of honor."

"Take care of her. She needs you." He pats my arm. "Donna, I'm serious: you don't have to do anything you don't want to."

I nod. I know he means kowtowing to Babette.

And going to Salem.

Or anything else that hurts the ones I love most.

MARY SITS STILL. HER EYES ARE RED, BUT THE TEARS HAVE stopped.

She waits until I'm seated beside her before asking, "Why did you say yes to her?"

"Because…Ryan asked me to."

She nods slowly. "So, if you were to be honest, this has something to do with your job, and nothing to do with any obligation you feel to Babette."

"Yes, of course! Mary, I think it's obvious I'm not friends with the woman. As much as she despises me, I was shocked she even asked to take it on—"

"Wait…so she asked you, not the other way around?"

"Of course, I'd never ask her! And I was a fool to mention it to Ryan. Had he not known, that would have been the end of it."

"I told Ryan about it." Jack is standing behind us. Kneeling, he adds, "So blame me, not your mother. I knew how much she wanted you as her maid of honor, and how much you wanted to do it."

"Glad you've finally manned up," Mary retorts. "I know just how you can make it up to me, too."

"Anything," Jack promises.

Mary rewards him with a devilish grin. "Driving lessons. And not in Mom's SUV either. In the i8."

Jack's eyes open in mock horror. "Anything…but that."

Mary crosses her arms. There will be no further negotiations.

He sighs. "Great. But we start after the honeymoon."

Mary puts her arms around my waist. "If it has to be Babette, I understand. Thanks for leveling with me...finally."

I kiss her cheek.

"And be sure to bring my driving instructor back in one piece from the honeymoon."

Jack and I howl with laughter.

"There's not much you can do to kill your partner in bed," I sputter.

"I'll bet there are plenty of ways, and I'm sure you know every one of them," Mary retorts. "And by the way—*too much information.*"

Arm in arm, we walk inside.

16

Giving Away the Bride

The tradition of giving the bride away goes back hundreds of years. Usually, it was her father who did the honors by approving her betrothed and hosting a formal matrimonial ceremony. The bride was considered her father's property (let's bandy about the term "chattel," why don't we?) to be acquired by the husband, along with the added incentive of cash, land or both, serving as a dowry.

Today's bride is likely to have a job, and make her own living. Hopefully her fiancé does as well, and they can pay for their own wedding—although, considering the cost of weddings these days, help from one or both families may be needed, and will certainly be appreciated.

The man who raised her—be that her father, stepfather, uncle, big brother, or mother's significant other—will find it an honor to walk her down the aisle as a token of their mutual adoration. In other words, any very close loved one who takes pride in her accomplishments will do just fine.

In the modern era, no father has to pay a man to take his

daughter off his hands. Her personal and professional accomplishments are adequate proof that she can take care of herself.

Guests should feel free to peruse the blissful couple's wish list of wedding gifts on their preferred online registries. Being a self-made woman doesn't mean she would object to a little help in feathering her nest.

Look at it this way: anything you give them is a drop in the bucket on what they'll spend, per guest, during the wedding. My God, do you know how much these things cost these days?

"THIS IS FOR YOU!" TRISHA, MY LITTLE TROJAN PONY, COMES bearing a gift for Janie: a birdhouse in the design of a two-story Williamsburg cottage.

After an ear-piercing squeal, Janie squeezes Trisha's neck with a heartfelt hug.

It doesn't raise an eyebrow from Zeb and his posse.

Jack, acting as heavy lifter, kneels so that Janie can see inside. "Can we put it up now?" she begs.

Jack turns to Janie's au pair, Frannie. "Perhaps I can set it up for her, on the playroom terrace?"

She nods. "Yes, of course. Follow me."

She includes me in the offer, but I shake my head. "I've got to meet with Babette. Is she around?"

"Mummy is in the study. She has a headache." Janie shrugs. Apparently, nothing new there.

Trisha frowns. "There's a mummy in your study? Is it all wrapped up in bandages? Can I see?"

Janie shakes her head. "I meant *my* mummy—my

mommy. She prefers I call her that." She stops to think a moment. "But, yes, she had bandages on her back. I think they're off now."

Interesting. But from what I now know of Salem, I'm not at all surprised.

I trot off in the direction of Babette's wing. Something tells me the next conversation won't be as appreciated.

"I DON'T THINK BABETTE IS EXPECTING YOU." NARCISSA, WHO had been thumbing her way through the latest issue of *Vogue,* sits on a settee outside the door of Babette's personal study at Lion's Lair. Noting that her words don't slow me down, she stands up in order to block me.

"It's important that I speak to her—*now.*" I'm smiling, but she can read between my fists: *Don't push me.*

Narcissa grimaces at my obstinacy. "She's asked not to be disturbed. She's seeing to some very important affairs of state. You can set an appointment." She opens the calendar app on her iPad. "How about tomorrow? I can squeeze you in between seven-ten and seven-twenty in the morning."

"Nope, don't think so, no. *That's my wedding day.*"

"Ah. Yes, of course. Which means that the first lady has a lot on her plate between now and then in preparation for it, since she will be its most important guest. Did you know that both *Vanity Fair* and *People* are bidding for the exclusive rights to Mario Testino's photos of your wedding? Not just of the event, but Mrs. Chiffray's preparation leading up to it. Everyone else is trying to climb the compound's walls. There are already helicopters circling overhead! POTUS may insist the NSA deem it a no-fly zone. Still, between the paparazzi and the Secret Service, Chantal is beside herself." Seeing my shock at all of it, she adds, "The proceeds will go to charity, of course. Babette has chosen supporting the local libraries—FLOTUS's pet cause. So you see, that specific ten-minute window is the only one that works—"

With my arm across her throat, she has nowhere to go but against the wall. "There are many ways in which I can imply my sense of urgency. Would you like me to show you?"

"Not necessary." Narcissa is gasping so hard that I can barely hear her.

I may have bruised her hyoid bone. She got off lucky.

She can barely breathe. Now she knows how I feel.

THE DRAPES ARE DRAWN. THE ROOM IS SO DARK THAT AT FIRST I don't see Babette. She is lying on the couch, her eyes closed. There is a cloyingly sweet smell in the air.

Something is terribly wrong.

I'm practically standing over Babette when she mutters, "I thought I told you to leave me alone."

"I think we need to chat." I take the chair closest to her head. My God, she looks pale. "Babette, are you okay?"

"Who the hell…" One eye pops open. "Oh, it's you. What do you want now, Donna?"

"I don't want anything. In fact, I never did." I take a deep breath. "Babette, I want you to bow out as my matron of honor."

"How dare you!" She struggles to right herself on the

couch. "After all I've done to make it the wedding of the decade—"

"That's just it. I never wanted it to be 'the wedding of the decade.' All I wanted was for it to be *my* wedding—surrounded by those who love me most. No celebrities, no heads of state, no paparazzi in helicopters circling overhead—"

"No. Sorry. It's not your decision to make at this stage." She glares at me. "Who do you think you are, anyway?"

I lean in so that she hears me loud and clear: "I'm the only one who matters. *I'm the bride.*"

"You're also an ungrateful bitch!" She shoves me back into a chair. I let her. "All this time, I've been extending an olive branch to the very woman who is destroying my marriage—"

"I'm doing no such thing!"

"Oh, please, Donna, quit acting coy! Don't you think I know what you're up to? First, there's your ongoing affair with my husband—"

"That's a lie!"

From the despair etched in her face, she refuses to believe me. Why is that?

Lee. "Is that what Lee told you?"

"He doesn't have to! I'm no fool! I see how he looks at you!" She practically spits in my face. Her breath is rancid. "And now you're going after my…my very close friend—"

Enough of this crap. "Don't you mean your lover?"

Realizing I know her secret, she blanches. She can't deny it.

All she can do is throw up—

On my shoes, no less.

Groaning, she leans back on the couch.

Then it hits me: "You're…pregnant."

She nods. A long sigh is followed by wracking sobs.

"Is it Lee's?"

She throws up again. This time, I'm able to move quickly to avoid the last vestiges of her breakfast.

She sobs even harder. I move onto the couch beside her. I lay my hand on her arm.

She acknowledges it by taking it in her own. "I hate my life! It's…it's like living in a fishbowl!" She chokes out her words in fits and starts. "I can't breathe, I can't think…I can't hide…and now this."

"When will you tell Lee?"

"I don't know. I was thinking about waiting until after the summit."

"Will he…know?"

"Know what? That it isn't his?" Her upper lip lifts into a snarl. "Dear Donna, if there's one thing Lee Chiffray can do, it's count." She closes her eyes, as if the thought of his reaction exhausts her. "He'll want to pretend it's his, if only to save face. But I won't let him. Salem needs a male heir to continue his legacy and enjoy his family's largesse. If I'm carrying a boy, he'll banish all of his other wives at my behest. I'll be his one and only princess. And my son will be prince." She smiles at this fantasy.

Stupid Babette.

Poor Lee.

Neither of us says anything for a long while. Finally, she whispers, "Can I trust you to keep your mouth shut until then?"

"I've said it before and I'll say it again, Babette. I have no desire to involve myself with Lee's personal affairs, or yours."

She nods grudgingly. We both know she will never trust me.

Well, it's her problem, not mine. "And I meant it when I said I'd prefer that you withdraw as my matron of honor. It was kind of you to take on the wedding planning—far beyond the call of our…friendship." I wince when I say that word. "But even before you insinuated yourself into that role, I had already asked Mary. I cannot go back on my word to my daughter. Surely, you understand that."

"Turning me down, for a brat teenager who will probably embarrass you? I think you're a fool." She shakes her head in disbelief. "But if you're set on doing this, so be it." She flicks her wrist toward the door. "Just be prepared: the minute Chantal puts out the word that I won't be attending your quaint little shindig, don't expect anyone of importance to show up either."

Boo hoo hoo. "Duly noted." I turn my face so that she doesn't see my relief.

"That goes for Lee too."

"If that's his decision, I understand perfectly."

As I start toward the door, she calls out, "Oh, and Donna, when you see Salem today, for your own sake, I hope you don't blurt out my news. It may earn you more pain than you bargained for."

Her warning stops me cold. Salem told her about me? What a romantic guy.

She drops her robe off of one shoulder so that I can see her back. It is crisscrossed with belt buckle welts.

Noting my shock, she giggles. "Never mind. The moment

he puts the ball gag in your mouth, you won't be able to say anything about it anyway."

I walk out before I'm tempted to give in to the urge of also throwing up.

~

"Don't go." From Jack's tone, I know it's a demand, not a request.

He's on the bed, watching me put on my makeup as I get ready for my date with Salem. I don't feel the need to dress for the role of submissive: that is, as demure schoolgirl, or in flowing virginal white. And certainly, the last thing I have to do is look like a call girl. Instead, I've chosen an outfit of elegant simplicity: flare-leg dark gray pants and a matching fitted long-sleeved jacket over a burgundy long-sleeved crewneck top.

"Let's go over your fears, one by one." I am using my kindergarten teacher voice. It is soft and slowly modulated. There is no emphasis on words that may cause alarm—the primary word being, *fears*.

He holds up a hand with his index finger raised. "He reserved the Presidential Suite. It's on its own floor in the Beverly Wing. In other words, there is no one to hear you scream should he...when he..." Jack balls his fists at the thought of any and all of the fun and games Salem has in store for me.

"It won't come to that. *I swear*."

"How can you be so sure?"

"I'm not a ten-dollar hooker on the clock. He's trying to seduce me. We'll have drinks first, at which time I'll drug him, remember?" I hold up my hand in order to point to an antique diamond ring. "As discussed, liquid Rohypnol, ready and accounted for. One twist and it's in his drink. Nighty-night, Salem! I'll then take the microdot from his ring, scan his cell, and I'm out of there. Arnie is covering the security cams, in case I need…well, a quick exit."

"A quick exit, with bodyguards at the door?"

I shrug. "I'll sashay out as if I don't have a care in the world."

"Yeah, right, we'll see about that." He lifts a second finger. "What if he doesn't take a drink?"

I sigh mightily. "If he doesn't go down one way, he'll go down another."

To prove my point, I lift up my crewneck top, revealing my Glock 43, tucked in my FlashBang bra holster. "Talk about cleavage, right? It both lifts, *and* separates."

By the frown on Jack's face, he's still not convinced.

Next, I put my right foot on the bed beside him so that he can admire my tall, gray stilettos. A second later I pull, quite literally, a stiletto from one of the heels.

A third finger goes up. "You're presuming that he won't make you strip, or tie you down. If he does, you'll have no way to defend yourself," he counters.

I shrug. "Don't I always come up with something?" To be honest, he's hit on a brain tickler, but I don't need to let him know that.

"That's not an answer."

"Okay, how about this? Did you know that the Tiffany lamps on the bedside tables in the master bedroom of the Beverly Wilshire's Presidential Suite each weigh sixteen pounds? One crack over the head, he's out like a light." I lift my hand to my mouth in mock shame. "Oopsy, bad pun."

"Donna, have you forgotten what a sadist this guy is? If he has you tied to the bed, it's game over."

"Not necessarily."

"Oh no? Explain."

"I can…" *I can what?*

"Thought so." He's now pacing the room. "Look, let's say you get out of that room alive. What if he's got body-guards, either in the suite, or posted outside? If they have even an inkling that something's gone wrong, are you going to turn the Beverly Wilshire into high noon at the O.K. Corral?"

"You're mashing up two different westerns. *High Noon* was a fictional incident, and starred Gary Cooper, whereas *Gunfight at the O.K. Corral* depicted a real shootout, with Doc Holliday, Wyatt Earp, and his brothers on one side—"

He rolls his eyes. "You're specifically avoiding my question."

"No, I'm not…okay, maybe."

"That's it. I'm going too."

When I sputter my objection, he holds up his hand. "Don't worry. It's your op. I'm just there for backup. I'll book the room directly below Salem's suite. I'm bringing Dominic too."

"Sure, what the hell? The more the merrier. But if he walks in on me in a compromising position, one smart-ass remark and his twenty-thousand-dollar pearly white grill will get kicked in."

"He'll be duly warned." Jack celebrates his victory over

my stubbornness with a faint smile. "Are you wearing your surveillance lenses?"

"Yes, of course."

"Good." He tosses me my jacket. "Let's get this over with."

~

"I THOUGHT YOU'D STAND ME UP." SALEM CIRCLES ME AS IF I'M the last musical chair in some game in which there is only one winner: him.

And he's willing to sit on me to prove it—possibly with a saddle, a bridle, and a Rainbow Pony tail butt plug.

If he does, the three bodyguards outside the suite—one in front of the door, and the other two standing sentry at each end of the hall—will pretend not to hear my screams. It's not like they haven't heard anything like that before, right?

At least the one who frisked me didn't cop a feel. He knows his boss isn't into sharing, let alone sloppy seconds.

"Shall we take a tour?" Salem suggests.

I nod. "Sure, why not?"

I stifle a shiver when he places his hand on the small of my back as he guides me through the penthouse.

The rooms are modern and sumptuous in their appointments: thick rugs over hardwood floors, deep modular couches, and wall-to-wall-windows with views of Los Angeles from every direction.

Our first stop is the suite's luxury kitchen. "I hear you are quite the chef, Mrs. Stone."

I nod. "I do know my way around a kitchen." And I'm

relieved to see that this one is fully equipped—not that I plan on impressing Salem with my culinary skills, but because of what it offers me: lots of deadly devices.

Something Salem may find out the hard way.

He comes up behind me and murmurs in my ear, "There is an apron hanging in the pantry—white and trimmed in lace. All day, I have been imagining you naked except for it"—He looks down at my shoes—"and perhaps your heels…Ah, but no! I bought you a pair I like even better, from Yves St. Laurent."

He opens a cabinet and pulls out a shoebox. He drops to his knees. Gently, he lifts my right foot and unstraps my shoe, replacing it with one of the two hot red four-inch designer sandals, adorned with a bow.

Okay, now we're talking: swag! And Saint Laurent, no less. I'll be sure to take them with me when I leave.

Soon, I hope.

He places his hand on the countertop. "Marble—so cold to the touch. Come, feel it for yourself."

I place a hand on it.

"The other as well," he cajoles.

I see where this is going. Still, I comply.

He bends his body into mine, pressing down on me until I'm flat against the counter.

"When you are naked, your nipples will harden." His hands move between my legs. "You'll dampen even before I touch you—"

His buzzing cell phone interrupts his flight of fancy.

He holds me down with one hand even as he pulls a cell from his coat jacket with the other. The Caller ID elicits an annoyed sigh from him.

"Excuse me," he murmurs, moving away.

As I right myself, he turns his back to me and starts speaking in a rapid Arabic dialect.

"Holy shit," Abu murmurs in my ear bud. But of course, he can hear Salem too. I'm dying to know what is happening but I can't ask, what with Salem standing ten feet away.

I take these precious few moments to pull a steak knife from the butcher-block stand.

Just in case.

A second after I slip it into the sleeve of my top, Salem is off the phone. He seems distracted.

Worse yet, his mood has darkened. "Time to tour the bedrooms."

This time, when he takes me in hand, it is by the elbow. He holds it so tightly that I want to scream out in pain, but I won't give him the satisfaction.

SALEM STOPS IN ONE OF THE SUITE'S LONG HALLWAYS. "I WANT you to choose which of the three bedrooms we should use for our inaugural tryst."

"Surprise me," I suggest.

"No, no. You see, each holds specific pleasures—a theme, if you may."

He opens the door on the right. The curtains are drawn. The room smells of incense. The sound of a Japanese lute comes from a speaker.

Laid out on the bed is a red silk kimono, a white kabuki mask, ten-inch-high platform shoes, a silk Shibari bondage rope, an open brocade box containing two stainless steel

Ben Wa balls, and a black wig with hair piled high in a bun.

Salem picks up the Ben Wa balls with one hand and shuffles them so that they click as they hit against each other. "Geishas are elegant and submissive. Should you choose this room, I will bind your hands, and then draw the cords to your feet. It is one way to make you bend to my will. And then I'll insert these," he chortles.

Wishful thinking on his part. I stifle a yawn. "Shall we continue?"

In the next room, two spreader bars lay on the bed: one near the head, the other toward the foot. There are chains on the opposite ends of the poles, each attached to Lycra cuffs. Also laid out on the bed are three dildos, each a different size, girth, and stiffness. An anal hook, nipple clamps, crotchless black panties, and a studded leather breast harness complete the scenario of a good time had by one: Salem.

"Classy," I murmur.

"Each accouterment provides a unique pleasure," he assures me.

For you, maybe. Then again, you're one sick fuck.

He jerks my arm behind me in such a way that if I pull away, he can wrench it out of the socket. "Maybe the master bedroom will be more to your liking."

The way he goose-steps me down the hall, my guess is no.

⁓

OF THE THREE BEDROOMS, THE MASTER SUITE SHARES THE BEST view with the living room: one facing downtown.

Sliding doors open to a large terrazzo tile terrace.

There is no bed in the room: only a cage with chains dangling from bars on each side, and a bench with leather buckle restraints.

A ball gag is on the bench, along with a mask, a leash, and a collar.

The wall is lined with hooks, from which paddles, whips, and floggers dangle.

I circle the room to peruse his collection of instruments of pain. "This is quite a mini-bar of torture! Speaking of mini-bars, aren't you going to offer me a drink?"

"Such libations are against my religion."

"It's not against mine," I point out. "I can't imagine that Allah will frown upon you and your progeny for toasting our union with a glass of water."

He picks a flogger off a hook. "I will enjoy breaking you of your will, then mounting you."

"I take it that's a no to the drink?"

He lashes me across the shoulder. I wince, but I stay put.

He smiles. "Everyone has a crutch. I fear yours is alcohol. It makes most women silly—or worse still, sad." He raises his arm again—

Bringing it around to my backside. The slap is just as loud as it is painful—*which means it hurts like hell.*

My grimace makes him chortle with glee. "Ah! You liked it."

"No. I did not." I start for the door.

He beats me to it, blocking it. He's no longer smiling. "I did not give you permission to leave."

"Out of my way," I mutter.

This time, when he raises the flogger, I elbow him in the gut.

When he doubles over, I punch him in the kidney.

He falls with a thud and curls up in the fetal position.

"Well done," Jack murmurs into my ear bud.

I walk over to the bench and pick up the ball gag. It's a start, anyway. The leash and collar may be fun too.

I'm contemplating whether to leave him in the cage or to bind him, spread-eagle to the spanking bench when I feel a slight sting on my calf.

I turn around to find that Salem has managed to crawl over. He's pricked me with something—

And, suddenly, my leg is numb.

Before the rest of me goes that way too, I pull my gun from its holster under my shirt. I'm somewhat dizzy, but I can still aim and pull the trigger.

And, besides, if I miss the first time, I've got six other bullets.

I'll need them, because first one misses him completely. Thank goodness the master bedroom is down a hallway far enough from the front door that his guards can't hear the shot. Even if they did, I would imagine they've heard enough strange noises during Salem's exploits to stay put.

But this is no ordinary sex play. Salem knows he must fight for his life. Coming in close again, he trips me and I fall on top of him. He rolls on top of me as we wrestle for the gun.

Still, I hold on with all my might and pull the trigger one more time.

The next bullet's the charm: right to the heart, and muffled by his chest.

I can barely breathe as I shove him off my body.

"Donna, hang in there, I'm on my way," Jack calls out.

"But…how…?" Jack's O.K. Corral scenario comes to mind.

"The terrace."

I'm woozy, but I bend down anyway so that I can twist Salem's ring off of his finger. Then I rummage in his jacket pocket until I find his cell. I place both items in the secure pocket of my jacket.

I stumble out to the terrace, just in time to see a rappelling hook attached to a nylon cord fly over the banister.

Shit, I think, does he really think I'm climbing down in these heels? No way…

Not to worry. Jack tosses me over his shoulder. Thank God my eyes are too drowsy to stay open. Otherwise, I might barf.

Thinking of doing so brings Babette to mind. What will she do when she hears about Salem's death? Her exit strategy from the White House just went up in smoke.

She'll hate me even more for knowing I killed him.

Before I pass out, I hear Dominic. Despite the fact that he sounds a million miles away and under water, his voice still grates on me, especially when he declares, "I say, Jack, before we take off, would you mind if I clamber up and grab a few of the old boy's sex toys? I doubt he'll be needing them now…"

____

17

Wedding Bell Blues
____

Whereas the whole process of planning and holding your wedding should be blissful, in most cases it is stressful and, let's be honest, scary. You wonder, "Have I made the right decision about the day/the venue/my bridesmaids/(and, most of all), the man with whom I'll be spending the rest of my life?"

That depends on how you answer these three questions:

- *Question #1: Are you looking forward to your wedding day, despite all the things that could—and inevitably will—go wrong?*

Think for a moment. You're having an outside wedding, and it rains. A groomsman gets drunk and tosses his cookies onto your mother's shoes. You rip your veil on the heel of your shoe. Despite the fact that all of these things may seem frustrating at first, if your answer is "yes," good for you! You get the big picture: that, as time goes by, even those things that went wrong now add to the laughter and memories you'll have of the day.

- *Question #2: Are you ready for "the big day" to be over, so that you and your beloved can move on to the rest of your life? If you answered yes, then congratulations! Certainly, a lot of time and effort has been allocated for this one day of celebration of your lives together. Still, you realize that it dwarfs in comparison to the time and effort that will go into a marriage that will hopefully last to the end of your days.*

- *Question #3: Will you ever question the love you have for your betrothed? The right answer here is "yes." If you never question it, the relationship never grows. There should be misunderstandings and disagreements, because love isn't a fairy tale. It is a challenge—and sometimes a struggle—to shape two lives into one.*

If a third person gives you reason to question his love, don't settle it by wrestling with her in a tub filled with scented lube. Better to end your misery in a game of Russian roulette—for him.

(Helpful Hint: Load the gun for him. And yes, the more bullets, the better the outcome.)

"Rise and shine, sleepyhead." Jack's voice nudges its way through the brack and brine of my drugged slumber. "It's our wedding day, remember?"

I bolt upright so fast that my shoulder slams into his face. "Oh, my God! How long have I been out?"

"Jesus, Donna! Slow down! Both of us have to be there

for the I Do's, or it doesn't happen," he growls, as he places his hand over his eye. "You slept for twelve hours."

"Let me look at your eye," I insist.

He hesitates before moving his hand away.

I wince. "No shiner...I hope."

"If one appears, you'll officially be a husband beater."

I shrug. "Ha! Trust me, that rumor has been circulating for years! Why else would you have hung around, if not afraid of what I'd do if I caught you?"

And why else would the real Carl have up and left me, and our family, in the first place?

If only my neighbors knew the truth.

I grab Jack's arm. "How was the reaction to Salem's death?"

"There hasn't been any. The second Arnie broke the encryption on his phone, Abu texted Salem's bodyguards to stand down until further notice. They were last seen headed to the Silver Rein Strip Club. They're under the assumption that he's having too much fun with his new concubine." Jack grins slyly. "In the meantime, the cleaners have taken care of the Beverly Wilshire suite, and Emma deciphered the microdot. It contains a detailed floor plan of Lion's Lair, including all security codes, panic rooms, and the locations of armament caches kept within the compound."

"Why?" I wonder out loud.

"From the directive also embedded in the microdot, a full-scale jihadist invasion is to take place during the Middle East summit at Lion's Lair, which starts the day after tomorrow."

I leap out of bed and head to the window. Lion's Lair

looms over Hilldale, crowning the summit of its tallest bluff. "Has Ryan informed Lee of this?"

"He won't do so until he's positive Lee wasn't the owner of the cell phone used to contract Catherine's assassination."

"It makes sense, since the person who put out the hit and may be sabotaging the summit are one and the same," I murmur.

Jack holds up a finger. "Speaking of which, Arnie just texted me. Thanks to the false cell phone tower in Janie's birdhouse, the cell's GPS signal has been picked up within Lion's Lair."

"Good. Let's go." I hop into a pair of jeans and throw on a T-shirt. "Have Arnie link us to the cell's GPS so that we can track the user."

"Um...yeah, sure." Jack looks at his watch. "Hey, what do you think, should I take your dress and my tux along—you know, so that we don't have to run back home and grab them before the wedding begins?"

I lift onto my toes in order to kiss him on the nose. "Silly man. There's been a change in venue. Emma and Mary have it covered."

"Smart move. My tux is a rental. Considering all that's going down at Lion's Lair, one bloodstain and I own it."

He grabs my hand and out the door we go.

JACK AND I HAVE JUST ENTERED LION'S LAIR'S FOYER ROTUNDA when we hear Arnie's voice in our ear buds. "The signal is coming from the roof terrace."

We start down the hallway and leap into the elevator.

When the doors open next, it is on an idyllic tableau of a full breakfast *alfresco*.

Lee is at the head of a wrought iron table that seats eight. The chair opposite his—Babette's—is empty.

However, Todd is there, as are Eileen, Janie, Frannie, Narcissa, and Trisha.

Seeing us, Narcissa stands and starts our way. She's not smiling. "Oh! Since it's a sunset wedding, we weren't expecting you for several hours." She purses her lips, "In fact, I'd hoped to save you the trip of coming at all. Babette isn't feeling well, and won't be attending."

"It's not her cell," Arnie mutters in our ears.

"Good to hear," I say.

The others stare at me. "Oh! I don't mean Babette. I hope she feels better soon. But, yes, we talked yesterday—when she was feeling under the weather."

Lee leans back. His head is cocked, as if he doesn't believe me. Not that I blame him. He is quite aware of my opinion of his wife. Hey, can I help it that, by coincidence, my outburst describes how I really feel about Babette's absence?

Very slowly, Jack circles the room one way, while I go in the opposite direction. As I pass Eileen, Arnie murmurs, "No go."

I nod. Perhaps keeping my mouth shut is best.

"As such, and because of the preparation needed for the summit taking place the day after tomorrow, the wedding has been cancelled," Narcissa continues.

Lee frowns. "This is all news to me."

She purses her lips. "Sorry, sir, but it was Mrs. Chiffray's wish that we do so. In fact, last night Chantal sent out the cancellation missives to all the guests."

While she blathers through this weak excuse, I walk by Todd. "Arnie says, "Also clear."

I know I should take it at face value, but I whisper back anyway: "Are you sure?"

"Positive," Arnie replies.

Narcissa is finding it hard to hide her annoyance at my obliviousness. "But of course I'm sure! Ask Chantal yourself," she smirks. "Quite frankly, she found it a fairly easy task, since none of the guests who RSVP'd were close, personal friends of yours anyway."

At that moment, Jack passes Lee. Arnie mutters, "In the clear."

"POTUS is now free to know the status of this mission," Ryan reminds us.

I'm relieved for him. Lee's world is crashing down upon him in other ways.

Jack shrugs his disappointment, but shakes his head, to warn me off any sudden revelations to this roomful of suspects.

I'm now walking by Janie and Trisha—

"Donna, it's next to you! There!"

"No…Can't be." I shake my head adamantly.

"I swear," Arnie and Narcissa proclaim in unison. But whereas Arnie is being sincere, Narcissa mocks her declaration by crossing her heart.

"Okay, yeah, whatever," my response is to both of them.

Lee seems more taken aback than me. "This is bullshit, Narcissa! What the hell is wrong with Babette?"

"I don't…I don't know, sir. I'm only following orders."

"Not a good response," he warns her. "It didn't work at the Nuremberg Trials, and it doesn't cut muster here."

As she babbles through yet another weak explanation, I kiss Trisha on the forehead. "Good morning, sweetie. Ready to go home and get dressed for the wedding?" I'm angled in such a way that I've given myself enough cover to snatch Trisha's cell phone, which lies beside her orange juice glass. I lift it up and walk a few steps away with it.

Confused, Trisha's brow furrows. "But...But Mrs. Chiffray said it was called off."

"It's not the one," Arnie assures me.

"Yep... Well, we're just doing it differently," I tell my daughter.

Trisha frowns. "Can I still wear my dress?"

"But of course," I assure her, patting her head.

As I place it down, I reach for the one beside Janie's plate—

But it's gone.

"Janie, where is your phone, honey? Trisha was raving about it. Maybe I'll get the same model for her."

Janie giggles. "I never carry it because only Mummy calls me. Frannie must have it." She points toward the elevator door. "See?"

She's right. Frannie stands in the elevator. The phone, encased in a bedazzled pink and purple shell, is in her hand.

Her eyes meet mine.

She knows.

I run to the elevator—

The doors close in my face.

"Is there another way off the roof?" Jack asks Lee.

"A staircase, there." Lee points to the other side of the roof. "What the hell is happening?"

I'm closer, so I reach it first. "She has the phone that called Xia!" I shout. "Tell Secret Service to capture and detain her, not to—do anything else!"

The children's eyes open wide with concern. The last word I want to use is "kill."

I run down the stairs.

Jack is on my heels.

WE STOP ON THE NEXT LEVEL DOWN, LION'S LAIR'S FOURTH. "She could be on any of these floors," he points out. "We should split up. Take four and two. I'll take three and one." He's off.

Slowly, I open the door. I'm not packing heat, for obvious reasons: the Secret Service would have taken any weapon from me. They would have done the same to Frannie, so maybe we're on even footing.

Except for the scissors whizzing toward my face.

I duck in time. The scissors pierce the door behind me.

I grab them. "She's on four," I murmur into my ear bud.

From what I can tell, I'm in a foyer for the master suite. It contains a study, as well as a bedroom and an ensuite bathroom, both leading out to their own terrace.

I scan the study, ducking around the desk to make sure she isn't hiding there.

Nope, she's behind the door.

I realize this when a heavy book slams mid-center into my back.

By the time I right myself, she's run into the bedroom.

THE BED IS EMPTY. FOR SOME REASON, IT HASN'T BEEN made yet.

Frannie tries the bathroom door, but it's locked from the inside. If Babette is in there, I pray she stays put.

I have Frannie cornered. She crouches into a defensive position, ready for my attack.

"The Secret Service will be busting in here any moment now," I remind her. "Make it easy on yourself."

"They can't get in here. I locked the elevator, and the door to the stairs is bolted from the inside."

"Who are you, and why did you order Catherine's hit?"

She inches toward the terrace door. "Who I am is not important. Catherine's time was over. She was a threat. The same goes for Xia."

"As was the poor White House janitor. You ran him over with your car, then stole his cell phone."

She shrugs. "There is collateral damage in every war."

I strike at her with the scissors.

She dodges just in time. Her attempt at a sidekick misses my gut by an inch.

"You're Quorum, aren't you?"

"But of course!" She smirks. "The true masters of the universe, funding a world that thrives on commerce through chaos."

"Wow, now that's a truly snappy slogan." I swing the scissors again, this time drawing blood as I slice her thigh.

She screams and stumbles as she backs out onto the

terrace. Still, she riffs the party line. "You may stop me, but you know better than anyone that the Quorum is a thirteen-headed hydra. Each time you chop off a head, another grows in its place. I'm just one of many who have burrowed deep within the corridors of power."

I roll my eyes. "Get a grip, Frannie. At most, you're a pawn. Granted, a well-placed one. It was you who gave Salem the detailed schematic of Lion's Lair for the attack on the summit in two days, wasn't it?"

Her eyes grow big. "How did you—"

"Does it really matter—now that he's dead?"

"My Salem—*dead*?" Frannie's anguished cry is that of a lover's.

Make that two lovers: Babette's voice echoes hers from the far side of the terrace.

The first lady is dressed only in a silk robe. Her hair is disheveled and her eyes red-rimmed. She's been crying.

She must have heard our voices and come out of the bathroom to investigate the ruckus.

Now she knows Salem's fate as well.

Rage roils from her deep despair. Surprisingly, this time it is not aimed at me. She marches up to Frannie. "You were a nobody! I made you a confidant! I trusted you with"—Babette turns toward me, as if seeing me for the very first time—"with my child! And he was fucking you too?"

Frannie does the worst thing possible. She smiles.

There is something even crueler she can do: *taunt*. "You were much too easy a conquest, Babette, and much too needy," she sneers. "We laughed about it often."

Shamed, Babette lowers her eyes.

She doesn't need to raise them in order to throw an elbow into Frannie's stomach.

Frannie's gasp is sharp, but her scream is even louder as Babette, furious, shoves her over the balcony.

I rush to the edge. Four Secret Service men stare up at me.

Another three rush in through the battered door: Zeb, and others in his detail. Instinctively, he covers Babette. The other two tackle me to the terrace floor.

I'm not released until Lee shouts, "Stand down! *Stand down!*"

I am lifted up by Jack, who cradles me in his arms.

Lee is doing the same to Babette.

18

Old, New, Borrowed, Blue

Traditional weddings demand that every bride wears something that represents these four items:

- *Something old. Preferably, an heirloom. See if his mother isn't willing to part with any jewelry worth six figures or more. If she says, "Hell, no," take it as a broad hint to how the rest of your life will be, now that she is in it.*
- *Something new. This is where ditching your flannel nightie for brand-new lingerie comes in handy. (No, the Spanx you need to get into your wedding dress doesn't count.)*
- *Something borrowed. See "Something old." The fact that his mother won't realize you broke into her safe to get her antique ring until she sees it on your finger shouldn't deter you from at least trying to kill two traditions at once.*
- *Something blue. Should your groom be as upset as his*

mother at your light-fingered snatch, payback is obvious: a wedding evening in which the debauchery he longs for falls on deaf ears—thus the term, "wedding ball blues."

"I love weddings!" Aunt Phyllis exclaims. "All the men get soused—which means that they're easy too!"

"You have a one-track mind," I chide her.

My aunt shrugs off my admonishment. "At my age, having any mind at all is a blessing."

"So I take it that wherever this wedding takes place, it'll at least have booze?" I ask slyly.

Mary and Trisha snicker. Trisha wags a finger at me. "Mommy, we've already told you—it's a *surprise*."

Wherever they take me will be perfectly fine.

I'll be with those who love me most.

It's been an afternoon of laughter with my bridal party—Phyllis, Mary, Trisha, and Emma—who are here to assist me as I dress. I've never seen them lovelier.

Or happier.

I am blessed.

Each has her role. Trisha's assignment was to lay out all the items in Emma's large make-up case. She was determined to doll me up. "Glam, but not Goth, right? Like an Oscar nominee," is how Emma put it.

"Works for me," I assure her.

"Mommy, I know what counts for 'something new.'" Trisha points to my dress. "But what is your old, your borrowed, and your blue?"

"Ah, good point," I sigh. "I haven't even had time to think about it."

"I've got your blue," Aunt Phyllis declares. From her purse she pulls out a pale blue silk garter. "The boys at Meat Market Lounge were supposed to put this on the bride." She grins broadly at me. "Since you ran off so early, the honor was all mine."

I shake my head in awe. "That doesn't surprise me." As I slip it on my leg, I add, "You'll get it back after the honeymoon. That way it kills two birds with one stone: something borrowed and something blue."

Aunt Phyllis arches a brow. "So happy it'll be getting a little action."

"As for my something old"—I open my jewelry box and pull out the antique heart-shaped locket that was left to me by my mother. I hold it up to the others—"I'll wear this."

I put the locket in a safe place after Carl disappeared. It was too precious to wear, since it held the only picture I had of him. The locket's other side holds a photo of our children. When Carl came back to me under the guise of taking down the Quorum, I started wearing it again, but only on special occasions.

Long ago I should have replaced his photo with one of Jack. I'll do so on our honeymoon.

I now hand it to Mary, who clasps it around my neck.

Each step of the way, Aunt Phyllis and Mary have been taking turns capturing these special moments with my aunt's digital camera. The photos may not be as polished as the ones Mario Testino would have shot, but who cares? They'll be candid, which is the only way to truly capture the raw emotions of the day.

I can't wait to see the look on Jack's face.

I close my eyes to imagine it:

His eyes widening in astonishment of all that he finds beautiful about me—not outside, but within;

The catch in his throat as he stumbles to find the words to express his awe;

And, finally, the sly grin that promises fun and games when the dress comes off.

Aunt Phyllis scrutinizes me through my vanity mirror. "If I had your figure, I'd be beating them off with a stick."

At the very least, the past week of running around in search of the terrorist embedded in the White House has helped me drop a pound or two. My wedding gown fits like a glove.

Noting my bliss, Aunt Phyllis's gaze shifts to Mary. "I guess you'll soon be breaking hearts too, missy."

Mary, who has the honor of zipping me up, shakes her head. "Life is much too short to play those kinds of games." She blushes. No doubt she's thinking of Evan. Jeff has teased him unmercifully about the Bunnies' care and feeding of him. "The right guy for me will have to prove himself every step of the way"—she pauses when our eyes meet in the mirror—"like Dad does for Mom, each and every day."

Dad. These days, it rolls so easily off her tongue.

As it should. As hard as Jack works to prove his love for me every day, he has done the same for her.

"I think Evan is hot." Aunt Phyllis's declaration to Mary comes with a nudge to me.

Mary's cheeks pink up. "Obviously, I'm not his type. You saw that for yourself."

"A boob job does not a relationship make." My aunt's

advice is cockeyed, but sage in its own way. "He'll grow out of it. They all do. Sort of." She looks down at her own ample bosom, which looks smashing in her gown.

The dress she chose was enthusiastically approved by Mary and Trisha: an ice blue Kay Unger column gown boasting a bateau neckline and three-quarter length sleeves, with sequins embedded in its full-length lace overlay.

The final touch: Emma does my hair. First, she sweeps it into a low topknot—loose, with tendrils falling on either side of my face.

Gazing at my reflection in the mirror, Trisha whispers, "My mommy is beautiful."

"I'll second that." At the sound of Lee's voice, everyone freezes.

His eyes find mine in the mirror. The depth of their sadness breaks my heart. Neither of us regrets our friendship, just the circumstances that put us together.

And keep us apart.

We were drawn together by a mutual enemy. Carl was the face of it. He may be gone, but the Quorum lives on.

Our allegiance only survives on our trust. It is why Lee is here, now.

Emma taps Mary and Aunt Phyllis on the arm. "We still have some last minute details to call in to the venue," she reminds them.

"Oh…yeah, right!" Phyllis tries to sound convincing, but knowing her, the moment she heard Babette ditched on the wedding, I'm sure she pulled out her trusty Rolodex and called in some favors.

I fully anticipate that Jack and my I-do's will be shouted over "B Sixteen…again, B Sixteen…" and "N-Four…I said,

N-Four…" in one of the many bingo parlors between here and Pasadena.

Yet another great memory we'll share.

I wait until the door is closed before teasing him: "You do know it's bad luck to see the bride before the wedding, don't you?"

"That bit of bad luck is only reserved for the groom." The regret in his voice hangs heavy between us.

"I'm glad you'll be attending, Lee. It means so much to me."

The fact that I don't mention Jack in the same breath is not lost on Lee. He chuckles. "Attending? I'm marrying you and Jack. I think you realize how special you are to me, Donna. Frankly, I wouldn't have missed this for the world." He is now close enough to stroke my head. Very gently, he wraps a tendril of my hair around his finger. He waits until it uncoils, then sighs. "I wish I could have waited until you got back from your honeymoon for your debriefing of Operation China Doll, but as you can imagine, I'm curious about your findings, what with Frannie's death this morning."

I nod. "I know." Other than my vanity stool, the only chair in the room is piled high with the sweaty clothes I wore earlier today, as I chased around after the very evildoers that are now on his mind too. I can only offer him the bed for a place to sit. I nod toward it. "I think you should take a seat."

"That bad, eh?" He plops down, but leans forward, fists clenched, as if preparing for the worst.

A punch in the jaw wouldn't hurt half as much. We both know it.

Lee Chiffray is ready to take his lumps.

"YOU ASKED THAT ACME CONDUCT A THOROUGH AND unhindered investigation," I begin. "Thank you for that."

He shrugs. "It was the only way it would publicly pass any sniff test. And, personally, I knew it was the only way you'd ever trust me, from this point forward."

"You were right." I smile. "The good news is that both you and Babette were cleared as suspects in the contract killing of Catherine Martin."

"Babette too?" He seems relieved. "I'm glad to hear it. As for me"—he allows himself a sly grin—"I could have told you that. In fact, if I remember correctly, I did. I presume I have your trust now."

"Yes, Lee. But don't get cocky. Believe me, you were prime suspects for quite a while."

He frowns. "How so?"

"On the night of my engagement party, I lifted one of the cell phones that was in your pocket."

"Seriously—you did that?" He laughs so hard that he's choking. "Pickpocketing the president? That takes nerve."

"Tell me about it. I was nervous as hell. The last place any woman wants to spend her honeymoon is the Federal Prison Camp in Alderson."

He raises a brow. "I take it that the cell didn't contain what you were looking for."

"On the contrary. It was the one used to correspond with Xia about the hit on Catherine."

"But how could that be? If the hit was contracted by Frannie—" He thinks for a moment, then his eyes open wide. "I think I have the answer. That night, the battery on

Babette's phone died. She borrowed Jamie's cell so that Narcissa and Chantal could keep in touch with her while she entertained guests."

"The last mystery solved, then." Now, for the hard part. I come over to sit beside him. "You were once on the executive board of Salem's Company, Graffias International."

He frowns. "You're right. It was years ago. Why would that be a problem?"

"Lee, Graffias is a front for the Quorum. We've known for some time that the Quorum launders its money through Graffias."

He leans back, stunned. "Oh…hell."

"In fact, Salem's ring—the one with the black crest with the number thirteen—confirmed his allegiance to the Quorum." I take a deep breath. "Salem was terminated yesterday, by me."

"During your rendezvous with him." He tries to keep all emotion out of his voice, but it cracks at the end.

"Believe me, Lee, I would have avoided it at all costs, except for the fact that Acme's covert analysis detected a microdot secreted in a hollow pocket beneath the ring's crest. It was crucial that we retrieve it."

Lee nods. "Ryan has already filled me in on its full contents: the details of the Islamic State's planned attack on the supposedly secret summit of Middle Eastern leaders that is being held at Lion's Lair, the day after tomorrow. Talk about getting rid of all the obstacles standing in the Islamic State's way, in one swift blow!" He shakes his head, stunned. "Ryan also informed me that the ring's intel includes the locations of safe houses for jihadist cells that are currently embedded in the U.S. The NSA is rounding them up now.

Still, as we speak, jihadists are attempting to breach our border with Mexico. More have been arriving by private and commercial flights all week. The NSA is deploying Special Forces swat teams to stop them before they reach the Los Angeles metropolitan area. Checkpoints are already set up within a ten-mile radius around Hilldale." He grimaces. "We're ready for them."

"If they show up at all," I reply.

He looks at me sharply. "Why wouldn't they? Word of Salem's death has yet to get out."

"One person knows of it," I counter. "Babette."

"And you suspect Babette?" He shakes his head, confused. "But—but you said Babette was cleared from any wrongdoing!"

"Yes, she was—in regard to owning the phone that negotiated the hit on Catherine Martin by Liang Xia. But we also know that Xia's correspondence with Frannie was forwarded to a third party. The GPS showed the location as the White House, but because it was a dark device, there was no way to trace the cell."

"Donna, if Babette were Quorum, why would she have pushed Frannie off the balcony?" he argues.

"With Frannie cornered, she was a risk to the mole." I hesitate, then add: "And then there's the fact that Frannie was also Salem's lover."

He bows his head as that sinks in.

When finally he raises it again, it's to mutter, "I…I can't believe it."

I reach for his arm. "But, Lee, there are too many coincidences." I count them down on my fingers. "Number One: are you aware that Babette's first husband, Jonah Breck, was also on the Graffias board—in fact, the same year as you?"

"What? ...No!"

"You never met him at any board meetings?"

Lee shakes his head adamantly. "The meetings were held annually. During the year I was on the board, my father was dying of cancer. It was one of the reasons I chose to leave the board after only a year." He paces the room. "I can see how this all seems. No wonder Jack finds it so hard to trust me."

I have nothing to say to that because it's true.

As for Lee's claims, they can be easily checked. I know Jack well enough that he'll do so. I hope it'll clear Lee in Jack's mind once and for all, and that's a good thing.

"Number Two: the man the Widow Breck chose to liquidate Jonah's assets—Carl—was a Quorum hit man. He chose you as the potential buyer. Not only did you buy Breck Industries—including Fantasy Island—you met and fell in love with Babette."

"Lucky me," he says dryly.

"Number Three: her name is currently listed as a Graffias board member."

"She can't be! She knows better." Rather than facing me, he stares out the window.

"And, four: her most recent lover was Quorum as well as Graffias's chief executive."

The blood drains from Lee's face as the implication sinks in:

The first lady of the United States may be a terrorist.

"Lee, another known Quorum operative was listed on Graffias's executive board along with Babette and Salem. Do you know an Eric Weber?"

He thinks for a moment, then nods slowly.

"How are you acquainted?"

"Salem met him right after we graduated from college. Eric helped Salem diversify his holdings by convincing him that the Middle East was too unstable for the amount of money and assets Salem had there. Out of the diversification came Graffias International. What does Eric have to do with anything?"

"He was Carl's first handler. And out of Graffias came the Quorum," I murmur. "Oh, what a tangled web the Quorum weaves."

"Oh…shit. You mean to tell me…" He hits his fist in frustration. "He was the 'Mr. Weber' you and Jack found in France, who could have testified against Carl's terrorist acts?" This knowledge hangs so heavy on Lee that he must sit down again. "At one point, Salem approached me about a merger between Graffias and my company, Global World Industries. I'm glad I trusted my gut and turned him down." He shrugs. "Not that it matters. My purchase of Breck Industries put me in bed with the Quorum, quite literally. It's my cross to bear."

I nod. "I can say the same."

"Well, I, for one, am tired of being tied up in it." He shakes his head angrily. "I'm sure you are too."

Now, the telltale moment: "Will you authorize the further investigation of your wife?"

He closes his eyes. "I can't, Donna, because Babette— well, she's pregnant."

Ah, so she finally told him. "Have you considered the possibility that it's Salem's baby?"

He nods. Lee and I are beyond any reason for pretense.

Finally he says, "I'll let Ryan know he has the authorization to do…to do what is necessary regarding Babette."

"I'm sorry, Lee."

His eyes seek out mine. What he finds there relieves him, because it is not pity but concern.

Gently, he kisses me, but he knows better than to let his lips linger on mine. He stands, honoring me with a slight bow. "I'd better hit the road. I've got a wedding to officiate."

"Oh, really? Where is it taking place?" I ask innocently.

"You won't get it out of me, Mrs.…well, soon to be Mrs. Craig. Like the rest of the wedding party, I've been sworn to secrecy."

He leaves without looking back. It's for the best. I pat away my tears before my bridal party comes storming back in to whisk me away for parts unknown.

19

Happily Ever After

Yes, you will live happily ever after.

But not before some fighting, screaming, and crying.

There is no gain without pain.

And there is no make-up sex either.

So that you don't extend the inevitable (in this case, the make-up sex), here are a few tips to move things along:

- *Tip #1: Don't go to bed mad. However, if he insists on doing so, make sure the gun is under your pillow, not his.*
- *Tip #2: When you make up, kiss. In fact, hug too. And fondle, which may lead to undressing, which gets you to home plate with a smile on your face in record time.*
- *Tip #3: Choose your fights wisely. Frankly, "sex" is just as fun as "make-up sex." Skipping the barbs and accusations may not get your heart rate spiking as fast, but a cardio workout—say, running naked around the*

house as you play Chase Me, Kiss Me—will have
exactly the same effect, and is much more fun.

I WILL NEVER BE HAPPIER THAN NOW, AS I WALK THROUGH THE sand to join my beloved by the water's edge.

I'm sure Aunt Phyllis feels the same way, since she had Dominic walk her down the aisle to her seat of honor in the first row, center, for my sunset wedding on Crystal Cove beach, in front of the Sand Dollar Café, off Newport Coast Road.

It is where Jack and I had our first date.

Later, we'll have our reception inside the restaurant.

My party planners, Emma and Mary, have done well.

The way the chairs are set up, there is no bride's side or groom's side. Everyone here knows of the tenuous lives we lead. Certainly Ryan and the whole Acme office, but also Coquette, Lady Dannie, Katy May, and Maria as well.

Even one of Jack's oldest and dearest friends, Anton Gregorescu, is here. Anton and Jack once loved the same woman, albeit at different times—Valentina, Jack's first wife. Anton can also claim that he risked his own life to save those Jack loved most: her and me. It wasn't easy for our wheel-chair-bound friend to make it here from Paris. His friendship has no bounds.

I am preceded by Trisha, who tosses hydrangea petals of all different hues into the air. They dance in a brisk breeze over the heads of our guests before floating down.

Janie, who sits on the first row beside her mother, blows kisses at her best friend. She has elected not to wear the same frock as Trisha. Perhaps that was Babette's decision, since they are dressed like twins: from their hot pink designer lace sheaths to their white gloves and shoes, and down to their tiny clutch purses.

My maid of honor, Mary, is walked down the aisle by Jack's best man: Ryan. They are followed by Emma, who is accompanied by Evan. Bringing up the rear is our ring bearer: Nicky Locklear, in the arms of his father, Arnie. The toddler holds a satin pillow with two rings tied to it. One I had admired that day as we stood in front of the Tiffany window: the two-and-a-half carat diamond that sits above a band inlaid with channel-set diamonds on each side. Jack's wedding band complements it in its design.

My man doesn't miss a trick.

With my son's arm in mine, I make my way toward Jack. When we reach Jack's side, Jeff shakes his hand then kisses my cheek before joining Mary, Emma, and Trisha at my side.

Our eyes meet once more. I mouth *I love you.*

My son answers me by making a heart with his hands and holding it at his chest.

As I turn to face Jack, Lee begins with a few words on the things that should matter in a union between two people who love each other: honesty, devotion, passion, and love. He speaks from the heart with examples of those traits, personally observed by him in either Jack, or me, or both of us.

Jack looks surprised at his reminiscences. Not me. I have yet another reason to call Lee my friend. I hope Jack now feels the same way.

When the time comes for us to voice our commitment to each other, Jack does so first. As I listen to his vows to love, honor, and cherish me, I suddenly feel the presence of those who are here in spirit only.

My father, who walked me down the aisle to my first husband, loved my mother so deeply that her untimely death from breast cancer broke his spirit, and drove him to drink.

My mother's death was the catalyst for my own loss of innocence and fierce protection of the lives nearest and dearest to me.

Just over Jack's shoulder, my very first love, Robert Martin, smiles proudly at me. His needless death, orchestrated by his power-hungry wife, Catherine, will never destroy his great works on behalf of others less fortunate. For once, I don't feel his longing for me, only his boundless joy on my behalf. My way of honoring his loss at the hand of Carl is to keep my vow to protect his son, Evan.

Even Valentina is with us. She smiles, but her essence is filled with regret. Had she loved Jack more than Carl, I wouldn't be standing at his side today.

And yes, Carl is here, too. As the waves churn and crash angrily against the shore, I vow my everlasting love to Jack Craig in a clear and steadfast voice.

Fidelity. Trust. Eternity.

I never had it with Carl. Then again, had he been able to provide it, I would have never met Jack.

It is enough reason to forgive Carl for leaving me.

Finally, he can rest in peace.

And now, enveloped in sweetness and promises of Jack's first kiss as my husband, I will go on with the rest of my life.

～

OUR GUESTS' CONGRATULATIONS ARE HEARTFELT. OUR CHILDREN and Aunt Phyllis are the first to gather around us, in a group hug. Mary makes sure that Evan is included in it, grasping his hand firmly and drawing him in with her. When he pulls back shyly, she simply says, "Evan, it's okay! *You're our brother.*"

From the look of longing on his face, I know he is both touched and disappointed. Their mutual attraction grew into a shared adoration. Now, only through time and random acts of trust, can it ripen into a love fueled by an everlasting passion.

"Give it time," I whisper into his ear as we hug.

He blushes at the realization that I've read his thoughts. It's a shame he can't read mine.

When the group hug breaks away, Aunt Phyllis hugs Jack, as if she'll never let him go. "I guess we're stuck with this one after all."

I wouldn't have it any other way.

FOR ONCE IN HIS LIFE, RYAN HAS NO QUALMS WRAPPING ME IN A bear hug. "It's about damn time," he growls.

I frown up at him. "What, you mean you actually had doubts that Jack and I would ever marry?"

"Hell no. He was gaga over you years before you even knew he existed. All of this"—he motions at the guests—"was inevitable."

"It must be wonderful to play God," I retort.

He laughs. "Best gig ever. You should try it some time."

Abu moves in for a kiss. I accommodate with that, and a hug. "You know, you've always been like a sister to me."

I pat his arm. "And you are the brother I never had."

"You know I'll always have your back, right, Donna?"

"And you'll be duly rewarded with any pie of your choice."

He lights up. "I still think there's a business in it."

"It's a bandwidth issue," I remind him. "Too many terrorists, so little time."

My declaration erases the smile from his face. He knows this better than anyone else. Still, ever the optimist, he shrugs. "Not forever. In the meantime, I'll finesse our business plan."

Emma and Arnie are laughing with Jack about something. I poke my head into their threesome. "Was it something I said?"

"It's more like everything you do," Arnie blurts out. "Emma said that when she grows up, she wants to be just like you."

Emma frowns. She doesn't like being outed as my fangirl.

To show her the feeling is mutual, I hug her, but also whisper: "Be careful what you wish for." Her smile fades as she glances over at Nicky, who is now wrapped in Mary's arms. I know what she's thinking: would the trade-off be worth it?

I ask myself that every day of my life. Every night, I say a prayer of thanks that, as of yet, I have nothing to regret.

Dominic's congratulations are delivered with a full-on open mouth kiss.

After shoving him off, I gasp, "What the hell are you doing?"

He smiles knowingly. "Allowing you one last chance to give in to your erotic fantasies about what might have been, had I not jilted you."

Wiping his spittle from my lips, I growl, "Remind me again: on what occasion was I quote-unquote jilted?"

He rolls his eyes. "Are you off your chump? Why, on the way to Fantasy Island!" Noting my blank stare, he sighs mightily. "Nipped in the bud during our Mile High Club hijinks. As I recall, you got somewhat more possessive than agreed upon." He clicks his tongue. "Not that I blame you, my dear. I've been blessed—or shall I say, cursed? No, no, blessed is truly the apt description—with the profile of a Greek god. Happens all the time." He turns sideways so that I may admire it.

"That wasn't me, Dominic. You were tag-teamed by a couple of flight attendants."

"Oh?" A faint smile rises on his lips as the memory corrects itself. "By Jove, you're right! Well, blow me down!"

"I'd prefer to blow you up," I mutter.

"Ah, very well. Then consider our little congratulatory kiss my wedding gift to you," he proclaims magnanimously. "It's one you'll never forget, eh?"

"I'll say," I mutter. "The memory of it will haunt me for a lifetime."

Dominic doesn't hear me. Lady Dannie's seductive wink has the same effect on him as a dog whistle on a mongrel: he's panting.

I'm still shaking my head at his audacity when the Chiffrays approach us. This time, Lee's congratulatory kiss is quick and formal. "May you share a lifetime of love," he says to Jack.

Babette leans into me. I'm expecting a couple of perfunctory air kisses. What I get instead is a real hug.

Her statement to me is just as heartfelt, albeit somewhat off-putting: "I don't envy you."

For what, the job I do? Marrying Jack? For whatever tribulations are yet to come my way?

I could say the same about her, but I don't.

She'll find out soon enough.

ANTON'S HUG IS STRONG AND LONG, AS YOU'D EXPECT FROM A former gymnast. His hold on me lingers, as if somehow he is channeling Valentina. "Jack's happiness is now complete."

"How about yours, Anton?" I ask.

His shrug is not Gallic shorthand, but his personal resignation to a lifetime of loving a woman who didn't, and couldn't, love him back. "Life gets easier with each passing day," he assures me.

Maria, Katy May, Coquette and Lady Dannie have bonded during their time together. Besides flirting outrageously with all the single men at the party, they take turns toasting us—or I should say roasting him—with one exaggerated story after another about Jack's cleverness under fire. Unable to crack his façade of memory loss to all of his supposed derring-do, they turn their attentions on Dominic, mercilessly teasing him to pick up the gauntlet of lover-spy and run with it.

"I say, old boy, had I known how many old flames you'd

left flickering in your wake, I would have encouraged the two of you to tie the knot in a more timely manner." He fans the hotel security cards each of these lovely ladies has slipped him sometime during the evening.

"So, what's your guess?" Jack asks, as Maria entices Dominic to dance a samba with her. "Do the cards belong to empty rooms?"

"More than likely, rooms that have been assigned to drunken sailors on leave, who won't appreciate a dandy Brit in a tux snoring in their bed."

Jack laughs until he falls on the floor. "God, I hope you're right." He holds up a glass of wine to toast the women now referred to as his Jack Pack.

JACK MUST HAVE REMEMBERED THE NAME OF THE TRIO THAT played here at the Sand Dollar on the night of that first date, because they are here now. The lead singer, Andrèe Belle, is as lovely as ever. Our first dance as husband and wife is to the same song, too: *At Last.*

"Happy, Mrs. Craig?" he murmurs in my ear.

I chuckle. "Ecstatically so, Mr. Craig. Especially when you call me that."

Jack shakes his head in wonder. "You know, at some point, I'll have to go back to using your given name." Jack takes me out on the deck.

"Perhaps after our one year anniversary," I replay. "If it's any consolation, I waited twice that long for you to say it."

"Good point. Anything to make you happy." He dips me.

I hang upside down for only a moment—

But, it's long enough to see a ghost.

He stands out by the shore. It's too dark to see his face, but his height and stance are familiar…

Oh, my God. He's here.

At least, I think it's him.

I'm tapped on the shoulder by Mary. "Mind if I cut in?" she asks me.

"By all means."

She gives me a peck on the cheek before Jack whisks her away.

When I turn back around, the ghost is gone.

At least, that is what he wants me to think, but I know better.

JACK IS SUCH A GENTLEMAN. EVERY WOMAN IN THE ROOM GETS a dance with my handsome groom.

Babette got her dance immediately after Mary. It was my daughter's idea. She should intern with the United States Diplomatic Corps. I'll put in a word for her with Lee.

Eventually, Jack gets down to asking Lee's secretary, Eileen. In order to dance with Jack, she left her clutch purse on the table. Maybe because of Lee's attempts to relax and have fun, she's been on her cell phone constantly, fielding calls on his behalf. I presume some of them have to do with the jihadist sting going down right now.

She comes back to the table, breathless.

"I'm going to the lady's room," I say, handing her the purse.

"I think I'll join you," she replies with a sigh. "Tiny bladders and boogying down don't really go together."

In the restroom, there is only one stall. "You're the bride. You should go first," she declares.

"Are you sure?" I ask.

"I insist." She turns to freshen her lipstick.

I hurry, and she makes small talk. "What a day you've had!" she exclaims. "First Frannie, and now your wedding! And I thought my job was crazy."

"I'm sure Janie was upset."

"Ironically, she seemed relieved that, as Babette put it, 'Frannie left us so suddenly.' I think she is starved for her mother's attention, don't you?"

If she thinks I'm dissing on Babette, she's wrong. "I'm not around them enough to say. But, every girl needs more mommy time."

I've barely flushed and exited the stall when she runs inside.

I don't realize she's left her clutch on the lavatory counter until it buzzes yet again. The clutch is partially open, so it's easy to see the Caller ID lit up on the display:

It is my long-lost ghost.

"It's not polite to snoop," Eileen hisses in my ear. I feel the barrel of her gun in the small of my back. "Shall we head out the fire exit? Let's take a walk down the beach. My gun has a suppressor and the waves are loud enough that no one should hear anything. They may not find you for quite a while."

I nod, but say nothing. Despite all the Secret Service and Acme agents in the building, I'd rather disarm her somewhere out of the sightline of my children.

The same goes, should I get shot.

The hallway is empty. She beckons me to move in front of her. "Walk quickly," she commands.

"In this dress and these heels? You're dreaming," I mutter.

The next thing I know, she gives a gasp.

I turn around in time to see her collapse in Lurch's arms.

A tiny syringe is sticking out of Eileen's neck. Her eyes flutter for a moment, then close.

Apparently, forever. I don't find a pulse on her wrist.

"Thank God," I murmur. "Aconite?"

Lurch nods.

"How did you know about her?"

"I've suspected since I was first given this detail." He shrugs. "Watching the president gives you an opportunity to watch those around him. She'd been with him for so long that he took too much for granted. And besides"—he glances away—"Babette never liked her."

Babette?

So, he's the Secret Service agent whom Babette's trainer, Walton, saw kissing her in the limo.

He's in love with her. But surely he knows of her trysts with Salem.

Does he know about the baby too?

The hopelessness in his eyes tells me that Babette's new and unusual circumstance won't change his feelings for her. He confirms it when he says, "Mr. al-Sadah's extermination was necessary for everyone involved."

"Lurch, did the president suspect Eileen too?" I ask.

"After Frannie's death this morning, he noticed that Eileen was too antsy. I suggested surveillance. It paid off.

We've been tracking her calls, as well as her data transmissions from this."

He unpins the dead woman's brooch from her chest and tosses it to me.

"Quite a little souvenir." As I toss it back, I pocket her cell phone, handing back mine instead.

He's too busy calling in a cleanup crew to notice. By the time he does, I'll have what I need from her phone.

I head out down the hallway, but duck out onto the deck then toward the beach before hacking her phone with the scanner.

When the cell opens, I read the last text message. It shows the coordinates to a spot just a quarter-mile down the beach.

Soon, my ghost and I will be face to face.

HE HAS HIS BACK TO ME AS HE WATCHES A TUMULTUOUS TIDE: *Sturm und Drang* created not by the pull of the moon, but the geopolitical turbulence soon to hit our shores.

After all this time, I'm surprised I recognize him at all:

Eric Weber.

His silver mane flows straight back in the blustery wind now coming off the ocean. In fact, it is blowing too hard for him to hear me approach.

But, spies have uncanny instincts. When I'm twenty feet from him, he turns around. His disappointment shows itself only for a moment before his mouth molds into a smile. "Ah! The blushing bride comes to greet me"—he feigns a glance in either direction—"and without an entourage bearing arms, I see."

"You're an unexpected guest." For tickles and giggles, I dimple up. "Should I pretend that your invitation got lost in the mail?"

"We are beyond game playing, you and I." He loses his smile. "I take it Eileen has been taken into custody."

"You could say that." No need to tell him of her untimely demise. Let him sweat it out.

He shrugs. "A pity. But life always provides an upside. Salem's untimely death, for example."

So, he knows. If so, the invasion of the summit has been called off.

Thank God for that.

"It leaves an opening on the board of Graffias International. Your resume is a bit spotty in places, but you do provide an interesting skill set."

"Seriously, Eric? You're turning this into a job interview?"

He grins. "I realize my timing is less than ideal. But isn't that the case with all of life's opportunities?"

I shake my head, awed at his chutzpah. "I guess I should be flattered, but I can't say I am. I'll take a pass."

"I don't give up easily," he promises.

Or perhaps it's a threat.

He walks down the beach.

I'd follow, but I'd never catch him.

Besides, I'd ruin my dress, and I've already promised it to Trisha.

Hopefully, he'll be picked up in a dragnet that begins the moment I get back.

____

20

How You Know the Honeymoon
is Over
____

The time leading up to the wedding seemed interminable.

The actual day of the big event went in the blink of an eye.

Now that the hoopla is over, can the marriage itself keep you enthralled?

Sure it can! But you must:

1. *Remember all the wonderful reasons you married him. Granted, it has nothing to do with his smelly feet and occasionally bad breath, but everything to do with his random acts of sweetness and great sex. (Helpful hint: Stock up on mouthwash, and make sure he changes his socks every day.)*
2. *Remind him of all the reasons he married you, too. Just because he's around twenty-four-seven doesn't mean you should forget to work out, wash up, dress up, and put on make-up. (Helpful hint: You took him off the open market. To ensure both of you stay off, retain the magic as well as your gym membership.)*

3. *Practice showing your love—every day, and in every way. Yes, S-E-X. But also with kindness, patience, and giving him the benefit of the doubt. Unless, of course, another woman's panties show up in your bed. (Helpful hint: Have the kindness to give him a head start, and the patience to aim before firing.)*

JACK IS IN NO RUSH TO TAKE OFF MY DRESS.

I follow his lead. Slowly, I pull one end of his tux bow. When, finally, it unravels in my hand, I toss it to one side.

He licks his lips in anticipation of my next move.

I don't keep him waiting too long. Before twisting off his cufflinks, my fingers stroke his wrists. Before unbuttoning his tux shirt, I massage his nipples.

At that point, he pulls me down onto the bed with him. His attempt to release me from my gown is a comedy of errors. Finally, he gives up on the futile effort of inching it up over my breasts.

"How did you get into this contraption?" he growls.

I lift my left arm, revealing the zipper under it. "Try it with your teeth," I taunt him.

"To hell with that."

A second later, it's off.

He groans at his next challenge: My Spanx.

To make it up to him, I unbuckle his belt, and yank down his pants.

As I'd hoped, it revives his efforts to leave me solely in my birthday suit.

Mission accomplished, he declares, "From here on out, we stay naked," he declares.

He'll have no argument from me.

My kiss proves it.

"You promised to stay naked," I remind him.

"I forgot about water."

I point toward the honeymoon suite's mini-bar. "In there, along with stuff that will give it a kick—like scotch."

"Which brings me to a second reason to cover up the family jewels: ice."

I sigh mightily. "Okay, but make it snappy. Satisfaction was guaranteed to the Now Mrs. Craig. I'm holding you to it."

If Jack's kiss is a precursor for what is to come, there will be no reason to ever trade him in for a new model. And I certainly won't be giving in to my body's pleas for sleep.

Besides his tux pants, he puts on his dress shirt. At least he doesn't button it up. Any woman walking the halls is in for a cheap thrill.

It's my gift to her.

He whistles as he goes out the door.

If I'd fallen back asleep, I would not have thought to wonder what the hell was taking him so long.

The hotel bar has a piano. After he saw the bill for the wedding, he may feel he has to play for tips.

Need I remind him that he's got a much better way to be spending his time?

I now feel the need to break our cardinal rule, and slip into something. Unlike Jack, I dig through my suitcase for yoga pants and a T-shirt. It's not exactly the sexiest attire for a wedding night, but it'll do for traipsing through the hotel in search of my husband.

THE BLOODY PATH STARTS TWO DOORS AWAY.

I run to the elevator. I pray as I push the button, but of course he won't be in there.

It comes up empty, except for one of the buttons from his dress shirt.

It too is smeared in blood.

Oh…*Fuck!*

I've lost another husband.

To the Quorum, no less.

EILEEN'S CELL IS IN MY CLUTCH PURSE. I'D PLANNED TO HAND IT over to Arnie to scrub. He'll get it, one way or another but first things first.

It beckons me to do what I know I must, if I'm to save the man I love.

When the cell comes alive, I hit the most recent call.

Eric doesn't say my name, he just laughs. "You didn't waste any time."

"Just tell me what it will take to get my husband back."

"But I have told you, my dear."

Despite knowing that every second matters, I count to ten. Finally, I whisper, "Okay, I'm in."

"Easier said than done," he warns me. "There will be a series of initiation tests. Should you pass them with flying colors, your husband lives."

He rings off.

As I stare down at the phone, I think, *What have I done?*

I've given Jack a chance to survive until I find him. Or perhaps a chance to escape.

In the meantime, I must be a traitor to my country.

Now I am married to the Quorum.

—THE END—

Next Up for Donna!

The Housewife Assassin's Husband Hunting Hints

(Book 12)

There is only one way for housewife assassin Donna Stone to save her husband and mission leader, Jack Craig, from torture and termination: become a traitor and act as a double agent for the terrorist organization known as the Quorum.

Other Books by Josie Brown

The True Hollywood Lies Series

Hollywood Hunk

Hollywood Whore

The Totlandia Series

The Onesies - Book 1 (Fall)

The Onesies - Book 2 (Winter)

The Onesies - Book 3 (Spring)

The Onesies - Book 4 (Summer)

The Twosies - Book 5 (Fall)

The Twosies – Book 6 (Winter)

The Twosies - Book 7 (Spring)

The Twosies - Book 8 (Summer)

More Josie Brown Novels

The Candidate

Secret Lives of Husbands and Wives

The Baby Planner

How to Reach Josie

To write Josie, go to:
mailfromjosie@gmail.com

To find out more about Josie, or to get on her eLetter list for
book launch announcements, go to her website:
www.JosieBrown.com

You can also find her at:

www.AuthorProvocateur.com

twitter.com/JosieBrownCA

facebook.com/josiebrownauthor

pinterest.com/josiebrownca

instagram.com/josiebrownnovels

9 781942 052210